PRAISE FOR

THE DEVIL HATH A PLEASING SHAPE

"Roberts's superb third whodunit featuring Stephen Robbins (after *My Mistress' Eyes are Raven Black*) finds the PI investigating the mysterious death of a college girl at the hotel where he used to work.... Roberts matches evocative historical detail and genuinely surprising twists with top-shelf character work, cementing Robbins's spot in the troubled PI hall of fame. Fans of Ray Celestin's *City Blues Quartet* will adore this."

—***Publishers Weekly Starred Review***

"If Hercule Poirot had been born in Appalachia instead of in Belgium, he would be Stephen Robbins."

—**Daniel Wallace**, author of *Big Fish* and This Isn't Going to End Well

"Gripping and gorgeous... Those who dive into this deliciously crafted mystery will find themselves submerged in such evocative mood and detail that they will not want to come up for air. Terry Roberts cements himself as the master of Appalachian noir."

—**Denise Kiernan**, *New York Times* bestselling author of *The Last Castle* and *The Girls of Atomic City*

"Terry Roberts has crafted another classic noir mystery rich with sensory details, brisk pacing, crackling dialogue, and escalating tension. I tore through the pages of this newest Stephen Robbins novel, completely immersed.... [It] swept me along so powerfully that I became just as desperate as Robbins to see justice prevail."

—**Heather Bell Adams**, author of *Maranatha Road* and *The Good Luck Stone*

"Roberts delivers with another novel [that] explores privilege, power, corruption, racism, and the cost of redemption. The historical setting may be illustrious, but everyone's morals are in question."

—**Leslie Logemann**, Highland Books, Brevard, NC

"If you want a needle-threading, button-popping literary crime novel that you can't put down, then pick this one up. Quickly."

—**Clyde Edgerton**, author of *Redeye*

"A gripping story with an unflinching view of Asheville in 1924, it echoes Thomas Wolfe, John Ehle, and Robert Morgan, and looks forward, we hope, to another Stephen Robbins mystery."

—**Wayne Caldwell**, author of *Cataloochee*

"Terry Roberts proves once again his distinction as one of our finest novelists, in a narrative of sinister danger, enduring love."

—**Robert Morgan**, author of *Chasing the North Star*

"You'll hang on to every word and read long into the night in this superbly crafted historical mystery."

—**Mark Kaufman**, owner of Story & Song Bookstore Bistro

"Corrupt officials, sultry dames, and a world weary but tenderhearted detective combine to create a cracking story replete with secrets, twists, and characters who linger in your mind long after the story is over."

—**Amy Tector**, author of the
Dominion Archives Mysteries Series

"Terry Roberts writes the best of historical fiction: his novels show us the complexities of our past and present selves while at the same time entertaining the hell out of us."

—**Julia Franks**, author of *The Say So*

THE DEVIL HATH A PLEASING SHAPE

ALSO BY TERRY ROBERTS

That Bright Land
The Holy Ghost Speakeasy and Revival
The Sky Club

THE STEPHEN ROBBINS CHRONICLES

A Short Time to Stay Here
My Mistress' Eyes Are Raven Black

THE STEPHEN ROBBINS CHRONICLES

THE DEVIL HATH A PLEASING SHAPE

TERRY ROBERTS

Keylight Books
an imprint of Turner Publishing Company
Nashville, Tennessee
www.turnerpublishing.com

The Devil Hath a Pleasing Shape: A Novel

This is a work of fiction. All the characters and events portrayed in this book are either products of the author's imagination or are used fictitiously.

Cover design by Emily Mahon
Book design by William Ruoto

Library of Congress Cataloging-in-Publication Data
Names: Roberts, Terry, 1956- author.
Title: The devil hath a pleasing shape : a novel / Terry Roberts.
Description: First edition. | Nashville, Tennessee : Turner Publishing Company, 2024.
Identifiers: LCCN 2023046216 (print) | LCCN 2023046217 (ebook) | ISBN 9781684420346 (hardcover) | ISBN 9781684420353 (paperback) | ISBN 9781684420377 (epub)
Subjects: LCGFT: Detective and mystery fiction. | Novels.
Classification: LCC PS3618.O3164 D48 2024 (print) | LCC PS3618.O3164 (ebook) | DDC 813/.6—dc23/eng/20231017
LC record available at https://lccn.loc.gov/2023046216
LC ebook record available at https://lccn.loc.gov/2023046217

Printed in the United States of America

For Robert Morgan
historian, novelist, poet
and
friend

"Life and death are twins in league together."

—John Ehle

THE DEVIL HATH A PLEASING SHAPE

THE BEGINNING

THE MAN IS STANDING BESIDE THE TOUSLED BED. He stares down at the woman in the shallow glow. The one lamp he has allowed her to light casts more shadows than illumination.

Still, he can see the lipstick smeared on her face.

"I'm sorry," she says plaintively. "I thought we almost had it the second time."

He shakes his head brutishly, as if to shed her words. Shed even the thought of her words.

"I can try again," she says and rolls toward him. Sits up on the side of the bed. She remembers that she is supposed to whisper.

She reaches out to touch him there, between his legs. He steps back uneasily, so she slips forward onto her knees. The rich carpet is thick and surprisingly soft.

"I can use my mouth," she whispers. "It will be like nothing you ever felt before."

"Where did you learn to do *that,* Rosie?" he says and takes another step back, away from her in the direction of his clothes strewn over the Roycroft chair. "You whore."

"College," she says dreamily. "Let me show you."

"I'm not going to pay you," he mutters. The sound of his voice is hard now, raspy in his throat.

"Please," she says. Just that one word.

He turns his face away, sickened by the sight of her on her knees. Moves toward his clothes.

"But you promised," she says. "When you brought me up here, you said . . ." She calls him by his name.

He twists around, his trousers in his hand. "What did you say?"

She says it again, tentatively. His first name. Why is he surprised? she thinks. Anyone, everyone, knows his name.

"Stand up," he mutters. "Get dressed." And after a moment, "You're disgusting."

"Please," she says again, a catch in her voice. "You don't have to give me anything. We didn't—"

"Don't worry," he says. Now there is something threatening in his voice. His name! Why did she have to say his name? His name in her mouth is dirty.

He pulls up his trousers, hiding his shrunken piece, and buckles his belt decisively. The buckle is silver and quite old.

When he pulls on his shirt, the touch of truly fine cotton soothes him. He fumbles in his pocket.

"You don't owe me nothing," she says, standing up. "Let me get my skirt, and I'll . . ."

He has the derringer in his hand now. His father's little pocket plaything. Pearl grips and oh, so hard in his hand.

His father would approve, he thinks. The one thing he will do in the dark of this night that his father would approve of.

PART I

CHAPTER ONE

IT WAS IN OCTOBER THAT THE LETTER CAME, THE FIRST FEW days of October 1924. Slashes of ink on fine stationery that translated into words, words into sentences. All the way from the famous Grove Park Inn in Asheville, North Carolina, to our tiny Hot Springs, thirty miles downriver. From the massive inn built to last decades to the Hot Springs post office. The letter meant to drag me out of hiding and return me to the streaming world. The first time it came, I wadded it up and tossed it in the fireplace. The second, more insistent, time, it arrived in the form of a strongly worded telegram. I showed the telegram to my oldest friend, Prince Garner.

"Who's this Benjamin Loftis?" he asked, after running his eyes down the Western Union sheet.

"From what I've heard, he's related to Old Man Grove."

"He own the place?" He glanced back and forth from the paper to me. "Newspaper says the Grove Park is the finest pile of rocks ever built."

I shrugged. "Him or Grove. You know how families are. Maybe they split it down the middle."

"Mr. Loftis sounds a little high and mighty. Says here 'your presence is required due to a matter of some urgency.' You gonna get down on four legs and run into town with your tongue hanging out to do his bidding?"

"What do you think?"

Prince chuckled, which was a fine, deep, bass-noted sound indeed.

I TELEGRAPHED BACK UPRIVER TO ASHEVILLE TO LET MR. Loftis know I wasn't interested. Nothing for a few days. And then, lo and behold, Loftis came to me. Or rather his car and his driver navigated the steep, winding roads down to Hot Springs, with Loftis perched in the back seat. Seems that his "matter of some urgency" was enough to hazard the wilds of Madison County.

Since the death of my wife, Lucy, in childbirth, my son Luke and I had lived alone at Rutland, the Rumbough family mansion up on the hill above town. I was paying my friend, Johnny Rumbough, the youngest son, a little bit of rent, most of which he gave back to me to spend on the house. Johnny only lived a few hundred yards away in the old Mott house, and we enjoyed seeing each other from time to time. In truth, I was more caretaker than lodger at Rutland, and that suited everyone just fine, so long as you didn't consider the rest of the Rumbough family, most of whom had abandoned Hot Springs by that point.

So, Luke and I had made something of a home in the mansion. I was chewing my way through the library, one old book after another, and Luke—at three years old—was learning to talk. I suppose you could say that we were equally unsteady on our feet and both trying to stand up straight and make some sense of the world.

What helped was the fact that Prince and his wife Dora lived only a hundred feet away on the street behind Rutland, in a house that Old Man Rumbough had built for them. All four of us—Prince, Dora, Luke, and I—went back and forth between the two places in a relaxed and happy way, and I'd come to think that we might just all live to see Luke dance his first dance and kiss his first girl.

So when Mr. Benjamin Norwell Loftis suddenly appeared in town that October morning, and the chauffeur got out to ask around for me, the local folks sent them on up to Rutland, where we held our conference on the broad front porch.

What to say about Benjamin Loftis in the fall of 1924? Newspaperman, chemist, pharmaceutical manufacturer, self-styled architect, and—this is important—hotel man. When he showed up in Hot Springs, he was as neat as a pin in a light-gray linen suit with matching tie and socks. White bucks that were so spotless, you wondered if his driver had carried him from the car to the porch. Wire-rimmed spectacles and a receding hairline over a pale, watchful face. He was making the effort to smile at me—a stranger—right up to the point where I insisted that Prince—a fine, stocky, expansive Black man—sit with us. Imagine a Mexican bandit with skin the color of ebony. It seemed to me and to Prince it was the dark hue of his skin that Loftis didn't much like, although he seemed to recover quickly enough.

Prince and I looked downright shabby in comparison to Loftis. We weren't expecting company that nice crisp morning, and even if we'd known he was coming, neither of us could have matched his sartorial splendor and wouldn't have done much to try. So there Prince and I sat, looking like we belonged in that beautiful place on that beautiful morning. There lay my old dog, King James, occasionally thumping his tail on the floorboards when something amused him. And there sat Mr. Loftis, anxious to tell his story.

We plied him with good coffee and encouraged him to say his piece, which began almost like an advertising brochure.

"Gentlemen," he intoned, "the Grove Park Inn is among the very finest hostelries in the entire world. Certainly, one of the finest on this continent. Its size and construction are nothing short of magnificent, and yet, it presents a wholesome simplicity for the weary man and his family. It invites the public man to escape the busy world outside, to rest awhile and rekindle his moral and physical energies. It—"

I interrupted him. "We get the picture," I said. "No offense, but that's the same kind of blather I used to write for the

Mountain Park back before the war. Question is, Mr. Loftis, what has interrupted the flow of *wholesome simplicity*? Put another way: what the hell are you doing here?"

Not being permitted to finish the standard pitch for his inn before getting down to business seemed to throw him off a bit. But after stumbling and stuttering for a moment, he recovered. "Almost two weeks ago, someone was killed in one of the rooms on the third floor." He stopped and stared at us as if this revelation alone were so shocking, he need say no more.

"And . . . ?"

"And we're at a very delicate point in the development of the inn and its reputation. We can't afford to have word get out that the peace and quiet our guests crave might be interrupted in any way, let alone that . . ."

"One of them might end up at the coroner's office. Was the victim a guest?"

He shook his head. "No. A local college girl. Rosalind Caldwell."

"Age?"

"What?"

"How old was she?"

He stared helplessly while his mind seemed to spin for a moment. "Twenty, I suppose. Maybe twenty-one."

"White?" Prince asked.

Loftis nodded. "She wouldn't have been . . ." He paused, staring at Prince.

"In one of the rooms if she was a Negro." Prince smiled at him, although the irony was obvious. "I understand."

"Unless she was a maid, and you didn't say she was a maid." This from me.

Loftis nodded. "And I said she was a college girl."

"So, in sum, you have a murder on your hands, and not just a murder, but the worst kind—a supposedly innocent young woman. The publicity is killing you. Two weeks have gone by, and the sheriff hasn't been able to nail anybody for it, and you're getting desperate."

"That's right, and the story is on the front page of the paper every single morning."

I shrugged. "You do have a problem." I stared at him. "Why me?"

"I didn't know what to do. I've never been through anything like this before." He sat up straighter in his chair. "So, I consulted with my old friend, William Jennings Bryan. Do you know who—?"

Loftis was looking at me, but Prince cut in. "Sure. The secretary of state, the Great Commoner. Ran for president."

"I doubt if the Great Commoner has much experience with murdered girls in hotel rooms," I said, "but you never know. What did he advise you to do?"

"Mr. Bryan advised me to call the Bureau of Investigation in Washington and to use his name in reference." Loftis was obviously proud of this bit.

"And?"

"And I spoke to someone at the top. At the *very* top. So high in rank that he declined to give me his name. And he . . . he sent me to you."

I laughed. "Oh, I know his name."

CHAPTER TWO

"WHAT IS IT EXACTLY YOU WANT ME TO DO, MR. LOFTIS? IN A former life, before my wife died, I found things for people. In particular, I found things for the Bureau of Investigation. But this doesn't sound like that."

"He said you could do whatever needed doing."

"Our nameless friend?"

Loftis nodded. "And that I was to pay you whatever you requested and not ask any questions."

"Chances are I can do whatever needs doing, but chances also are that you might not like the results. Just to be clear, what *do* you want done?"

"I want the murderer caught and punished, so that the inn's reputation will emerge unsullied."

I glanced at Prince. "Did he say *the* murderer, not *a* murderer?"

"He did say that."

"What?" Loftis looked nonplussed.

"There's a difference," Prince rumbled. "Big difference. Most men in your position would be satisfied if the police hung this on just about anybody, hustled them down to Raleigh, and got them executed double time. Get the whole thing over with and off the front page of the paper. But you didn't say that. You said *the* murderer."

"What if it's one of your wealthiest clients? Or most famous?" I asked.

"That's impossible."

I shrugged, and Prince guffawed.

Again, Loftis recovered his composure; this time, though, it took him a bit longer. "Will you do it?" He was looking directly at me, half pleading, half challenging.

"He'll do it," Prince said decisively.

I glanced at Prince, eyebrows raised. I hadn't made my mind up, but apparently, he had.

"How much do you charge for . . . detective work?" Loftis again.

I grinned. Here was my way out. I suggested a price per day that I knew would bring Mr. Gray Linen Suit to a full stop. Plus, I'd be staying as an anonymous guest at his hotel, and there would be other expenses in addition.

But I'd underestimated just how desperate Loftis was. This time he didn't pause. "I'll write you a check before I leave today," he said. "When can you be there?"

"WHAT THE HELL YOU MEAN, *HE'LL DO IT*?" I PUSHED my voice as low as it would go to mimic Prince. It was evening, and the two of us were walking down through town to the river, leaving Luke playing with Dora after supper. "Maybe I hadn't made my mind up."

Prince took his pipe out of his jaws just long enough to reply. Pointed the stem at me while he did so. "Here's what I got to say. If you stay around here much longer, pretending to be retired—whatever the hell that means—and going fishing every other day, you will wither away. It's time for you to get out in the world again. Time for you to find a new life."

"This is my life. You and Dora and Luke."

We reached the bench down by the riverbank where we occasionally snuck off to smoke. Prince his pipe, me one of my two or three cigars a week. Once we were both of us lit up and the smoke was drifting into the azure evening sky, I repeated myself, for good measure. "This is my—"

"Ain't much of a life," he interrupted me. "How the hell old are you anyway?"

"You know how old I am, you old coot. Forty-four a few weeks back."

"A young man."

"Don't feel so young." I was exaggerating somewhat, just to aggravate Prince. That summer, I felt better than I had since Lucy died. That evening, Prince and I sitting on our bench, I felt something akin to human. Still shaky at times, but human.

"I been knowing you a long time," Prince said finally, blowing a stream of smoke out in the cool air that flowed off the river. "And you don't have much tolerance for just sitting and doing nothing. I got a gift for doing nothing and enjoying it. You do not. You need to move. Need to think and do. Make a mark. Time for you to get up and get on with it. Your life, I mean."

"You might be right. But here's the thing, Prince among men. Maybe I am ready for something, but what about Luke?"

My son, Luke. Dark hair and chocolate eyes like his mother's. Skin a café cream color that turned easily brown in summer sun. Having grown so used to him, I wasn't sure I could leave him. Not even for a few days or weeks.

"Do you trust Dora?" Prince asked, after several moments had passed.

Dora was Prince's wife. Quiet, Bible-reading Dora. The illegitimate, half-African daughter of Jack Rumbough. Her fine features and mahogany skin were beautiful in any light.

"Of course I trust her. You and Dora, along with Luke, are the only family I've got . . . About the best family anybody could ask for."

"Well, then, you already know that Dora has wanted a child of her own since the beginning of time, and now she has one.

Don't get me wrong, she knows that Luke is yours and belongs with you, but it would give her nothing but pleasure to have Luke stay with us for a few weeks, maybe even through the winter if that's what it takes. I might even manage to keep an eye on him too, from time to time."

"What about King James?" My constant companion, half-shepherd, half-husky. "He's getting old, you know, and requires a little more care than when I've been gone before."

Prince grunted. "I'll take care of the damn dog myself," he said. "We'll be old together."

I grinned at him around the stub of my cigar. "Prince Garner, babysitter."

AND IN THAT WAY, IT WAS DECIDED. ON MONDAY morning, I would catch the train south, upriver, toward the bustling town of Asheville, North Carolina. Show up at the Grove Park Inn as a mysterious guest from . . . where? New York, perhaps? I had lived there long enough to know the city.

I would find Benjamin Loftis's killer for him and spit in the devil's eye.

CHAPTER THREE

I ARRIVED IN ASHEVILLE ON OCTOBER 6TH, JUST AS FALL began to wrap its cold hands around the mountains.

Midmorning when the taxicab from the train station dropped me off in the parking lot of the fabled Grove Park Inn. On instinct, I stepped back rather than in, walking to the far end of the lot to gain some perspective on the place. How to say what the famous inn looked like that morning? If you'd never seen it, it'd be hard to imagine a structure that large made entirely out of stone.

There was a large, central block of perhaps six stories high, say 120 feet long, with an equally long wing on either side, neither of which is as tall as the central block. As I stood facing it, there was to the right—toward the north—yet one more smaller wing, not matched on the left where the end of the building butted up against the mountainside. The whole structure ran north to south, and I imagined that the far side must face west over the golf course toward the sunset. Each wing, including the central block, was topped off by an astonishing, curved red roof, made of poured concrete designed to look like the slopes of the surrounding mountains. How in God's name they had managed to pour concrete six stories off the ground, I couldn't say, but there it was.

I was used to huge structures from my years of working and managing the old Mountain Park Hotel in Hot Springs, which was, if anything, even larger. Or at least it was before it burned down in the winter of 1920 while I was in New York. And I had spent one fateful summer and fall hunting down a congregation of killers on Ellis Island, through a sprawling complex of buildings, of which the large, ornate main hall was only a small part.

So, it wasn't the size of Grove's inn that intimidated, that seemed to almost shove me back into the trees. It was something else. It was only eleven years old, but it seemed ancient. What hit you between the eyes when you stood face-to-face with it was the incredible weight of all that rock. I knew that it was constructed out of granite boulders—that's the only word that does them justice, boulders—that had been blasted out of the sides of the surrounding mountains and hauled to the site using trains of heavy wagons drawn by a gasoline-powered truck. But it didn't feel constructed. It felt as if the whole massive structure had stood long before time and human habitation, the puny beings come along only recently to honeycomb its interior with some rugs and lamps and bedsteads.

Even though I stood staring in the blare of morning sun, the thought occurred to me that this edifice was more a creation of night than of day, spun out of darkness more than light. It was itself shadowy, even when bathed by the sun.

I picked up my bags and walked toward the broad front door, slowly, keeping my eyes on the face of the building, watching it grow broader, older as I approached. I nodded to the one bellman—a young Black man with a crisp mustache—who stood just at the door. He nodded back but didn't take my old leather valise and my stained carpet bag seriously enough to help me with them. And then I was in the lobby for the first time, where my initial sense of darkness and weight was confirmed. A cave, I thought, or a cathedral built inside a cave. The ceilings rose up and up for at least thirty feet, supported by huge pillars, sheathed in oak but surely made of the same granite, boulder stacked on boulder into the darkness above. A flagstone floor with what seemed acres of chairs and couches formed around thick, blood-red carpets, which Loftis later told me were made in France specifically for this room.

At either end of the long lobby, one on my right and one to my left, loomed massive fireplaces so large it would have been easy to walk inside either standing erect. A log fire had been laid in each and was burning against the chill in the air. And by logs, I mean lengths of tree trunk split into what looked like fence rails that had been trundled somehow into the fireplaces' maws like you would throw splits of pine into the belly of your stove.

At that moment, I realized the size and scope of the world I'd entered. Loftis had said that since the murder, the average occupancy per night had slowly fallen, so that the place was now only a third full during the week and half full on the weekend. All this despite the fact that autumn weather usually packed the inn with guests.

But those were just numbers—rooms, customers, visitors. The place was so big and so sprawling it shrank any number down to a cipher. It would, if it could, shrink me down to a cipher as well.

AT FORTY-FOUR YEARS OLD, I'D ALREADY LIVED A HALF-dozen lives. Childhood runaway from a cove buried so deep in the southern mountains that it was hard to get to except in your imagination. Or get out of except on foot.

Ran away to Hot Springs, which was then a bustling town on the mighty river, and found my way to the great hotel there, where I became a stable boy, then a golf course caddie, then a waiter, then a front-desk man in a tie, then a night manager, then . . . a son-in-law.

Taken in by the mighty Rumbough family, who owned that magnificent hotel. Educated in an offhand way by Mrs. Carrie Rumbough using the library at Rutland. Taken hold of by old Major Jack Rumbough, who trained me up through all those jobs. Married by one of their daughters, Sadie, who found me sufficiently entertaining for a few years, until we lost our little boy, Jack, to infant cholera, and I refused to be Sadie's tame house pet anymore.

Times in that marriage I'd felt like a sideshow oddity—the runaway mountain boy who'd actually learned to read and write. Like a two-headed rooster or a cat with six toes.

After the divorce, I became the general manager of that sprawling hotel by the river. With Major Rumbough's profane blessing—and to spite his daughter—I became more even than manager. I was the spirit, the soul, the will that kept the Mountain Park moving and breathing. It was where I shot Bird Shelton's husband to save her life and so stood trial for murder the first time.

And so continued through the war, the Great War, when my Mountain Park became the centerpiece of the Hot Springs German internment camp. Where, by default, and despite my drinking, I became inspector general of the largest camp for German noncombatants in the country.

The war—that pageant of bloodlust and stupidity—was when I met her. Anna Ulmann . . . *her*. The answer to my tattered life, or so I thought. The war, wherein she and I fell in love. I don't hesitate to say the word: *love*. Love for a woman. Though it is alien to me now, I once knew what it meant. The war, our war, when the sheriff was killed, and I stood trial for my life for the second time. When acquitted, I chased Anna all the way to Manhattan, New York City, *her* home and *her* refuge.

One life, two lives, three lives, and then New York. Where Anna and I, so tightly bound, fell not together but apart. Where the pressure of her art and her reputation and her ambition broke us. Broke me. Where in my misery, I went to Ellis Island for Jack Durand, the nameless man from the Bureau of Investigation. Where I met Lucy Paul with her warm, café au lait skin and raven eyes. Where together we hunted down and destroyed a coven of killers. A congregation of sanctified racists, for whom Nordic purity justified anything, even the slaughter of the innocents.

Lucy, who saved me in the end. Brought me, barely alive, back to North Carolina, to my mountains. *My* place and *my* refuge. Gave me a son. Luke. And in giving him to me . . . died. Clouds passed before the sun, and the peritonitis that came after Luke's birth cast its frigid shadow over me and buried her.

What do you say to all that, friend? In those forty-four years, I'd been married twice, once divorced and once widowed. I'd stood trial twice for murder and twice been acquitted. I'd fathered two children, of whom Luke survived. I'd killed three men, but only three. Someone else shot the sheriff. I'd been pistol-whipped once and nearly killed twice.

But each time, each blessed time, I'd risen from the nightmare and the deathbed. Each time, I had sat up out of the shallow grave prepared for me and walked away. Scarred, angry, edgy . . . and alive.

And now Prince was determined I should rejoin the human race.

When I signed in the leather-bound registry on the ornate desk in the Grove Park Inn lobby, I scribed my own, my real, name: *Stephen Baird Robbins.*

CHAPTER FOUR

"LET ME BE THE FIRST TO WELCOME YOU TO THE GROVE Park Inn, sir. As I imagine you know, all our guests are preapproved by Mr. Loftis himself, and you, sir, are to be accorded every privilege." The young man behind the desk was meticulous. His gray uniform suit was carefully pressed, his white shirt immaculate. His hair and even his teeth gleamed.

"Say again."

"You are to be—"

"No, before that. Preapproved . . . ?"

He smiled. "Every guest, or in the case of a family, the head of the family, is preapproved by Mr. Loftis himself before registration. You see, sir, the Grove Park Inn operates as a haven, a respite from the busy world. And, as you can imagine, a certain . . . class of clientele contributes to that sense of relaxation. Something that I'm sure you will come to appreciate during your stay." That said, he handed me a sheet of Grove Park Inn stationery, with a list of some sort scribed on it.

I glanced down the list and whistled. "What's your name, son?"

"Edwards, sir."

"Your first name?"

"James, sir."

"This a joke, right, James? I mean, it says that there will be 'no children, no dogs or animals of any kind, no loud or intrusive behavior, no unseemly conversation in the lobby after seven o'clock in the evening, no gambling, and no writing except in the writing room.' What the hell, James?"

"And no cursing, sir. Point number seven."

"Like I said, James. What the hell?" I stared at James, and he stared back at me, slightly appalled. "So, it's not a joke?"

"Oh, no, sir. Mr. Loftis believes that public austerity and personal discipline are the keys to a fulfilling and productive life. He believes that—"

"He believes a lot, apparently. Or at least there's a lot that he doesn't believe in. Why no writing?"

"The rugs, sir."

"You don't write on rugs, James. Or at least I don't."

"No, sir. But during the early years, Mr. Loftis discovered that some of our patrons could be rather careless with their ink bottles."

"And spilled ink on the rugs?"

"Precisely, sir. Thank you, sir. The rugs are very expensive, sir. From France," he added helpfully.

"James?"

"Yes, sir."

"Why would anybody in his right mind want to stay here?"

"Oh, sir! Because it is full of rest and . . . wholesomeness." He positively glowed at the mention of wholesomeness.

It was on the tip of my tongue to ask him just how in the hell could anybody manage to get themselves killed in such a place. But I thought I'd save that question. A question I would have to answer for myself.

I HAD REQUESTED A ROOM NEAR WHERE ROSALIND Caldwell had been murdered. I wanted to learn about the layout of the place, where and how people came and went, and who those people were. After glancing at a note clipped to an envelope, my wholesome friend James had assigned me room

340 before handing me the envelope. "It's a corner room on the Palm Court," he explained. "Third floor if you want to take the elevator."

Given that I was carrying my old leather valise and a heavy carpet bag, I took James's suggestion about the elevator, which was buried within the chimney at the south end of the lobby. The elevator operator was an older white gentleman with a waxy, close-shaven face, also wearing the inn livery. He didn't have much to say, but then neither did I. I was starting to feel my way around and into the place, and I was more interested in watching him run the elevator than chatting about the weather. I wondered if someone could have brought the girl up by elevator the night she was killed. Not unless they'd had a lot of practice with the controls, I decided, which meant an employee. Or a former employee.

Room 340 was in the corner of a large, open court on the third floor. Directly above the lobby if I hadn't lost my bearings. According to the newspaper reports I'd read on the train that morning, the Caldwell girl had died in room 341, which was also a corner room but on the opposite side of the court, across from my room rather than beside it. I sat my two bags down beside my door and, since the Palm Court appeared to be empty, strolled all the way around, pausing before the door to 341 but only briefly. It appeared perfectly normal, as if nothing unusual had ever happened behind that solid oak door with the room number affixed on a small brass plate. So normal that I wondered if indeed it was the room.

Once inside my own 340, which was more than comfortable with thick, heavy furniture and windows that opened out to the west, I sat for a moment to read what was inside the envelope James had given me. The first sheet was yet one more copy of the inn rules. Just for me, someone—Loftis himself, perhaps—had meticulously underscored the edict against alcohol. I wadded up the rules and tossed them in the wastepaper basket. The second sheet was a letter addressed to hotel employees, introducing me and asking that they answer any questions I might have. It was so ambiguously worded that I might have almost been a health inspector or a fire marshal rather than a hired dick. It mentioned the Caldwell girl but so obliquely that if you didn't know better, you'd think she fell down the stairs.

> *GROVE PARK INN*
>
> *Sunset Mountain—Asheville, North Carolina*
>
> *To Friends & Employees of the Inn:*
>
> *This is to introduce you to Mr. Stephen Robbins. Mr. Robbins is here at the particular request of myself to aid us in our recovery from the unfortunate events of several weeks ago, specifically the death of Miss Rosalind Caldwell on our premises. Please accord him every courtesy and answer any questions he might have concerning that regrettable evening.*
>
> *Please make note as well that Mr. Robbins is a guest of the Inn and should be accorded every hospitality.*
>
> *Sincerely,*
>
> *Benjamin N. Loftis*

I FOLDED UP LOFTIS'S NOTE AND SLIPPED IT INTO MY INside jacket pocket, figuring it would come in handy over the next few days. Then I began to unpack. Clothes into the chifforobe and the dresser, both solid oak. Shoes under the bed. The disassembled shotgun I'd brought along just in case on a towel laid over the coffee table. The gun was a fine ten-gauge Parker side-by-side that Jack Durand, aka the Nameless Man, had sent me as a present when it became obvious that I would survive my injuries from Ellis Island.

So, there I was, sleeves rolled up and necktie tucked into my shirt, when someone knocked on the door. I folded the towel over the pieces of the gun and opened up.

CHAPTER FIVE

THE KNOCKING TURNED OUT TO BELONG TO THE ASSISTANT day manager. Just to be clear, he explained, Mr. Loftis himself was accounted the official manager of the inn. There was an assistant for the day, one for the evening, and one for the night. And this guy, Andrew Miller, was day.

He was there because Loftis had warned him about me and, indeed, had sent him to show me around. Answer any questions. Which was both good and bad, of course, because it meant he'd only show me what Loftis wanted me to see and tell me what Loftis wanted me to hear. Not that I didn't trust Loftis or his day manager at this point; just that I wanted to see behind the walls, talk to the people who really made the place run, peer into dark corners and jimmy open locked doors. It wasn't that the place itself killed Rosie Caldwell, but the dark corners knew who had.

I invited Miller to sit. He asked me if I'd like coffee brought up. Sure. He stepped to the door and spoke to a bellman waiting in the court. Sat himself back down, crossed his right leg over left, and adjusted the seam of his trousers. He wasn't dressed as finely as Loftis—I got the feeling that wasn't allowed—but I still felt a bit threadbare by comparison.

Interestingly, he looked like a slightly less self-assured, less elegant version of Loftis himself. Pale face and pale eyes, with carefully brushed hair, his shoes polished, and his suit tailored. It was as if the whole place was run by a tribe of male librarians who seldom saw the light of day.

We traded pleasantries for a few minutes. He was from Atlanta, where he'd known Loftis before. A lifelong hotel man, he was recruited specifically for this post. Why? I asked. He was discreet, intelligent, extremely detailed, devoted to his work in every way. All of which he didn't mind telling me while we waited on the coffee.

"I meant *why* did you decide to take the job?" I smiled.

There was a quiet knock, and the bellman came in with the coffee—a silver pot, of all things, on a silver tray. China cups with saucers, with matching sugar bowl and cream pitcher. Ever so delicate. Especially when you considered that I had to push a towel-covered shotgun aside so the bellman could place the coffee tray.

The bellman closed the door quietly behind him. I took a little cream. Miller took his black. I sat back and nodded.

He crossed his legs again. "You were saying . . ."

"Why did you decide to leave Atlanta and come up here, Andrew? Andrew, right?"

"Oh, that's easy. Mr. Loftis is very persuasive. He's a Christian gentleman in every respect. He cares passionately about how things are done, and he believes that a hotel like this one should be an oasis of peace and tranquility in the storm-tossed sea of modern life. My values and his values are one and the same."

"Big raise, huh?"

He grinned. "And yes, I got a significant raise."

"Good for you. I bet you earn every penny of it." I didn't pause. "Tell me about the girl." I watched his face over the rim of my cup.

He paused for a long moment. As if there were a lot of girls I might be referring to.

"Rosalind Caldwell."

"Oh. Her."

I nodded. "Were you the one who found her?"

Suddenly, I caught a glimpse of why he was the day manager, a little bit of backbone behind the milky exterior. "I was not. Unfortunately, a guest who was checking in the next day unlocked the door to 341 and found her. At first, he thought he had the wrong room and that there was a woman asleep on the floor beside the bed. But then he saw the blood."

"What did he do?"

"Pulled the door closed, left his luggage, and walked back down to the front desk."

"Walked?"

"Well, ran actually. He alerted the desk clerk, who called for me. I ran up with a bellman who was on duty. Our man carried the guest's luggage back down to the lobby, and I used my passkey to gain access to the room."

"What did you find?"

"It's all in the police report," he said. "I told it countless times that day, when it was fresh in my mind."

I shrugged. "Well, the police haven't made any arrests yet, have they?" I said. "You know this place and these rooms better than anyone. Even Loftis. What did *you* see?"

He shifted uncomfortably and paused to pour us both some more coffee. Even added cream to mine, which bespoke his attention to detail.

"I saw a woman lying on her back at the foot of the bed." He paused and took a deep breath. "She was nude and lying in a pool of blood. Congealed blood, almost black. One elbow was down in the blood, her forearm and hand over her stomach. The other arm was flung back over her head and was clutching some of her clothes . . . Her underwear and her slip, I believe."

"She'd been shot, is that correct?"

He nodded. "Twice. Once low in her stomach."

"Did the police take photographs before they moved her?"

He nodded. "It was the sheriff's department. I just wanted her out of there, but they insisted."

I made a mental note to track down those photos. Find out about the bullets. "I understand. You wanted things back to normal as soon as possible."

He crossed and uncrossed his legs. And just as before, straightened the crease in his trousers. I was in my shirtsleeves, and he still hadn't unbuttoned his jacket.

"I did want things back to normal. But, of course, there were sirens, an ambulance. We had them remove her body through the basement to cause as little commotion as possible, but still."

"Tell me about the bed."

"What?"

I shrugged. "The bed." I couldn't tell if Andrew Miller was stupid or if his mind just automatically returned to hotel operations after every single pause. "Was it still perfectly made? Had it been slept in? Was it tousled in a way that suggested sex or wrestling or—hell, I don't know—a troop of wild animals had trampled through?"

He glanced down at the toe of one polished shoe and actually blushed. The man was older than I was, and there he sat, turning pink. He muttered something under his breath.

"Sex?"

He nodded without looking up.

"Was there blood anywhere other than under the girl? On the bed, on the walls, in the bathroom?"

"No." His hands trembled a bit with his cup and saucer. Apparently, he didn't like blood. Even the thought of it.

"Can I see the room?"

"Now?"

"Sure."

"Mr. Robbins, I'm not . . . I know Mr. Loftis has engaged you in solving our problem, but just what do you want . . . intend to do?"

I smiled at him. Earlier, I had set my empty cup and saucer on the tray. Now, I leaned over and casually lifted the end of the towel as an answer to his question. Even disassembled, the shotgun looked exactly like what it was. Beautifully made, finely crafted, but still just a tool with only a very few uses.

CHAPTER SIX

At first, Andrew Miller didn't especially enjoy showing me room 341. But the more compliments I paid him and the more questions I asked, the more he seemed to relax and maybe even relish his role.

Inside the room, a narrow hallway allowed space for the bathroom and closet on the left hand. Then it opened out into the bedroom itself. I gripped Miller's arm once we were inside with the door closed behind us.

"Now," I whispered to him, "I want you to pretend it's the morning you told me about, when you found the girl. From here on out, I want you to move as you moved and stand where you stood. As you go through the motions, I want you to tell me what you saw and when you saw it."

"Why in the world—?"

I cut him off. "Because what you saw depends on the angle you saw it from. How much light was in the room. Where you were standing, and just how fast your heart was beating when you looked around you. Unless you were in the war . . . ?"

"I wasn't."

"Right. Unless you were in the war, a dead body will send your heart racing and put tears in your eyes. Cause your brain to spin out of orbit. So I want you to think. Explain to me what you saw and when you saw it. Go slow."

"Well." He cleared his throat. "The guest who found her had already turned on the light switch beside the door." He touched the two buttons in the wall to his left.

"Good. Go ahead and turn on the same light."

"From here, I could see part of her on the floor."

"Part of her?"

"Her leg. One of her legs pointing toward the window."

"Go on."

"I walked forward like this, fast. But when I came here, to the end of the passage, I could see . . . everything. All of her."

"All right. Stand here for a moment. Right where you are. I'm going to lie down on the rug, with my body just where hers was. I want you to tell me just how she lay, with her arms and legs just where they were."

"I'm not sure I recall just . . ."

"Of course you do. It's burned into your memory." I stepped past him and lay down on the floor with my legs aimed at the window and my head pointing back toward Miller. "Like this?"

"Her legs were further apart."

I spread my legs. "Like this?"

"Yes. And like I told you, her arm was . . ."

"Which arm?"

"Her right arm was down beside her in the blood, except that . . . except that her forearm and her hand was up over her stomach." He actually stepped forward then and placed my arm where he'd seen hers.

"Good. Now the other arm."

Which turned out to be flung back over my head toward the bathroom.

"Her head? How was her head?"

"Turned toward the arm that was flung backwards, almost as if turning away from . . ."

"And that was the hand, the hand above her head, that held . . . what? Her bra and her slip?"

I looked up at Miller. He was nodding. "Yes, but it was

her . . . panties and her slip."

"Where were the rest of her clothes?"

He shook his head. "I don't remem . . . her skirt was on that chair, by the armoire. I don't remember anything else."

I nodded to him, from where I lay on the carpet. "All right. Be still for a moment and let me think." I let my head fall back against the floor and half-turned my face toward my upflung arm. Let my mind go blank, or as blank as it would in that uncomfortable position, with a relative stranger looming over me. "Go stand by the chair near the window," I suggested to Miller. And when he did, I felt a sudden shiver, as though a splinter of light had penetrated my brain, and my stomach convulsed involuntarily, as if in a momentary and sudden cramp.

I sat up, more than a bit lightheaded. Looked around the room. "If it's all as you remember," I said to Miller, "then that's where he shot her from. Standing beside the chair. Or perhaps a bit closer." I stood up, again more lightheaded than I would have expected. "Show me how the bed was. See if you can make it look like it looked that morning when you first came in."

He hesitated.

"Christ, Miller. Are you worried about having housekeeping in to remake it?"

He smiled ruefully and shrugged. "The maids are gone for the day."

"Just do it. I'm going to need to come back in here tonight to see what I can feel, see, smell. They can make it up again in the morning."

And so he dug into the bed, friend Miller, assistant day manager of Grove's exquisite inn. Tossing the coverlet against the wall and throwing the covers back, rumpling the sheets, one pillow against the Arts and Crafts headboard, one on the floor. Then he paused and stepped back to regard his handiwork. After a moment, he leaned forward again and, with his hand, flattened the middle of the headboard pillow to show . . . what? Where a head had lain against the soft down.

Then he stepped back, and we stood side by side.

"What do you think?" he asked after a moment.

"I don't know yet," I admitted. "I don't know." But that didn't seem quite fair to him, who I sensed had tried his best. "I think they came in together. Which means that either the door was unlocked or one of them had a key. I think they had sex or at least got far enough along that she was naked when he shot her. The fact that she had her panties and her slip in her hand probably means that she had picked up some of her clothes to start getting dressed. Two shots and nobody heard them?"

"Nobody was staying on the Palm Court that night. There had been a reception earlier in the evening, and so we didn't rent these rooms." He pointed at the ceiling. "Several guests on the fourth floor told the police they heard what sounded like champagne corks, one after the other. Around two in the morning."

"Small-caliber pistol."

"That's what the police said."

I shook my head.

"It's not a lot to go on, is it?" Miller asked.

"There's what we don't know," I said. "Sometimes that's the most important thing."

"What we don't know?"

"Why the hell didn't she scream?"

CHAPTER SEVEN

MILLER AGREED TO LEAVE ROOM 341 UNLOCKED UNTIL the next morning. He didn't like it, it felt messy to him, you could tell, but when I suggested the alternative was that he give me a passkey, he almost choked. A passkey was too much access for this stranger with the scarred face and the rough ways.

I also didn't let him straighten the bed. I wanted to come back in that night—late—and get a feel for what the light was like, the shape and feel of the room. I wanted to sit and listen to the shadows. See what the ghost of Rosalind Caldwell could tell me, if anything.

I FINISHED UNPACKING, ASSEMBLED THE SHOTGUN, AND placed it carefully up on the shelf behind the spare blankets. Secreted the box of ten-gauge shells behind my underwear in the bottom dresser drawer. Rolled down my sleeves and threw on my jacket. Went out to meet the world—the world inside the Grove Park Inn, that is.

I spent most of the afternoon walking. In the years before and during the war, when I managed the Mountain Park Hotel down in Hot Springs, it was my habit to roam the halls when I was restless. Just walk up and down stairways, back and forth in the long hallways, climb to the uppermost floor and even gaze into the high, groaning attics. Especially in the winter, when the old place was mostly empty of guests, I felt like I owed it to the building itself, for I loved the Mountain Park unashamedly.

It felt natural just to spend an afternoon walking, poking, exploring, trying door handles to mysterious rooms, sitting for a few moments in the smoking room or the writing room. I stayed away from the lobby because, in the middle of the afternoon, I imagined it would be smeared and blurred with human traffic. Loud with voices and cart-clatter and laughter. Not that I was opposed to laughter—God knows I needed regular doses of that—but rather I wanted to hear the inn itself. I wanted to know what the rocks could tell me, what the long splits of wood in the fireplace muttered into the dark air as they turned to ash. I wanted to hear the place itself late at night.

I did stop to chat with a maid or two, once to a bellman way up on the fourth floor who was returning from delivering towels and ice to a couple in the north wing. I rode up and down both elevators and from the first to the fifth, chatting aimlessly with the operator of each about this or that . . . the most famous person he'd ever hauled up or down, the drunkest person, the sexiest woman. The answers? Henry Ford. That man who got down on his knees to pray and fell asleep. Ella Loving.

"Who's Ella Loving?" I asked, and for that got only a knowing smile.

Right about five o'clock, I did wander back to the Palm Court to sit for a bit. My stomach was growling, as I'd eaten almost nothing since a hard roll on the train that morning. And my head was yearning for a drink of something strong, something to unknot this odd day. I decided that I needed to know about the party that night, the night the girl was killed. It was too much of a coincidence for the light and sound and music to have flowed back and forth in waves through this long, public room and then something hot and naked and angry to have then taken place so close by . . . just behind that door over there. On the same night, breathing the same air.

After all that thinking, I washed up a bit in my own room,

slipped a battered metal flask with homemade white liquor into the side pocket of my jacket, went in search of the restaurant on the first floor. Hungry and tired.

As I crossed the lobby from the south elevator toward the dining room, I met Benjamin Loftis for the first time in his native environment. He was standing in front of the registration desk, chatting animatedly with a tall man with light brown hair. The tall guy looked to be in his late twenties to early thirties, with a handsome, tanned face that was at once open and receptive. He was the kind of good-looking that said minor celebrity, and his careful grooming along with his tan said that he'd probably been playing tennis all afternoon and playing very well. Even Loftis, the master of all he surveyed, seemed to lean toward him as if soaking up some of the younger man's sun.

I meant to maneuver right on past, but Loftis saw me out of the corner of his eye and called me over. "Robbins, it's good to see that you finally made it. Here's someone I want you to meet. Madison Aycock, this is Stephen Robbins, a guest at the inn who joins us on the recommendation of our friends in Washington. Robbins, I want you to meet Madison Aycock. Madison is a local attorney for whom a number of us harbor the highest ambitions."

I shook hands with Loftis first—after all, he was paying the bills—and then turned to regard his companion. I was a head taller than Loftis, and the young god was half a head taller than me. He was smiling at me now, staring straight into my face and pumping my hand like I was the last vote in a close election. And I admit, the effect was charming, if charm can be measured in voltage. The tan was real, the teeth were perfect, the hair was casually but carefully combed back over his head, and the eyes were a warm, welcoming blue.

The whole effect was refined but masculine. Manly, even, in a self-conscious sort of way.

"Call me Madison" were the first words out of his mouth.

"And you're . . . ?"

"Stephen. Stephen Robbins."

"You look like you might just be headed for the dining room, Stephen. It's early, but would you care to join Mr. Loftis and me for dinner?"

It was on the tip of my tongue to decline, but Loftis beat me to it. "I don't think Robbins has . . . time in his schedule for us this evening, Madison. And there's a few things I need to mention to you about . . . that other matter before dinner." Loftis turned to me. "Perhaps another time," he said. "Several of us are hoping to convince Madison here to run for governor in a few years, and that sort of planning and preparation takes time."

"Of course," I said heartily. "I understand perfectly." Shook hands all around again while we muttered the standard variations on *pleased to meet you, glad to know you, again soon* and such, the whole time me suspecting that Loftis was glad to be shut of me so he could have Aycock all to himself. I was glad to be shut of both of them so I could eat in peace.

I ASKED THE MAÎTRE D' FOR A TABLE IN A CORNER OF THE large well-lit dining room, and because it was still relatively early, he obliged with something better than I could have hoped for. He sat me at a small table that was the last in a row along the west-facing windows, so that I could stare out over the golf course and watch the sun slip down the long slope of the October sky toward Mount Pisgah. Consider the evening as its darkening shadows consumed the day.

But just as important to me, at least to the thinking part of my mind, I could also watch the dining room and make some sense of what sort of people actually stayed at the Grove Park Inn. I knew I needed to come to grips with the smooth, polished skin of the place in order to imagine what went on beneath that surface.

My waiter was a handsome and well-dressed Black man

named Michael. After a few minutes' observation, it became apparent that all the waiters in the formal dining room—even on a Monday—were well-dressed Black men. Often tall, mostly handsome. Fair enough, I thought. Here's to good tips.

After a glance at the menu, I asked Michael what I should have. He was in and out of the kitchen, so he knew what was going on back there. I added, "The fish or the chicken?" He stared down at me for a moment and gravely shook his head.

"Bad?"

"On the contrary, quite acceptable." Michael had a voice like the baritone in a gospel quartet. "But I have something else in mind for tonight, since it's your first evening with us."

"How do you know it's my first evening?"

There was the faintest flicker of a smile. "It's my job to know, sir. Plus, you were seated in my section. When you return on successive evenings, this will be your table."

What he said made sense, if somehow, even in this period after the war, the inn still managed to maintain a clientele that stayed through the season.

"Fair enough. So, Michael, tell me what I should eat."

"The steak, sir. I observed it being seasoned myself."

"Well . . ." And suddenly, somehow, the way he said it, the rumble of his voice, made the thought of red meat an imperative. My mouth literally watered, and I had to swallow before I asked, "Medium-well?"

Again, the slight shake of the head. "Medium, sir. I will make sure they do it correctly."

I could only grin up at his handsome face. "Make it so, Michael," I said.

"Coffee or tea, sir?"

"Christ." After months down at the springs, I had forgotten that prohibition still ruled public places like the inn dining room.

"I'll see what I can do, sir," Michael intoned, and turned on his heel, as if *Christ* was a drink order.

In a moment, a middle-aged white man in a suit and tie emerged from the kitchen to ask me if everything was to my liking. I nodded, assuming him to be the dining room manager. He only glanced at Loftis's letter of introduction, and I got the sense that he already knew who I was. "This is my first evening," I admitted to him. "How are things laid out down here?"

Three dining rooms, all on the main floor. Three meals per day, limited menu with an emphasis on health. Every meal with fruit, including breakfast. "Mr. Loftis believes in the restorative value of healthy food, most notably fruit, especially prunes, as they are—"

"I get the idea," I said. "Who do you serve these three healthy meals a day to? Local people, guests, guests of guests?"

"We primarily serve local people on the weekends, Saturday night and Sunday noon. And, I might add, when we do serve local people during the week, they are usually someone who is meeting a guest or someone who is friends with Mr. Loftis."

"Friends of Loftis?"

"Only the very best of the local citizenry dine at the Grove Park," he said proudly. "We wouldn't want . . . the less socially astute interrupting your dinner, now, would we?"

Michael had been waiting patiently while his manager finished explaining things to me. As the suit slipped away to another table, he placed a china coffee cup and a small porcelain pot of what I assumed was coffee on the table, along with a basket of rolls. I grabbed a roll and a carefully pressed pat of butter, my first bite since breakfast.

When I poured from the pot to the cup, however, what came out was dark red, not black and definitely not hot. When I sipped from my coffee cup, it tasted like something from a jug in Little Italy, strong and earthy. "Jesus has changed this water into something fine," I muttered in surprise.

Michael smiled and held a finger up to his lips, signaling me to lower my voice. "We have our little ways. And you look like a man who can enjoy a sip of truly good wine with a bite of equally good beef."

"Does he know?" I asked, gesturing with my head toward the manager, who was working his way around the room, checking in with various guests.

Michael shook his massive head ever so slightly. "Only you and I know, sir, and one or two others in the kitchen."

I nodded. "One or two important people in the kitchen, I imagine. Thank them for me."

He nodded. "I asked the maître d', sir, your name, but since this is your first evening, you are Mister . . . ?"

"Robbins. But call me Stephen."

When he cleared his throat to object, I shook my head.

"Stephen will do. I prefer it. In fact, Michael, except for some extenuating circumstances, I doubt seriously if I would qualify for Mr. Loftis's list of preferred local folks."

Michael smiled and turned on his heel to head back to the kitchen.

The roll was brown and hard and delicious. The pale-yellow butter had been pressed into tiny rounds with the letters *GPI* on each, which didn't stop me from smearing it on the rolls and wolfing them down with a sip of wine to wet each bite.

Michael soon materialized with the steak he'd recommended steaming on the plate with mashed potatoes and broccoli. Butter already swam in the potatoes and a white cheese sauce hot on the broccoli. I may have groaned when I saw it, which turned Michael's smile into a grin.

CHAPTER EIGHT

After the pure pleasure of the first few bites of steak, I slowed down in order to savor the meat with the potatoes and the wine. Let it last, I thought, and between each bite, stared out over the long slope of the golf course and the river valley beyond to the high mountains in the west, where clouds tousled the fading light into layers of fiery pink and salmon.

Another bite of steak. A sip of wine.

I turned again to the dining room, half full of customers, most tables with two, three, four patrons. The waiters were on the move, filling orders, taking requests, making the whole operation run so smoothly, it was as if the food and drink appeared on the table by some invisible sleight of hand. I was pleased, but also a little puzzled, that no one close to me was enjoying a steak so thick and tender, and neither was there a teapot that might contain the wine God intended to go with it. Somehow, Michael had decided to bless me that particular evening, and I didn't resent the attention.

Another bite of steak.

As I surveyed the other diners, slowly chewing and sipping, a couple entered the dining room. He was casually but expensively dressed. Graying hair combed straight back over a high, thin forehead. Dressed for dinner in a suit, but unlike me and most of the men in the room, his clothes were immaculate, pressed and brushed. And he wore them easily, naturally, as if to the manor born.

He was in his mid-fifties or a few years older, and the woman with him had to be younger—perhaps even twenty years younger—and just as elegantly dressed, if perhaps just a shade flashier. Her face was also pale, but not like his, not Nordic. Something else, something more exotic, and her eyes were brown, like those of my dead wife. Her hair a light brown, cut to frame and accent her face.

They were seated at the next table for two by the west-facing windows, so that his back was directly to me. From my vantage point, I could catch glimpses of her face over his shoulder. Michael didn't offer them a menu, so they must be regulars, and the man quickly ordered for them both, speaking in gruff tones.

I remembered my steak and carved a bite. Whoever they were, this mysterious couple, they weren't more interesting than the taste of good beef chased with a sip of Michael's wine.

After a few moments, the man with his back to me unfolded a sheaf of newsprint he'd brought in with him, refolded it to the section he wanted, and laid it on the table in front of him. Began to read, ignoring the woman. She glanced out the window, savored the sunset for a long moment, and then glanced back at the man and his paper. She then did the oddest thing. She tilted her head ever so slightly so that she could see past her partner's shoulder, looked straight at me, and smiled ruefully.

Not flirtatiously but sarcastically. Barely nodded at the man and then rolled her eyes as if to say just what she thought of him and his newspaper. Even though I was chewing, I had to grin back at her. I could feel myself responding to the woman, warming to her humor, smiling to myself as I took another bite.

Later, when I stood up to leave and the couple were still at table, I made a point of nodding and smiling to her as I walked past them. The man didn't even glance up from his plate and his newspaper, but even so, the look she gave me—and the twitch of her lips—were secretive, something private between us.

Whoever she was, I was intrigued, but I doubted I'd ever see her again.

I NAPPED THAT NIGHT BEFORE VENTURING OUT IN THE WEE hours to see what I could make of room 341. I didn't undress and go to bed because I didn't want to sleep through the middle watch, the haunted time of night when Rosalind Caldwell died. Instead, I lay down across the covers in my suit pants and undershirt, comfortable enough to doze off but not so relaxed that I wouldn't wake until morning.

I had a visitor during that first night under the high, hard roof of the Grove Park Inn. Not a visitor in the flesh but something else, something spun out of memory and imagination. A visitor that troubled my dreams, who wouldn't leave even when I half woke to roll over to the cool side of the bed.

At first, she was silent and beckoning, but then slowly . . . whispering, gesturing . . . warning. Oddly enough, it wasn't Lucy, my dead wife. I often dreamed of Lucy when I was near Luke. Somehow, his presence down the hall as we slept in Hot Springs conjured Lucy into my dreams there, where the boy still tied us together.

But that night, he was thirty miles away, and I was alone.

No, that night the woman who slipped into my dreams was my lost lover, Anna Ulmann, the woman I'd thought was the marrow of my life before New York.

At first, as I lay sprawled across the bed, it seemed to me that she was in the room, that she sat calm and composed in the Roycroft chair just beyond the foot of the bed. Watching me. That's all, just watching over me, perhaps to be sure of something. That I was alive, that I was . . . aware.

Then she rose from the chair to come closer. Warmer and more real, as if there was some expectation between us. Some yearning that we shared. And in my dream, she sat on the side of the bed and reached out to me. Her ghostly hand toward my scarred face.

Which woke me. Not entirely, but raised me up. I must have groaned aloud and sat partway up on the bed. Rolled over then and pounded my pillow into submission before slipping back down.

Where she remained, waiting for me. Sitting almost primly on the side of the bed . . . impossibly there in the Grove Park, hundreds of miles from where I knew her to be. And this time, rather than reaching out, touching, she seemed to speak. Her lips were moving in the darkening dream and the words forming deep in my brain.

"Stephen." Her lips shaped my name. "Be careful. There's a devil here, Stephen."

I turned my dream face toward her. To be sure of what she said, what she meant.

"Nothing is as it seems, Stephen. Everything here is burning, but there is no light. Everything here is rich, but there is no . . ."—she paused as if troubled to say what was not—"love. Please be careful. My . . ."

Once more, she reached out her hand and, this time, touched my face. There in the dream, caressed my cheek, even though she knew it could only push me away from her, would only awaken me.

Which it did. With tears on my face to trace the path of her touch. Why her? Why Anna, when I had put her behind me?

And what in God's name did she mean, that *nothing is as it seems*?

So disturbing was the dream that it addled my waking senses, held onto me even as I splashed cold water on my face and neck. Most dreams fade with wakefulness, but not this one. This one hung in the air like smoke.

My watch told me that it was after three in the morning, and the image of the dream persisted like some sort of shadow in my mind as I dressed, slipped out the door to my own room, 340, and eased across the empty Palm Court to the unlocked door of 341. If felt as if Anna, wherever she happened to be on the daytime, sunlit face of the earth, was determined to go with me into the belly of that night. Into the dark place where a country girl named Rosalind—probably Rosie—had been killed.

As expected, the door to 341 was unlocked. I turned on all the lights the room had to offer—ceiling globes in the bedroom and bathroom, a lamp beside the bed and another beside the chair. Then, even though I knew the sheriff's deputies had combed through the place inch by inch, I still got down on the floor to feel under the bed and chair, still pulled the chest out from the wall to peer behind it, still touched almost every surface she might have grasped or he might have run his fingers over. *He*? I realized then and there that I was thinking of the killer as a man, imagining that only a man would be so cruel.

The bed had been left as I'd asked, tossed and tousled. How I wished I could touch and smell the sheets from that night, but even so, I imagined the sheriff's photos would say a lot. And perhaps one of the deputies had enough sense to save the sheets. And the rug . . .

When I first thought of entering the room at night and mentioned it to Miller, I imagined I would get some sense of who *he* was, some instinct about the killer. Stand where he stood, see what he saw. But as I worked my way more deeply into the place, I realized that what I felt more than anything was *her* fear and *her* desire. First desire, I thought, and then . . . at the last, shame. Shame and fear.

I gave up trying to inhabit his mind and began to consider her. I turned off the overhead lights and then the lamp beside the bed, which left mostly shadows thrown from the single lamp near the chair. Again, for some odd reason, I remembered my dream . . . Anna's soft touch and her warning.

I lay down on the floor again, just as I had earlier in the day, and let my limbs splay into the positions that Miller had described. My legs sprawled out toward the chair, my right hand over my stomach with the elbow on the floor. My left hand thrown back over my head, my fingers clutching something . . . a slip, a pair of plain cotton panties.

I half closed my eyes and let my face relax so that my mind could roam. It struck me—an odd, glancing thought—that it was easier for me to imagine being a woman than to imagine being twenty years old again. What was twenty but innocence? Trust . . . excitement . . . shock?

My slip . . . my panties.

There was a hot, stinging burning in my chest, but the wound, the real wound was down low, below my waist, where my hand was reaching to cover it. Protect it. Stop the bleeding.

A man's name floated briefly on the edge of my consciousness. Some name I was meant to say or had said. Should not have said. The name was . . . gone. Had skittered across the face of my mind, choked me briefly, like blood, and was lost.

My whole body twitched, and suddenly, I was very, very cold.

I sat up, coughing. My chest still burned, like heartburn but deeper, beneath the breastbone.

What did I know?

I knew that they had almost done it. Almost had sex. That she had wanted it. They both had. But something interrupted them, something gone badly wrong.

I knew that he had stood in front of me, or rather her, by the window chair, probably where his clothes were. And he had taken a step forward and shot . . . her. I could taste her surprise at the sudden pain. It was like the metallic tang of blood on my tongue. He had taken another step and shot her again. This time with the pistol held right up against her, I thought, muffled against her chest.

And then what?

Then, as cool and callous as a gravedigger, he had gotten himself dressed, stepped right over her, carefully avoiding her blood pooling on the carpet, and walked out, closing the door behind him.

He hadn't brought her there to kill her—at least not consciously—but then, when the time came, he didn't hesitate. Something unexpected had bruised him, and he struck like a snake.

CHAPTER NINE

THE BUNCOMBE COUNTY SHERIFF IN 1924 WAS NAMED "Mitch" Mitchell. He was everything you ever imagined about Southern sheriffs, if your imagination ran toward the nightmare end of the spectrum. Meaning that he had a reputation for toughness but not necessarily fairness. Medium height, running to fat, nearly always gnawing on a hard twist of apple-flavored chewing tobacco. Most of the photos I'd seen showed him in a wrinkled dark suit that didn't show stains over a white shirt that did.

He employed a number of deputies, nearly all mountain born and bred, most of whom were a good deal smarter than Sheriff Mitch but less colorful. These included his younger brother, Brody, who I'd heard of but never met.

The sheriff's offices were in the basement of the old brick courthouse. Right across the square from the previous jail where I'd spent Thanksgiving in 1917, awaiting trial for murder. When I showed up there on Tuesday morning, my second day on the Grove Park Inn job, I got a fine reception... right up to the point when they ushered me in to see Sheriff Mitch himself. Then things got testy.

He invited me to take a seat in one of his office chairs, a rock-hard, wooden piece, and told the uniformed deputy who'd shown me in to shut the door. The uniform didn't leave but slammed the office door closed and then stepped up behind my chair. Good old Mitch himself strolled around his desk, leaking a thin trail of tobacco juice from one corner of his mouth down to his second or third chin.

There was one other man in the office, a deputy, I imagined, dressed in a suit. Thin, closely shaven face, eye patch. Young, late twenties. I was glad he was there as a witness, even if he only had one eye, because Sheriff Mitch seemed perturbed, and the good sheriff had a reputation for using his fists in conversation.

"What in the red hell do you want?" This the sheriff's opening query.

I handed him the half-page letter from Benjamin Loftis, addressed specifically to the sheriff and requesting his cooperation. He glanced at it long enough to digest who it was from and then read it more carefully before tossing it into my lap.

"Does Loftis know just who in the hell you are?" he grumbled.

I shook my head, smiling pleasantly. "Doubt it," I said. "Not in the way you mean."

"I mean, does he know that you shot Roy Robbins down in cold blood five years ago and walked clean away? Right here in this courthouse."

I kept smiling and fingered the scar on my face, the scar the Madison County sheriff had given me right before he died. "It was seven years ago," I said. "And I doubt if Loftis's put all that together in his head. But right now, he's getting nervous up there on his private mountain, and if I can help you and him find out who killed Rosalind Caldwell, he won't much care who I am or what I did."

"Shit on you," Sheriff Mitch said. "I don't need no help."

"Got a suspect?"

"Several." Sheriff Mitch tended to spray a little juice when he got close, and he was getting closer all the time.

"Any of them guilty?"

"One of 'em is likely to confess any day now." Which meant they'd been applying two or three feet of heavy hose to some poor soul's back and rib cage by means of interrogation.

"That's great," I offered. "In the meantime, while your suspect is composing his confession, you mind if I have a look at the case file? Talk with the deputies who first saw the girl? Mr. Loftis would certainly appreciate the cooperation."

Sheriff Mitch grinned, which was itself a horrible thing to behold. Snuff-colored horse teeth. "Sure, sonny. We'll cooperate. Stand yourself up."

Which I did, bracing myself for whatever the old man meant by cooperation. "I'll share with you that the murderer first shot her right here," he said. And sucker punched me with his fist just below my belt buckle. Not so low as to ruin my day, but low enough.

I let myself fall back into the chair to get some distance from him. "And then the son of a bitch shot her right here." I caught the second punch half on my forearm, right over my heart. "How's that for some good old-fashioned cooperation, you little shit?"

Even though I'd been expecting the second punch, it still caused me a gasp or two. He was leaning over me and put his weight into it.

"Mitch?" the deputy in the suit offered. "You might go easy if he's working for Loftis. Public relations and all..."

"I just might," Sheriff Mitch said and laughed, which caused him to have to cough and spit... mostly in the cuspidor near the door. "Get the hell out of here, Robbins," he said as he hefted his bulk back around his desk. "Go someplace where I don't have to look at you." He paused. "And tell Loftis that if he's going to waste his money bringing in an outsider, to make it someone I can work with."

THE SHERIFF'S BOYS LET ME SHOW MYSELF OUT, WHICH at that point was fine with me. I stopped off in the washroom to scrub some of the tobacco spittle off the shoulder of my suit coat. I was swiping away with my handkerchief when the younger deputy who'd been in Mitchell's office found me. He leaned against the sink next to mine while I washed up and, when I was almost done, pointed to his cheekbone to signify a spot I'd missed. He was right. There were brown stains on my face as well.

"Thanks," I said. "It's a wonder he didn't spit in my eye." And was immediately sorry that I said it, given that the deputy only had one.

"He's getting old," he offered. "Aim isn't what it used to be."

"And you are . . . ?"

"Brody Mitchell."

I looked more closely. "I don't see the resemblance."

He nodded. "Thanks. I don't always see it either. You still want to take a gander at the case file?"

I gave him my own twisted version of a smile. "Sure."

"Follow me," he said.

Brody Mitchell's office was on the first floor, not far from the front door. It was barely large enough to hold a desk and chair, but it was adjacent to a small meeting room, where he left me to go fetch the files. When he came back, he locked the hallway doors to both his cubicle and the room, so that we could look and talk undisturbed.

I read the fine print quickly and then, in a few places, more slowly. Here and there a detail that seemed to almost leap off the pages. "No vaginal penetration," I commented to Brody. "Was the coroner sure that . . . ?"

"He was sure."

"But the inside of one thigh was bruised and slightly . . ."

"Abraded. I think the word he used was abraded."

Then the photographs. As hardened as I was from what I'd seen in New York and elsewhere, I wasn't quite ready for the images. Rosalind Caldwell's legs sprawled wide. The wound in her lower abdomen almost where Mitch Mitchell had punched me, just at the upper fringe of her pubic hair. The second wound an inch or two above her left nipple, surrounded by powder burns that stained the upper half of her breast. That was bad enough, but her face . . . her face made it all real. Sudden and agonizing. One eye mostly closed and the other starkly open. The lipstick smeared across her chin and cheeks.

"How do we know which shot was first?" I asked Brody. "Your sainted brother seemed to imply that the lower wound was first and the one to her chest came second."

"Mostly speculation," Brody admitted. "Powder burns on the chest wound must mean he was holding the pistol literally against her skin, which makes you think that she . . ."

"Was down and defenseless." I finished the thought for him. It matched my own intuition when I lay on the floor of room 341.

He nodded. "Plus if he'd already fired into her heart, why would he then step back and shoot her . . ."

"Down below?"

Again, he nodded.

"What do you think happened?" I asked him. After all, he'd seen the room the next morning, when the girl's body was still sprawled on the floor.

Brody shrugged. "Didn't look like rape. I mean, it didn't look like he forced her in there at gunpoint. The bed—"

"Looked like a little love nest." Again I finished his thought. "Maybe she changed her mind at the last minute, and it enraged him."

"That's what I thought, too, but there's a problem."

I raised my eyebrows. "Problem?"

"There was a twenty-dollar bill in the blood beside her." He nodded at the photos spread out on the table. "Look again."

I looked again. In the three photos taken of her whole body to show her in relation to the layout of the room, there was a crumpled bill beside her left hip, soaked in black blood, probably all but glued to the carpet. "Damn," I said. "That changes things."

Brody nodded. "Maybe she had it in her hand and dropped it when he shot her."

"Wrong hand," I muttered. She had her slip and panties in her left hand, probably getting ready to put them back on. "Maybe he dropped the bill or . . ."

"Or?"

I felt a chill run up my spine. "Or he threw the money down on his way out."

CHAPTER TEN

THE CARPET, THE CLOTHES, THE SHEETS FROM THE BED, even the twenty-dollar bill immersed in the pool of her dried blood. The sheriff's department had all of these things, and Brody told me that if I came back in a few days, he'd arrange for me to see them without his brother being any the wiser.

I agreed, and we shook hands on it.

I had more questions for Deputy Brother Brody, like why he was helping me when Sheriff Mitch told me to take a hike with his fists. But I figured those questions could wait as well. The twenty-dollar bill had spooked me. I hadn't imagined it before and couldn't quite make sense of it now.

After I left the courthouse, I bought the morning paper from a boy hawking them on the corner. I carried the folded newsprint around the corner of the Jackson Building and down the stairs to the lunchroom in the basement. I wanted coffee and quiet and time to think. I found a nice spot in the back corner booth, and the waitress brought coffee without even asking. I smiled at her, and she asked if I wanted pie.

"What kind?" I asked.

She took a step back to regard me more objectively. "Mountain boy?" she asked, though she had already made up her mind.

I smiled again.

"Apple," she said. "And it ain't half bad."

She was right, of course. Late morning, cool outside. Coffee called for pie, and mountain-bred called for apple.

The Asheville paper was published twice a day: *Citizen* in the morning, *Times* in the afternoon. This was the *Citizen*, and it heralded the day with news about all sorts of local and national pabulum, but the thing that struck me was on the right-hand side beneath the banner, an entire section of print closed off in a box framed in black, the title of which was *Murder Investigation Ongoing*. I scanned it while I poured a teaspoon of cream into my cup and absentmindedly stirred the milky cloud into the black coffee.

The state crime lab had confirmed . . . The coroner was quoted as saying . . . There was a photo of the county coroner pointing with a pencil to two very small bullets displayed against a white piece of paper on his desk. *Sheriff Mitch Mitchell had not one but two suspects in custody in the county jail and, with the help of a crack investigator from New York City, was interrogating them around the clock.* Another photo of the crack investigator, who looked like a middle-weight boxer gone to seed. A crooked nose and a cauliflower ear, which somehow said to me that he was even harder on Mitch's suspects than Mitch himself. *Two men in custody . . . one an employee of the hotel and one a delivery man, one colored and one white. News that the case had been blown wide open was expected hourly. Stay tuned for the evening . . .*

Remember this, friend. I learned it in New York and elsewhere along the road. Bruises from a heavy hose don't show so much on black skin as they do on white. A broken rib or two in a Black man's body are neither here nor there if they come papered over with a confession.

The coffee was so hot that even with cream it burned my tongue, which made the waitress laugh when she sat the pie down in front of me on the newspaper.

"Careful," she said. "Boiling when it comes out of the pot."

I nodded. "What's your name?" I asked her. "In case I need to yell for help."

"LaVada." She nodded curtly. "LaVada Biggs from Weaverville. You?"

"Stephen Robbins. Hot Springs."

She cocked her head on one side. "Thought that was you," she offered. "Shot that sheriff back in '17."

"Christ. Will that never go—"

"Away? Doubt it. Shouldn't go 'round shooting people, 'specially sheriffs."

I considered. "Well, some of 'em need shooting."

She nodded. Leaned over to whisper. "Pie's on the house" is what she said.

She was right about the pie. It wasn't half bad. Not up to Dora Garner's standards, but then Dora could pick her pippins straight off the tree. And if you blew on the coffee before each sip, it wasn't dangerous.

Page three of the paper showed me something else that spoke to the Grove Park Inn and Mr. Benjamin Loftis—a photograph of Loftis with Judge Bishop Aycock, local bigwig, and Aycock's son, Madison. Madison Aycock was the pretty boy I'd met in the lobby at the inn with Loftis. Looked like he had just come in from winning at golf without even bothering to sweat. In the newspaper photo, he was standing between the two older men—his father the judge and Loftis the . . . what? Moneyman? Kingmaker? The article didn't say Madison was running for governor. It was far too coy for that. But rather, it claimed that our lad—Madison, the Christian gentleman and gifted barrister—had begun to exhibit signs of the political ambition that so many of us already had for him.

LaVada was back to warm up my coffee, which was still steaming. "What do you think of him?" I asked her and pointed at the younger Aycock.

She leaned over for a closer look. "Handsome as a yearling steer," she said. She straightened and made a face. "He could tickle my fancy anytime he felt like it," she added. "But then his kind don't come down to the Uneeda Lunch very often."

I laughed. "I've met the boy, LaVada. And trust me, he's not good enough for you."

True to her word, the pie wasn't on the bill, and the coffee was only a quarter. I hid a folded dollar bill under the saucer for a tip. Figured LaVada Biggs was the sort of friend a man needed in a town like this. Probably knew a hell of a lot more about what was going on at the courthouse than the reporter slinging words into his typewriter.

I CAUGHT A CAB ON THE SQUARE TO TAKE ME BACK UP TO the inn. When it dropped me off at the front portico, I paid the driver cash. As I got out and slipped the billfold back into my hip pocket, I did next what I always did automatically: thrust my hands into my front pockets just to be sure my pocketknife, change, and keys were still there, not buried in the cabbie's back seat.

When I did, I touched the key to my hotel room, a simple enough item attached by a ring to a wooden disk, which had "The Grove Park Inn" stamped on one side and the number 340 on the other.

My own room key reminded me of *the* key. The key that would access 341 where the murder took place. Were there master keys held by certain staff? Andrew Miller had what looked to be a passkey on his key ring, the one he'd used to let me into 341 the day before. How many were there? Who had them? Were any missing?

I hurried over to the front desk to ask for Andrew and was directed to the maze of small offices in the corner of the lobby.

You could tell Miller was not all that happy to see me again, and when I asked about the keys, his mood didn't improve.

"The sheriff's deputies have already asked about this. You do realize that, don't you?" I had shut the door behind me when I eased into his office, but even so, he was whispering, and I realized that the walls within the office complex were paper-thin.

I nodded. "Sure. But then I met a number of the deputies just this morning, and they might not be the sharpest tools in the shed. Tell me about keys, Andrew. Where they're kept. How they're distributed and reclaimed from guests. Who carries passkeys? Everything you can think of."

He stared at me in frustration for a long moment and then sighed as if resigning himself to another hour or two with the boss's hired op. He led me out to the front desk and showed me a large wooden cabinet that sat against the outside wall between the front doors. The cabinet itself had been stained to match the dark cherry color of the rest of the furniture and blended in beautifully.

Miller opened the shallow cabinet and showed me the 150-plus hooks inside. Each of the hooks was labeled with a piece of paper pasted to the wood just above it; each tag had a room number. There was a separate row of hooks for each of the five floors that housed guest rooms, and a sixth, much shorter row that was labeled with names.

I reached inside the cabinet to touch one of the numbered labels. It was securely glued onto the wood, and the number was not scrawled on but carefully—even beautifully—inscribed in black ink. Perhaps a third of the hooks were either empty or held only one key.

"Does an empty hook mean that those rooms are occupied, and the patrons have the keys?"

Miller nodded. "Exactly."

"And if there's only one key on a hook, then there's only one guest in the room?"

"Yep." He reached out and touched the hook labeled 340. "There's your room," he added. "One guest, one key out. The other always stays here." The second key had exactly the same ring and embossed tag as the one in my pocket.

"Housekeeping doesn't use these? Or room service?"

"Nope. Housekeeping has a set of master keys, one for each floor. Those keys are only released midmorning to the head housekeeper for each floor and returned as soon as the rooms are done. Room service never enters unless the guest is in the room, so they don't need keys."

I pointed to the sixth row at the bottom of the cabinet. I counted eight hooks. They were labeled in order: *Loftis, Miller, Stoneman, Barnes.* Then set slightly apart: *Fireman, Security West, Security East, Physician.* Loftis's hook and Miller's hook were empty, plus both Security West and Security East.

"Stoneman and Barnes?" I asked Miller.

"Evening manager and night manager."

"Fireman and physician?"

"Both on call twenty-four hours a day, but don't carry their keys with them."

I glanced at the hook for room 341. Both keys were there, which meant the room was empty. Knowing Miller, he'd had the bed remade and locked it again as soon as he came on duty that morning.

"Any of the guests ever ask you to hold their keys for them?"

"A few, but not many. Most like being able to come and go anytime they like. Don't want to have to swing by the desk and show identification."

"Who has the extra master passkeys?"

"What do you mean 'the extra masters'? There are no—"

I grasped Andrew Miller firmly by his elbow and dragged him out from behind the desk and over to a couple of rocking chairs around a low table in the lobby. I wanted to ask him hard questions and hear some private answers.

He didn't like it. Neither my hard hand on his arm or me dragging him around inside his own lobby. "What the—!"

"Sit down, Andrew, and talk sense to me. I've got a couple of items for you. Item one, I saw the crime scene photos this morning. They're enough to peel your eyelids back. Benjamin Loftis can pretend all he wants to that what happened in 341 is no big deal, nothing to interrupt business as usual, but you and I know that girl matters. She will haunt this place until her killer gets his. Item two, you and I also know that there's got to be more master keys to an operation this large than the eight that get hung up in that little cabinet of yours. Who else has them?"

"Like I said, just housekeeping." He shrugged. "Plus, the head housekeeper for the third floor can only access that floor. None of the others."

"I'll talk to her. Who else?"

"Nobody. Nobody else."

I resisted the urge to slap him. Once hard across the jaw just to wipe that self-satisfied smirk off his face. "Andrew, damn it. Listen to me. When those keys were made, there had to be more than what you just showed me. What happens when you drop one, lose one, break one off in a lock? Look at me, Andrew. Where do you go for a replacement key?"

"You'll have to ask Mr. Loftis that question."

"Loftis, the paragon of virtue?"

"Yes."

CHAPTER ELEVEN

I TOOK A NAP THAT AFTERNOON.

I'd only been there one day, but the mystery of Rosie Caldwell's death was taking on a harsh sense of urgency, almost as if she were crying out to me. As if the walls themselves were whispering her name. And not just her name, but the things that had been said between her and her killer inside that room just across the way, the words grunted, groaned, and whispered just before and after he shot her.

So why stop to sleep when it felt as if everything was accelerating around me, the air vibrant with her loss? Because sometimes you have to go slow in order to go fast. And sometimes, you have to give your own mind time to work. To compare, sort, reconcile. Everything I'd seen and heard suggested that Sheriff Mitch and his cronies were going about this from the wrong direction. Whoever they had salted away in the cells at the courthouse were just as much victims of circumstance as the dead girl herself, and if Mitch managed to wring something like a confession out of one of them or place him near the Palm Court that night, then that "suspect" could end up just as dead as the Caldwell girl. The electric chair did that to you.

I'd find out over the next few days from Brody Mitchell who they had in custody, maybe even convince him to let me see one or both of them when Mitch went home for lunch. I couldn't shake the feeling that the sheriff's answer was the convenient one, not the real one.

Did Loftis care if the man Mitch offered up as the murderer had actually been in room 341 that night? No reason why he should. Even though he'd told Prince and me in Hot Springs that he wanted *the* murderer, not *a* murderer, the more time that went by, the more he must want to see the whole mess go away as far as the public was concerned. Particularly the tourist part of the public.

All this and I decided to take a nap?

I knew how my own mind worked, and it was already stuffed with sights, smells, sounds, and impressions of all kinds, and sleep let it search for what wove through it all, what webbed it together.

So I stripped down, took a hot bath to wash off the grime from my visit to the sheriff's department and to ease the soreness from Mitch's sucker punch. Soaked tired limbs while I tried to let my mind go blank. And just when the water started to cool, I got out, toweled off, and crawled between the sheets. Let all consciousness go.

I DOVE DEEP AFTER A FEW RESTLESS MOMENTS, BUT IF I dreamed, I don't remember it. When I woke an hour or so later, it was as if I swam lazily up from some midnight pool. As if I shed the vestiges of sleep ever so slowly, my whole body relaxed and my mind refreshed. In fact, when awareness first returned, I thought I was in my own bed at Rutland in Hot Springs, and I was listening for Luke to come romping into the room carrying morning in his chubby arms.

Then the fact that I was naked and the sheets crisp and freshly laundered reminded me of something else. Or rather somewhere else. It occurred to me that I wasn't home—as much as I might have wished it—but rather I was somewhere vaguely threatening. A moment later I realized I was in my room in Grove's inn, beneath all that granite and the even heavier weight of one dead girl.

When I finally opened my eyes and looked slowly around room 340, I had one clear, obvious thought. Sitting only a few feet away there yesterday, Andrew Miller had said that there had been a reception earlier in the evening Rosie Caldwell was killed so that none of the Palm Court rooms were rented for the night.

I thought the words and then said them aloud.

"Who was at that reception?"

I pushed myself up to sit on the edge of the bed, still drifty with sleep. Was she at the reception somehow? Rosie Caldwell?

I shook my head roughly and stood up. If she was, what the hell was she doing there? Who was she with?

I stepped over to the chest of drawers. Clean underwear and socks. A clean shirt from the wire hanger in the chifforobe.

And if she wasn't at the reception, then what was she doing at the inn? How did she even get here?

Nothing I had read, nothing I had seen or heard suggested that anybody was asking these questions, or if they'd asked, nobody was sharing the answers. And strangely enough—like who had a key to the room—they were the most basic questions of all.

I WAS STILL BEMUSED BY THESE SAME THOUGHTS WHEN I nodded to the maître d' and made my way over to the table where I'd sat at dinner the night before. Still muttering to myself about receptions and keys when Michael materialized at my side with his enigmatic smile.

When he started to hand me a menu, I shook my head. "I trust you more than that paper," I said. "What do you recommend? Or better yet, if you ate in the kitchen tonight, what did you have?"

He stared down at me for a moment. "I shall return momentarily," he said, spun on his heel, and slipped away.

I chuckled to myself. Michael spoke a more refined English than I did, unless I was mocking someone. Plus he came and went with so little fanfare that it was . . . what? Masterful? I wondered what he knew about receptions and keys.

Then he was back, with a basket of the same wheat rolls as the previous evening, the same pats of butter. The same small coffee pot, but when I touched the side, it was hot, not cold as I had hoped.

"Really coffee?" I asked.

He nodded. "Sadly, yes," he muttered.

I patted the jacket pocket where I carried my flask. "I'll doctor it a bit when no one's looking."

He smiled in response and nodded ever so slightly. Then, "What do you think about grilled onions in brown gravy over a thick pork chop?"

My stomach lurched at the way he described it. "Just the thought of it makes my mouth water."

Again, the smile. "A few of us had that this evening before the restaurant opened. I grilled the chops myself. There is one left, sitting in the pan."

"Not on the menu." It was a statement more than a question.

"Of course not," he muttered. "And it would be best if—"

"I didn't mention it to anyone."

"Just so."

"Lay on, Macduff, and damned be he who spares the gravy."

He chuckled as he turned away, and I got the distinct impression he recognized the line from *Macbeth*.

I poured a cup of coffee and added a splash of white liquor from the flask when no one was looking my way. The wheat rolls and butter were again delicious, aided no doubt by the anticipation of the chop and gravy. I stared out the window at the far mountains in the west, blue silhouettes against the orange and pink light cast by the setting sun.

One-half of my waking mind was taken up by food and drink, the taste of the bread with the salty, sweet butter. The sip of hot coffee with just enough tang from the liquor. The other half was back again to the questions that had emerged from my afternoon nap. What reception? Was she there? Was he there, the killer? All these thoughts swam together such that my tongue seemed to simultaneously taste the simple food and shape the harsh words.

I was still lost in this twin reverie when Michael reappeared with plate in hand. He smiled when he set it down in front of me. The smell alone of the gravy and onions was so potent that I could feel my stomach respond. "Good God, Michael," I muttered.

"That is the response I was hoping for, sir."

"Not sir. Call me Stephen. Which I think I said last night."

The bare, ironic twitch of his smile. "Yes, sir . . . Stephen."

"Can I ask you a question, Michael?"

"You may. But eat first, while it's hot. I'll be back around."

He was right, of course. He'd rescued the pork chop out of the cooling skillet, and somebody in the kitchen had probably heated the thick gravy back to bubbling so he could bring the plate out hot. It needed to be eaten.

I complied. Bite by glorious bite. The chop and gravy, the coffee and shine, the reception and the dead girl. Pairs of matched and mismatched impressions, tastes and textures, flowed back and forth inside me, but first and foremost was the food, warm and sustaining. I hadn't known how hungry I was until I tucked in, and the pleasure lasted right up until the last bite, when I used the remainder of a roll to sop up the last of the gravy.

When Michael came back around this time, he nodded at my plate. "Yes?" he rumbled in that baritone of his.

"Yes," I said. "I'm going to start coming around earlier, so I can just eat in the kitchen."

He nodded slightly at the window just beside my right elbow. "The view is not so fine from the kitchen," he said quietly.

"I understand." Equally quiet. "But the food is a hell of a lot better."

"What did you wish to ask me, Stephen?"

"I'm not here to rest and recuperate," I began. "I'm here to find out what happened to Rosalind Caldwell—"

"I know who you are," he interrupted me. He looked up from clearing the table to glance around the dining room. "And I know why you're here." He nodded toward one of the other waiters. "We all do."

I smiled and, following his lead, nodded.

"There was a reception in the Palm Court the night she was killed. What can you tell me about it?"

His eyes searched my face briefly, and then he turned on his heel and walked away, carrying my plate and used silver. Weaving his way through the other tables back toward the kitchen.

"Damn," I muttered to myself. Had I pushed him too far? Asked him a question that he couldn't or wouldn't answer?

At that moment, the man from the previous evening was ushered to the window table just in front of me. The man, but not the woman who'd smiled and shrugged while he'd ignored her for his newspaper. This time he sat facing me, in the chair she'd occupied the night before. And just as before, he gave a curt nod to the maître d', brought out his sheaf of newsprint, refolded it to the section he wanted, and began to read.

When Michael came to his table a few minutes later, the man looked up only long enough to shake his head at the menu still in Michael's hand and spoke gruffly, as if he were clearing his throat. "Chicken." That's all, one word. Michael didn't even glance in my direction, but I could have read his mind.

I poured out half a cup of coffee, and since the whole place had filled up while I was sitting there, busy and even loud, I could again add a quick splash from the flask to give the coffee some bite. There was something about the damn reception, I figured, that had turned Michael cold. Something that mattered.

But then he was back, with a round tray in his hand. From the tray, he placed a glass of iced tea on the table of the newspaper-reading man. And then turned to me. He didn't smile—the formality was back—but he did pause to put a dessert plate carefully down in front of me. A large slice of chocolate cake with chocolate icing. "May I warm your coffee, sir?" He was performing, back to acting out his role as the perfect waiter.

I nodded. Still balancing the tray, he topped off my cup from the pot on the table. And then, ever so quickly and without changing his solemn expression, winked.

The cake, of course, was delicious. Sinfully so. And when, after finishing it, I pushed the plate away, there was a folded piece of paper beneath it. Which I slipped into my pocket for later.

"Later" in this case meaning that I read the note while standing by one of the lamps in the lobby. *I get off at nine. If you have questions, meet me outside the bowling alley in the basement shortly after. We can find a place to speak that is not so public. Michael Joyner*

CHAPTER TWELVE

I HAD AVOIDED THE LOBBY EARLIER BECAUSE OF THE TIDES of people that seemed to flow in and out, the movement and noise. But this time around, I glanced at my watch after reading Michael's note to discover that it was only seven thirty or thereabouts. The cavernous place was quiet, except for a few subdued couples or small groups seated here and there, a few in rocking chairs before one of the fires.

There was a stack of newspapers at the registration desk, so I swung by and picked up the evening edition of the Asheville newspaper, the *Times*. Found a spot under one of the lamps where a group of deep, comfortable chairs had been situated around a coffee table. My back was to the fireplace at that end of the lobby so that I could watch much of the room while pretending to read.

The newspaper itself wasn't that interesting—repeated most of the same blather about our brave sheriff and his suspects in custody—but the room itself was fascinating. Dusk came early inside what the brochures insisted on calling the Great Hall. The ceiling floated high above with brass light fixtures hanging on long chains, providing something like a golden cloud of light fifteen feet overhead. Below on the flagstone floor, those expensive French rugs muffled the sound of stray footsteps. The pervasive darkness swallowed up what light there was except for islands of yellow lamplight that illuminated groups of comfortable Roycroft chairs, occasionally a small sofa. Here and there a murmur of conversation that almost seemed to float in the air as well, like a thin gossamer of cigarette smoke.

It was calm, it was quiet, and it was more than a little spooky. I rustled my *Asheville Times* just to make some noise, just to see if all motion inside the place would cease entirely in reaction to the crackle of real life. Nothing changed. I thought I could hear a fly buzzing. It was that . . . restful.

All that and then she showed up.

When I'd seen her the evening before at dinner, she'd quite obviously been with the man at the next table, the well-dressed, well-to-do gent obsessed with his newspaper.

But now she was alone. Well and stylishly dressed, she sported a kelly green hat that somehow accented her bobbed brown hair and a beaded purse over her shoulder that matched her darker green dress. She didn't stand out in the lobby at all unless you really paid attention to her posture and her face. Even though her movements were subdued, she managed to make the dress whisper something new and interesting. Her face was intent and watchful until . . .

She noticed me, and then that sly, ironic smile lifted the corners of her mouth. I supposed that, just as the evening before, that smile was all she had for me, but I was wrong. She wove through the clusters of chairs and lamps and presented herself in front of my coffee table. "Mind if I join you?" she asked. "I'm waiting for someone."

I nodded at the chair beside mine. "Please," I said. "And in case you're wondering, he's in the dining room reading his paper."

She laughed, and it was the oddest sound. Something like faraway chimes in the wind.

Those lobby chairs were low, but she managed to fall gracefully into the one beside me as if she were water flowing, and the pool of lamplight around us was suddenly warmer, brighter.

"You probably mean Frank," she said, "memorizing his *Wall Street Journal.* That was last night. Definitely not who I'm meeting tonight." And then after a pause, "What's your name, by the way? I admire the way you devour your food."

"Stephen Robbins. Yours?"

"I'm Ella Loving." She leaned forward and offered her right hand to shake, almost as a man would. When I took it, her palm was warm and dry, and she left it in my hand for perhaps two heartbeats longer than was absolutely necessary.

"I've heard of you, Ella Loving."

Her eyebrows went up. "Oh, indeed? What have you heard?"

"Elevator operator I chatted with the other day was telling me who was the most famous person he'd ever hauled up and down, the drunkest, the . . . sexiest, and your name came up."

She pursed her lips and tipped her head slightly to one side. "Which was I?"

"Not the drunkest."

"And not famous. If that, I might come to the attention of your Mr. Loftis."

"Loftis doesn't belong to me. And I sure as hell don't belong to him. Even though I work for him."

She stared more intently into my face for a long moment, long enough for me to notice on close examination just how pale was her skin and how dark her eyes. "Let me guess," she said. "You're the new house detective?"

"God, no. Not that. Although I am looking into something."

"The Caldwell girl?"

I nodded.

"So you're an independent operative?"

"Something like that. And you're the sexiest item ever to grace the south elevator."

Again, the sound of chimes or faraway bells. When she put

her head back to laugh, she exposed her throat, long and white, which was maybe why she laughed in the first place.

"So, what have you managed to find out?" she asked. "About the murder, I mean."

Normally, a question that direct from someone I didn't really know would have set off an alarm for me, but this exchange seemed natural, as if I already did know her after just a few minutes of eye contact and a bit of banter.

"I've found out just how much I don't know," I admitted. "And I have a lot of questions that no one but me seems to be asking."

For a moment, her face grew still—which seemed unusual for her—and her gaze almost pensive. "Such as . . . ?"

"Such as there was a reception in the Palm Court the night she was killed, so none of the rooms surrounding the court were rented out to guests. Then, five or six hours later, she dies in one of those empty rooms. But nobody seems to think that the two events are related."

"Except you?"

"Except me."

She smiled. "I was at that reception. Am I a suspect?"

"Not unless you were naked in room 341 after midnight."

Her smile grew bigger.

"And not unless you carry a sweet little pistol in that purse slung over your shoulder."

She shrugged. "No to room 341 and no to the pistol, although I sometimes think a little protection might not be a bad idea."

"Then you're not a suspect. But you can tell me about the reception."

She paused to consider. "I was only there for a few minutes, walking through with a companion, but it was big."

"Big as in lots of people?"

"Sure. Fifty or sixty maybe, but more than that, it was the kind of people who were there. Loftis was working the room. Hotel staff serving from platters. I saw a couple of judges, lots of lawyers. The kind of men you see in the newspaper doing this or giving that. The women were mostly country club wives decked out in their best jewelry and tottering around on their heels. Must have been some booze somewhere, maybe in the punch, because it was loud."

"You weren't tempted to stay?"

She shook her head and smiled. "My companion was from out of town, and we weren't invited. And with that kind of party, if you aren't invited . . ." She shrugged her shoulders.

At that moment, the tall, pretty man Loftis had introduced me to several evenings before made yet another appearance in the lobby, coming in from the parking lot, this time with a woman. He was dressed in another fine suit of clothes and laughing at something one of them had said. She was almost as tall as he and wearing a pale yellow dress that matched her hair. They paused for a moment beside one of the pillars that supported the ceiling, perhaps twenty feet from where Ella Loving and I were sitting.

For a suspended moment, it was as if we were watching something staged. She pirouetted, and he helped her off with her wrap and draped it over his arm. She smiled a shy but sweet smile, and he nodded, almost primly. Then he took her arm in a gesture that might have been protective, paternal, and they both paused to glance around the room as if checking for approval from an audience.

I was trying to recall his name—something other than "pretty boy"—when his gaze settled on me, and he nodded before turning his head to say something to the woman. With that, he led her in our direction, still with the firm grip on her elbow. It took them a moment, because they had to weave their way through the lobby furniture, but then there they were, and he flipped the switch on his smile. I climbed up out of my chair, as did Ella. I stuck out my hand, and he gripped it with enough force to hurt. Luckily, I remembered that trick from before and was ready for him.

"Mr. Robbins, I believe, an associate of Benjamin Loftis's. Am I right?"

"Stephen Robbins. And this is my friend, Miss Loving." Ella also extended her hand but, for some reason, kept her head down and didn't make eye contact, seemingly shy.

"Delighted, delighted. I'm Madison Aycock, and this is my fiancée, Beatrice Avery. We're on our way to a program at First Presbyterian tonight, and I convinced Beatrice to stop by for dinner first." He glanced with evident admiration at Beatrice, who was, if anything, even more . . . something. Nordic maybe. She was smiling faithfully at Ella and me, as if she had to endure this kind of chatter constantly but couldn't think of a thing to say. She was wearing an unusually large cross on a gold chain around her neck, and I glanced down at her hands, almost expecting a Bible.

"Beatrice's father is the minister at First Presbyterian"—Madison again—"and one of the finest speakers I've ever heard. If that man had become an attorney . . ."

"Daddy always says he's a lawyer for God," Beatrice finally spoke. Her tone was quiet but certain. Very certain. Beside me, I heard Ella Loving stifle a laugh.

"Would the two of you care to join us?" Madison asked. "We're just going into the dining room now."

"I've already eaten," I was able to say truthfully, "and Miss Loving is otherwise engaged."

"Well then, another time, another time." A second handshake, manly and firm.

"Have a blessed evening." This from Beatrice Avery. And they were gone—just as graceful, just as gleaming as when they first appeared.

"Christ," I muttered, "what was that?" This time, Ella Loving laughed outright.

We were still standing, staring after the two of them, when Ella reached out and touched my elbow. "I see my date for the evening," she said and nodded toward a gray-haired distinguished man, who was standing on the far side of the lobby. He was looking about, probably for her.

"Have a good time," I whispered.

She smiled enigmatically. "Something you should know," she replied, "before I go. That pretty little couple that just went into the dining room, Aycock and his girl . . ."

I nodded.

"They were at that reception you were asking about."

CHAPTER THIRTEEN

THAT NIGHT, I DISCOVERED THAT THE BASEMENT OF Grove's inn contained both a bowling alley and a swimming pool, as well as dressing cubicles outside the swimming pool—separate for men and women, of course—and one or two rooms designed for billiards or cards. It was dark down below. *Subterranean* was the word that came to mind, with many of the walls made of undressed stone and no windows anywhere.

I spent the hour or so before nine o'clock wandering around, sticking my head in this room or that, trying to figure out the lay of the land downstairs, beneath the showboat lobby and the other rooms on the first floor. Twice, inn employees stopped to ask me if I was a guest, and I answered by producing the key to my room, which satisfied them. Apparently, the recreation facilities downstairs were off limits to local people who came in for dinner or some other function.

There was a cluster of chairs outside the bowling alley entrance, and I stationed myself there a few minutes before nine, opened up the newspaper I had been carrying around with me and pretended to read. I had the creeping impression that I was being watched, even though that section of the basement was deserted. I could hear the clack of billiard balls down the hall, but that was it.

At a quarter past, my friend Michael appeared. He nodded at me, glanced around as if to be certain we were alone and, without speaking, gestured for me to follow him. A few minutes later, we found a large storage room roughly halfway between the swimming pool and the bowling alley that contained piles of linens on shelves and a couple of beat-up chairs. Once the hallway door was firmly shut behind us, this seemed to satisfy Michael, and he gestured to the chairs.

"Why are we hiding out?" I asked him as we sat down. "I'm a guest, and you're an employee."

Michael grunted as he sat down; I figured he'd been on his feet for hours. After settling into his chair, he replied. "In case you haven't noticed, employees don't talk to guests. Not outside their official service capacity."

"One of Loftis's rules?"

He nodded. "One of Loftis's rules, and it applies especially when the employee is a Negro."

"What difference does that make?"

Michael chuckled. "What planet that circles the sun do you hail from? It makes all the difference in the world. Most of the white people who stay here are wealthy, privileged. Most are not from here, even if they are from the South. And Mr. Benjamin Loftis figures that it would make them . . . *uncomfortable* to be addressed by someone who looks like me."

"The hell with that. Your English is much finer than mine."

He held up his hand, his *brown* hand. "It doesn't matter how I speak if my lips are black. You know that."

I shook my head roughly, then got up and fetched two crockery cups from an open box on one of the shelves. Handed one of the mugs to Michael and sat the other down on the arm of my chair. Then poured an inch or so of liquor from my flask into each. "Something strong to sip on," I said. "Made up where I'm from in Madison County."

"If it's against the rules for me to talk to you, can you imagine how bad it is for me to drink with you?" Michael asked with a smile, before taking a sip from his mug.

"Here's to breaking the rules, then," I said, and raised my cup to him.

"Without getting caught," he added in that deep rumble of a voice.

We both sipped—all you could do with straight liquor that was at least 100 proof. There was a pause while we each savored the sip, Michael likely tired after working a long shift being ignored or talked down to by most of the people he waited on.

"What would you like to know, Stephen?" he said finally.

"I'd like to know what the people who work in this place say about the Caldwell girl. Not when they're talking to the sheriff's deputies or the reporters or the managers. But when they're talking amongst themselves."

"I thought you just wanted to know about the reception that night."

"I do, but not just that. I want to know everything folded up and wrapped around that night. What was she doing here? Was she at the reception? How did she end up in that room? Why didn't she walk out alive?"

He took another sip, which I figured gave him a long moment to consider. "You know, this isn't too shabby," he said quietly, holding up his cup, "considering it was made by some cracker in a barn." Which gave him a longer moment before answering.

I smiled at *cracker in a barn* but didn't reply. Let him take his time.

Another sip, and while he held the liquor on his tongue, he nodded to himself, apparently making up some part of his mind. "I served at that reception, as I have at others like it. And I also recruited several of my colleagues from the waitstaff to work with me. When Loftis throws a party for his rich friends, he likes to turn the place out just so, and part of that is . . ."

"Elegant, refined Negro waiters?"

He nodded. "It's part of the effect, I imagine. Heightens the sense that the guests are special, set apart and set above. That night, the soiree was for Madison Aycock, the lawyer they have lined up to run for governor in two years. His father, the judge, was the host along with Mr. Loftis, and they were clear about the fact that at the end of the evening, everyone there was to contribute to the campaign. There was a crystal bowl on a table in the middle of the Palm Court, and you were expected to drop either a check or cash into the bowl during the evening."

"Who were the checks made out to?"

Michael shrugged. "The judge, I would imagine, but it was clear that the money was intended for the campaign. To send the boy around the state, stage interviews with all the major newspapers, and so on."

"I get the picture," I said. "Was Rosalind Caldwell at the reception?"

Another sip, another pause. "At some events here at the inn, like that one, there are a few young women present whose role is, let us say, decorative. They are not paid, at least so far as I know, but they help to keep the single men or the men who are present without their wives interested and entertained. Nothing illegal or untoward. They sip the punch, laugh at the jokes, smile, and circulate. My impression is that the Caldwell girl was there in that role."

"By herself?"

"No, there were a couple of other girls there as well. They were young and presentable, but not . . ."

"Flashy."

He nodded. "Plain, not fancy."

"How in the hell did the fact that she was there escape the notice of the sheriff's department, the newspapers, the management of this joint, and the entire rest of the world? It's ridiculous!"

"You don't believe me?"

"Of course, I believe you. But it's a highly publicized murder, and nobody—not even the reporters from out of town—seems to have noticed she was right there in the Palm Court three or four hours before she was murdered. Wait, you said nothing illegal or untoward. Does that mean that she and the other girls weren't for hire?"

"Keep your voice down, Stephen. And yes, that means that they weren't there to . . . perform after the party. At least I don't think so."

"Maybe. And maybe she was smitten by all the glamour and money and volunteered for overtime. But that still doesn't explain why nobody seems to be aware that she was there. The local newspaper can't go to press without ranting and raving about the murder."

"You're not that simple, Stephen. Think about it. First of all, the *Asheville Citizen-Times* is the local *white* newspaper. There are other newspapers out there saying something different. And second, there's not a single solitary soul who was either a host or a guest at that little reception who wants their name associated with that girl's death."

"Including Loftis."

Michael paused to turn up his cup and drain the last drop of liquor. "That's a hard one. I suspect that Mr. Loftis is torn between wanting this whole thing to go away and wanting it to go away without the inn's name being mentioned in any sort of negative way at a trial."

"And the others who were there, this Judge Aycock and the pretty boy barrister, his son, sure as hell don't want to be called as witnesses in a murder trial. Not while the golden boy is cranking up to run for governor."

Michael nodded. "Again, think about it. The people who were here that night were here because they had influence or money or both. None of them want to be dragged into this even if they know something. And one more thing . . ."

"The girls?"

He smiled. "Maybe you're not so simple after all. You think Mr. Loftis or anybody else involved wants it known that they make a habit of having some young local women in circulation during a private reception at the vaunted Grove Park Inn?"

"Even if they're only there for, what did you call it, decoration."

"That's right."

"Who finds the girls? Somebody has to spread the word around, make sure they're the right type, get them past the front desk, tell them how to act. Loftis?"

"Lord, no. Not his style at all." Michael paused to consider. "Just a guess, mind you, but maybe the evening manager."

CHAPTER FOURTEEN

I DIDN'T TRY TO TRACK DOWN THE EVENING MANAGER that same night. I wanted time to think through things first and figure out just how to work it, so that I got some semblance of truth out of him. Instead, I got five or six hours of sleep and began again on keys. Maids and keys . . .

Benjamin Loftis had insisted that the Grove Park Inn maids be available to the guests after six each morning but that they sit quietly—and I mean quietly—in the hallways, spread evenly along the rows of rooms where they could be summoned by any who needed them. They weren't to actually go to work cleaning the hallways and the rooms until nine, when they could begin to move about without fear of waking the guests. For all intents and purposes, they were like servants in some grand house, patiently waiting to fetch a cup of coffee or clean up a spill—obedient, efficient, and, above all, quiet.

I was able to see them all—the maids, I mean, white and Black, light skinned and dark—nod and smile at them as I strolled up and down the next morning. Because my shoes squeaked when I walked, more than one raised her eyebrows at me and a few shushed me outright. I stopped to chat up one middle-aged woman seated in the Palm Court. She looked bored out of her immortal soul with the sitting and waiting and was glad to step out into the stairwell in response to a crooked finger.

"Yes, sir?" she whispered in a definite mountain twang, not a lot different from my own.

"Do they pay you just to sit there?" I whispered because she was whispering.

She nodded. "Ain't it something? First time I ever got paid to do nothing in my entire life."

"How often does someone summon you?"

"Summon . . . ?"

"Call you into a room."

"Every so often. Maybe once a morning. Clean up something. Run fetch some water or coffee. Bring the newspaper."

"Anybody ever get fresh with you?"

"You mean, like the men?"

I nodded.

"No, we're supposed to leave the door open if we go in the room. Oh, I've had an old gent or two pat my bottom, but I got enough bottom to handle it. Now, some of them young gals . . ." She nodded back down the third-floor hall at several other maids and grinned. "I can't speak for them." She chuckled, and I followed suit.

"Who has the master key?"

"Hmm?"

"When you get ready to start cleaning rooms at nine, who carries the master key?"

"Head maid on each floor goes down to the desk and fetches it. But they won't give her the key until straight-up nine o'clock, and she has to turn it in again when we go home at noon. Ask Mildred, she'll tell you." She paused to point toward the far end of the third-floor hall, apparently to Mildred. "They's tight as a rooster's tail about them keys."

Mildred confirmed what my friend had said. "Nine on the nose by that big clock in the lobby, and even then, the keys have to be signed in and out like you was borrowing money at the bank."

So I learned . . . not much, except that Loftis ran a tight ship and that he liked his employees to be seen and not heard. Not unlike what Michael had said the night before.

After some scrambled eggs and several cups of coffee in the dining room, I went by the front desk and discovered that Brody Mitchell was good to his word. He'd phoned to say that he'd arranged for me to see Rosalind Caldwell's clothes and the sheets from the bed, but I needed to get there that afternoon, while brother Mitch was out of the office.

EARLY AFTERNOON. BRODY MITCHELL TOOK ME DEEPER into the first floor of the courthouse, past his own small office and the meeting room where he'd shared the case file. Down a maze of hallways to what looked like an interrogation room, at least the scarred table and rickety chairs suggested the sort of physical give-and-take you don't want to witness. He threw the deadbolt on the hallway door behind us and gestured at two cardboard cartons, one large and one small. They'd been taped shut, and somebody had written "CALDWELL, Evidence" on each in smeared black ink.

I pointed to the tape. Brody nodded and, using my pocketknife, I carefully slit the tape such that it could be put back neatly, with little suggestion that it had been opened. By chance, I chose the large box first, and it contained the sheets from the bed. I lifted them out slowly, and then, while Brody leaned against the wall and watched, his eye glittering, I laid them out as if the table were a bed: first the fitted sheet, then the top sheet pulled back as in the crime scene photo, the two pillowcases—one at the top of the table and the other on the floor—and finally, in the bottom of the box, the fancy GPI bedspread.

I recalled from what Andrew Miller had said, plus the photos, that the bedspread had been thrown completely off the bed and was strewn in a heap on the floor against the far wall. I left it in the box and set the box itself on the far side of the interrogation table to represent where it was found.

I leaned against the wall beside Brody and nodded at the sheets and pillowcases where I'd spread them out, mimicking the bed in 341. "What do you see?" I asked him.

He dug a box of Camels out of an inside jacket pocket and offered me one. I shook my head, and he lit up, using a kitchen match he struck effortlessly with his thumbnail. He blinked through the smoke and pointed with the cigarette. "I see two people who came in hot and bothered. Somebody, probably him, threw the bedspread off to get it out of the way. They're necking and pecking and groping, maybe standing beside the bed, and then they take a breather to take their clothes off."

"She took hers off and he took his off?"

He nodded as he took another drag on the Camel.

"How do you know?"

"Her clothes, except for her slip and panties, were laid out prim and proper on the chair by the head of the bed, bathroom side. They weren't thrown on the floor or tossed over a lampshade."

"And you figure his clothes were on the other chair? Near the window, where later he went for his pistol?"

Again, the smoke and the nod.

I shrugged. "Makes sense. So they reconvene after stripping and lie down on the bed. Maybe still in their underwear, maybe not. There's some thrashing around, heavy petting. They're both naked by now. He's even between her legs . . ."

"Bruised and abraded."

"Right. Her thighs were bruised and abraded. And then . . . no penetration. Why? What stopped them?"

Brody pushed off from leaning against the wall and stepped forward to stand by the table. I knew that in his imagination, he was staring down at the bed. That night, there, in the room. Trying to see Rosie Caldwell and the man.

"She didn't change her mind?" I whispered to his back.

He shook his head roughly. "Hell no," he muttered. "There wasn't a mark on her face or her neck, no bruises on her arms. No rough stuff. There was nothing under her fingernails. She didn't fight him off . . . Nothing to say she stopped it."

"Then he stopped it. Had a sudden crisis of conscience. Lost his nerve."

Brody turned his back on the table and stared at me. "Conscience! You really think that?"

"No," I admitted. "Not likely." I met his gaze. "Son of a bitch couldn't get it up. Flag at half-mast."

He nodded and sighed. "That's what I think too."

"And that's why he shot her?"

Brody shrugged. Then sighed. "It makes some kind of twisted sense, don't it?"

I opened the second smaller cardboard box and took out Rosalind Caldwell's clothes, piece by piece. Whoever had placed them in the box had folded them carefully, even neatly, which caused me to wonder briefly if Brody himself had been the one to place them there. Most of the other deputies I'd seen didn't seem capable of such delicacy.

I steeled myself and then laid the slip and panties on the cold concrete floor beside the table, more or less where they would have been according to the photos. Clutched in her left hand above her head. The bottom of the slip was stiff with crusted blood. Stepped over them to lay the thin blouse on a wooden chair approximately where Rosie Caldwell had left her clothes in the hotel room. I held up the skirt for Brody's direction.

"Folded and on the chair," he muttered. I placed the skirt.

"Bra?" I asked.

"No bra. She probably wasn't wearing one."

"Shoes?" There were no shoes in the box, but I figured I'd ask. She had to have been wearing shoes.

"One was under the bed and the other was by the bathroom door, as if she kicked them off when they came into the room."

"Having fun," I said. "Being playful."

He nodded and crushed out his cigarette butt against the bottom of his shoe, looked around for an ashtray, and, when he didn't see one, dropped it on the floor beside the door. The room suddenly turned hot, as if the air itself was thick, and I imagined Brody felt it too. "What do you think?" he whispered more than said. "Now that you've seen . . . ?" He waved his arm to indicate the sheets, the underthings, the clothes.

"I think she was poor," I said. "Her skirt, her blouse could have been bought off the sale rack at any cheap haberdashery. Hard to tell about the slip now, but her panties are plain white cotton, worn thin enough to read through."

"You think she needed the money?"

I nodded thoughtfully. "Sure. And there's something else. She must have thought he had money. Even if he didn't offer it up front, she must have thought he looked like he could pay for it."

"You think he was a swell, a party boy?"

"I think he was a nasty son of a bitch," I said suddenly, harshly. And then after a moment, more softly, "Who looked like a swell."

"Then what in the hell was he doing with her?" Brody asked. "Rosalind Caldwell? Why was he fooling around with some poor college girl from the country instead of sticking to his own kind?"

I shrugged. "Maybe his own kind don't like to play hotel room games. Maybe his own kind don't ruffle up the bedsheets in the middle of the night."

CHAPTER FIFTEEN

I HAD THE TAXI DRIVER DROP ME OFF AT THE FOOT OF MAcon Avenue, a half-mile or so below Grove's inn. I still felt like I was breathing thick dirty air from the interrogation room, and I wanted to walk. Wear out some shoe leather and let my body relax into its more natural rhythms after the electric shock of touching the dead girl's clothes.

The thinking part of me was spinning around inside room 341, back on the night the girl died. Had she gone in there expecting to be paid? Had she done everything she knew to earn a few dollars on her back and then ended up on her back forever? Something had stung her hot and sudden, that must have felt like a whip crack or a lightning flash. Something that burned and burned inside her.

Did that bastard in the room with her suddenly and instinctively shoot her down low in her belly because it was the only way he could . . . enter her? It was a horrible thought, one I didn't want to let circulate in my brain, but there it was. There it was.

"Scream, damn it," I said suddenly, out loud. To her. "After the first shot, when you still could, why didn't you scream your damn head off?"

I looked around me. I was standing on the sidewalk, partway up the broad thoroughfare of Macon Avenue, talking to myself. Or rather talking to a dead woman who couldn't hear a word I said. On the other side of the street, two children playing in their yard had stopped to stare at me. I smiled and nodded to reassure them, but I must have looked ghastly, my face contorted.

What kind of world contains a sister and brother across the street wearing silly hats and playing games of their own making . . . held up against the reality of that bloodstained slip and those worn-out cotton panties? What kind of animal is our kind when we feature play in a safe haven versus play that ends with two bullets and a blood-soaked twenty-dollar bill tossed down with contempt?

I made myself start walking again, even as I was choking over these questions. The sounds and images of those children led me to think of Luke, whose young and happy imagination could create a playhouse out of four tobacco stakes and a worn-out quilt. Whose faith and trust in those he loved was unstained, untroubled. How to protect him? How to keep him?

The clash of images also made me think of Anna Ulmann, the woman I'd found and loved, the woman who'd resurrected me from my own despair before we lost our way in New York.

It seemed to me then and there, as I wandered my way up that steep street in Asheville, North Carolina, that so much of human existence was as fragile as an eggshell, as tenuous as a spiderweb. And that what we did to each other was the worst of all. The hatred and the jealousy, the grasping and ambition—all of which led to such a tragic, foolish squandering of the scarce time we had.

I had thought because of my earlier dreams that the ghost of Anna had somehow found me in this bloodstained, wind-blasted Asheville, trying to warn me, perhaps even to save me. And I wanted her. But not here, where lamps flickered beside midnight hotel beds and bullets carved their way into flesh. God no, not here.

But rather at home. Our home in Hot Springs where we'd met and, in the old ways, came to love and trust each other. Me to save her from her barren, broken life and—God knows—her to save me. How we talked then, about any and everything. How we yearned for and sought each other. How we understood each other in the morning, the evening, the night. We'd even survived the shooting of Roy Robbins and the murder trial that followed. We'd even lived together past the loss of our baby girl, miscarried before I knew she existed.

Could we not go back there? Could we not return to what we were in Hot Springs years before, when we aided and abetted and loved one another? Could we . . . ?

But despite the sudden, fierce flicker of my desire for her to return, she was not there beside me on that empty street. Not even her ghost was present in the slant sunlight. Anna was hundreds of miles away, and I could only see her with my imagination, reach out to her with unreal hands. What was real was waiting for me. The massive stone structure of the inn and somewhere, lurking, the man who had shot Rosalind Caldwell when he couldn't have what he wanted.

CHAPTER SIXTEEN

THE EVENING MANAGER OF GROVE'S INN WAS NAMED Stoneman, Conrad Stoneman. According to the young guy at the registration desk, his shift ended at twelve, when the night manager came on duty. I figured I'd catch Mr. Stoneman late, an hour or so before midnight, when the whole place would be quiet and there would be time for some honest give and take.

"Call me Connie" was almost the first thing he said. "It's what my father called me, and I honor his memory."

Connie looked more like a hotel dick or a railroad tough guy than the evening representative for a classy place like the Grove Park Inn. He was my age or older, and while his nice suit seemed to fit him well enough, he'd discarded the jacket long before eleven o'clock and looked like he'd love nothing better than to kick off the dress shoes and prop his feet on the desk.

I showed him my letter from Loftis. He must have skipped to the last sentence because he tossed it back across the desk in record time. "You want to know about the Caldwell girl, then." It wasn't a question. "Double-check behind Mitchell and that crowd of deputies."

"Sure," I said and helped myself to the chair opposite him, the same chair I'd sat in to nag Andrew Miller during daylight hours. "I want to know what she was doing at the reception earlier that night in the Palm Court and why in the world she was still there hours later."

"You want to know a lot," he offered in a gravelly voice. "I can tell you why she was there, but why she didn't leave with the other girls, I got no idea."

If Andrew Miller looked and sounded like a junior version of Benjamin Loftis, this guy, Connie Stoneman, was cut from a different bolt of cloth. More street smarts, maybe more of a straight shooter.

"Why was she there, Connie?"

"She was there 'cause I asked her to be there. Her and two other gals from out at Weaver College. I got a contact with a woman teaches out there, and she'll send over three or four coeds for a party whenever we need 'em. You know what a coed is?"

"A woman student?" I was guessing.

He nodded. "Nothing hot and nothing fancy. Just some nice girls to keep the party lively. Especially if Loftis thinks it's likely to turn out mostly men and a few bored wives. Then he'll ask me to provide a few debutantes to dress up the place. Give it some feminine flavor." He pronounced *feminine* as if the last syllable were a number.

"Debutantes?"

"What he calls 'em. Society gals. Country club gals. But those kind a' gals ain't so easy to come by on short notice, so I call my friend out at the college, and there you are."

His voice was just a bit slurred and his grammar just a bit off, and I wondered if he had a bottle in the desk. Something strong for the long night hours. I had a feeling that if he did, Loftis would have something akin to a stroke if he knew.

"Did you pay them?"

He nodded. "A crisp ten-dollar bill and a taxi ride. I send the taxi after 'em and then pack 'em all into another taxi after the party." And then even before I could ask, he continued. "I sent the gals home that night, too, but Miss Caldwell wasn't at the front desk when she was supposed to be, and so I had to send the others on back without her."

"Surely to God, Mitch Mitchell asked you about all this."

He shook his head sadly. "Nope. Never come up. Not once. And when I asked Loftis about it, he said to 'keep my own counsel,' which I interpreted to mean . . ."

"Keep your damn mouth shut."

Stoneman grinned. "Yup. Keep it shut. Which I took to mean that he didn't want no newspaper reporters digging into the party girls. Didn't want no slur on the inn."

"So it would make sense if Rosie Caldwell thought she'd found herself a boyfriend at the reception, someone she wanted to spend a little time with or maybe meet later on? Someone who looked and acted like he had money?"

Stoneman shrugged. "Sure. If she was looking for a sugar daddy, that would have been a nice little pond to go fishing in." Then he did what I'd half been expecting all along. He leaned back to open a filing cabinet drawer behind him and came out with a small unmarked bottle of hooch and a cloudy glass. "I usually treat myself to a little snort about this time of night," he said, "once things get quiet. Care to join me? There's another glass or two on that table under the window."

There *was* another glass, a clean one, and I *did* care to join him. To keep him talking if nothing else.

After a sip of what might have been scotch, I slipped in my next question. "Were you there, Connie? At the reception, I mean?"

"I was in and out of it. Back and forth from the front desk down here and then back up to the Palm Court upstairs. Loftis wanted all the guests to feel like they was getting the red-carpet treatment, and one of my jobs was to escort some of the high and mighty up to the soiree, if you know what I mean. That and keep an eye on the money."

"The money collected for the campaign?"

"Yes, the point of this whole little get-together was to raise up some funding for the Aycock boy so he could crank up his run for governor. There was a punch bowl on a table in the middle of the Palm Court, and as the evening went along, first one and then another of the old gents made a little plea to the group and would throw in a hundred-dollar bill or a check or an IOU, that sort of thing. Well, as you can imagine, given the high and mighty that was in attendance, the cabbage in that bowl began to mount up, and one of my jobs as the evening wore on was to make sure none of it got lost."

Connie Stoneman was enjoying his might-be scotch, gulping while I was barely sipping, and he paused to pour himself another dollop. Which was fine with me: the more he drank, the looser his tongue and the more colorful his language. The thin veneer of Benjamin Loftis's civilization was wearing off the man before my very eyes.

"Surely nobody there would have dipped into the bowl," I urged him on. "They were all rich, right?"

"They were that, either rich or in"—a small hiccup—"fluential. But you're forgetting about the waiters. Them nee-gros. And the party girls. Them gals probably never seen three or four thousand dollars' worth of cash in a punch bowl before. Awful tempting, if you know what I mean."

I reached over and poured another inch or so of might-be into his cloudy glass. I was almost to the last question, the real question, and I wanted him well-lubricated when I tossed it out.

He hiccuped again and smiled at me for helping his glass. "Awful tempting," he repeated.

"What did you do with the cash at the end of the evening?" Not my last question, but I was still curious.

"I did what old Loftis instructed me to do. I raked it all into one of the canvas sacks we use to haul the inn's money to the bank, and I gave the sack to the judge."

"Madison Aycock's father, that judge?"

"Oh yeah." Another swig from his glass. "Superior Court Judge Bishop Aycock. I walked him out to his car, which was parked right by the entrance, and the old gent's driver took the judge and the sack on home."

"Who was at that reception, Connie? Is there a list somewhere?"

He opened his mouth to answer and then paused. I waited, hoping against hope that I hadn't pushed him too far or worded it the wrong way. "What?" he finally managed to mutter. "What say?"

"Who was at the reception?" I was almost whispering. "Anybody I know?"

He stared back at me, his eyes bleary, his mouth still half open. "Ain't nobody *you* know was there," he finally managed to say. "You son of a bitch. Trying to get me to talk, plying me with your damn liquor."

"Just making conversation to pass the time," I offered, trying to ease him back my way. "I was just curious."

He seemed mollified, at least a bit. Picked up his glass and was surprised to see one more sip nestled in the bottom. He sipped the sip. "Well," he offered. "I couldn't . . . shouldn't pass along that information. You'll have to ask Mr. Loftis about the guest list. His friends, not mine." He stared balefully at his empty glass and then at me. "What did you say your name was, bub? I'll pass it along."

CHAPTER SEVENTEEN

THE NEXT MORNING, I BATHED AND SHAVED CLOSE AND clean. Dressed as well as my meager wardrobe would allow and went down early for breakfast. It was time that I cornered Benjamin Loftis and had a little come-to-Jesus meeting over what was slowly emerging about Rosalind Caldwell's death.

I picked up the *Asheville Citizen* at the registration desk and carried it with me into the dining room. I asked for a couple of scrambled eggs and some toast, which I transformed into a sandwich to munch on while I guzzled coffee. I ignored the prunes that Loftis insisted be served to every guest at breakfast and lunch and glanced through the newsprint while I chewed and swallowed bites of bread and egg.

And there it was, in that black-lined box on the front page: *Sheriff Mitchell Promises Arrest in Caldwell Case Soon*. One suspect was to be released from custody, the other detained for further questioning. The second suspect was a Grove Park employee named Moore. All of that, and a photograph of our own sheriff standing on the front steps of the courthouse—his suit coat buttoned and his tie tight around his fat neck—smiling and gesturing to a crowd of bystanders as if to say that justice was being served and the public was once again safe to sleep in their beds. "When will there be an actual, honest-to-God arrest?" the reporters had demanded to know. "Within a few days," the sheriff assured them, "a week at the most."

What the article didn't say was that the suspect who remained behind bars was a member of Asheville's Negro community and that he'd been held for days on end without access to visitors or anything even resembling a lawyer. I'd been tried for murder in Asheville, North Carolina, seven years before—tried for a killing that everyone assumed I'd go to the electric chair for—but I'd at least been left mostly alone in my cell and allowed to commiserate with my own lawyer from time to time. In 1924, there was no pretense of equal treatment, and I couldn't imagine what this man, George Moore, had gone through at the hands of Mitchell and his "crack investigator from New York City."

It seemed clear enough to me that Mitch Mitchell was headed in one direction and taking the newspapers—at least the white newspapers—right along with him, and that I was headed in a completely different direction. And if Mitch, the high sheriff, was feeling the heat to get the murder solved, then Loftis was feeling heat as well, heat of a different kind, the dollars and cents kind. Which all made sense, but what didn't make sense was the direction in which Sheriff Mitch was headed—especially the Black employee who seemed destined to take the long, hard fall.

It didn't make sense unless for some reason Loftis or his high and mighty friends had let the sheriff know that they wanted it solved no matter who paid the butcher's bill. And they wanted it done fast.

AFTER ASKING AT THE REGISTRATION DESK AND BUTtonholing Andrew in the main lobby, I managed to make an appointment to confer with Mr. Benjamin Loftis at ten o'clock that morning in his office.

Loftis's office turned out to have a much finer setup than the small cubicles allowed for Miller, Stoneman, and the others. It sat in one of the fancier rooms on the first floor of the east wing, easily as large as two or three of the normal hotel rooms. In the outer room to this suite sat a secretary—a stern, middle-aged woman who didn't have a smile to share, at least not with me. Her name was Mrs. Rice, and she bore down hard on the *Mrs.* when she introduced herself, just to make certain I didn't confuse her with some younger woman who might exude a certain flair or charm. Neither flair nor charm there, but she did have a clock on her desk, and she steadfastly refused to rap gently on the boss's door until precisely ten.

What always impressed one about Benjamin Loftis was the way in which he presented himself to the world. When Prince and I'd first seen him in Hot Springs, he managed to show up fresh as a daisy, despite the hour or so he'd spent getting thrown around in the back seat of his roadster while his driver navigated the hairpin turns and steep climbs of Madison County back roads. I recalled a gray linen suit and a nice striped tie that somehow matched his socks. That's what I said . . . his socks. Something seldom seen in Hot Springs, North Carolina. We did wear socks, but not such that matched anything.

Well, that must have been his traveling outfit because that morning when I was finally admitted to his office, everything about him looked freshly pressed and freshly brushed, and this time, his dark pin-striped suit looked like he was on the way to get married.

Even though he'd made me wait, he still jumped up and came around his desk like he was glad to see me. Waved me toward one of two comfortable chairs positioned in front of the desk and then asked Mrs. Rice to bring us in coffee for two. A surprisingly short time later, she did so, and I was reminded of my first meeting with Andrew Miller. Apparently, coffee was one of the few strong drinks Benjamin Loftis approved of, and this was piping hot.

As soon as I'd stirred in my teaspoon of cream and Loftis had doctored his with sugar, he nodded and opened things up. "Tell me what you've been able to find out," he said. "I'm all ears."

I studied his face as I spoke, trying to judge his reaction as I took him deeper into the night of the killing. After all, I needed to know what he knew as well as the other way around.

"Rosalind Caldwell was at the reception that you and Judge Aycock hosted for Madison Aycock earlier that evening in the Palm Court. She was there because—"

"But surely that reception doesn't have anything to do with the murder!" He coughed as he interrupted me and came perilously close to spitting up some coffee on his immaculate suit.

"She was there because she was recruited, along with several other young women, by Conrad Stoneman at your directive. They were to dress up the party, laugh and drink and circulate and generally make everyone, especially the well-heeled men with fat wallets, feel good and generous."

Loftis was turning a funny color—pink, perhaps, and headed toward red. "I can't believe that Mr. Stoneman would . . . But what in the world does that have to do with what happened later?"

"Everything," I said bluntly. "Let me tell it. The girls were there to have a good time and to help everyone else have a good time, which in turn would help fill up the punch bowl with cash for good old Madison and his political ambitions. As far as I can tell, they weren't there to provide sexual favors or, at least if they were, nobody was saying it out loud. They might have interpreted it that way and, in particular, the Caldwell girl might have interpreted it that way."

Good old Benjamin was beyond pink now, and his face had taken on a splotchy red aspect. "Why do you think that?"

"I think it because of what happened later. She didn't show up after the reception when Connie Stoneman shoehorned all the other girls into a taxi to send them back out to the college sometime around seven, and everybody seems to have conveniently forgotten about her. Even Stoneman. But my guess is that she was still here, at the inn, meeting with someone who approached her at the reception."

"Why the reception?" Benjamin was whispering, and his color still wasn't good. His neck was close to purple.

"Almost has to be. Why else would she skip the ride home unless she had a reason? May have just been romance or an adventure at the grand and glorious Grove Park Inn, or she may have thought there was some dough in it for her. After all, she'd just watched a punch bowl fill up with cash. Likely more money than she'd ever seen before in her life. If you were her, what would you think?"

"I certainly wouldn't think that my sacred body was . . . for sale."

I had to stifle the urge to laugh. "No, Benjamin, you would not. But that night, in the Palm Court, I imagine Rosalind Caldwell saw pearls and diamonds hanging around the necks of the society wives who were there. She saw a mink stole or two and some silk and satin that she might never have seen before except in the pages of a magazine. Then, when things really got going, she saw bills, big bills, thrown casually into that punch bowl. Checks getting written with a flourish, checks that would probably pay her room and board for a year. Hell, Benjamin, as the temperature kept rising and the cash kept flowing in that Palm Court of yours, she probably thought that anything and everything was for sale."

"That's ridiculous."

I shook my head. "You say that because you're rich."

There was a pause, a long one. He'd gone pale again, more like his usual color. "Go on," he said.

"When she slipped into room 341 sometime after midnight, she wasn't alone. She was with a man, and she was there to fool around."

"You mean she was forced, against her will."

"No, not at all. It's tempting to think that, and my bet is that your friend downtown, Mitch Mitchell, is working along with that assumption in mind, but it doesn't fit the evidence. Why would she skip the ride home at seven, Benjamin, and wait around until things got quiet? So she could be picked up at gunpoint and forced into a guest room? I don't think so. And once there, why did she take the time to neatly fold her clothes and lay them out on a chair? If Mitch thinks he's going to roll this out as attempted rape, he's crazy."

"He thinks that—"

"Mitch reads the papers to find out what he thinks. That or he listens to some high-up muckety-mucks who come down from the country club to tell him what would best serve their interests. Here's what actually happened. Rosalind Caldwell talked with someone, presumably a man, at the reception, and sensing some interest, a mutual attraction, agreed to meet him later. Maybe he slipped her a few bucks so she could get something to eat or have a drink in the meantime."

"There is no alcohol in the Grove Park Inn."

"Sure, there isn't. Anyway, the reception ends, and she finds a handy nook to hide in, planning to meet her new friend in a few hours, let's say around ten or eleven. I'm guessing he has already offered her money or dropped a few remarks like *there'll be something nice in it for you* or *you won't need to worry about cab fare.* At any rate, they meet up later, flirt and exchange a kiss or two in a dark corner, and then he lets her into room 341."

"What do you mean, he lets her in?" You could tell the thought was especially worrisome for Benjamin. Even his suit seemed to be taking on a wrinkle or two.

"Unless the room was accidentally left unlocked for some reason, one or the other had to have a key. The door wasn't forced. My first thought was that it was somebody who worked at the hotel. Maybe, on that one point, Mitch could make the case that the hotel employee he's got locked up downtown fits the bill, but the more I worked my way through it and the more I found out about keys, the less likely that seems. You and your staff do a fine job of keeping track of the damn keys, and the two room keys for 341 were never missing as far as anyone can tell. So, it's a pass-key most likely, either for the third floor or the whole place. But here's the thing, Benjamin . . . Benjamin!"

He was staring at the coffee service on the low table in front of us, lost in thought, and I got the feeling that he'd stopped listening. I reached out and rapped on the tabletop directly in his line of sight. "Ben Loftis!" He jerked visibly and looked up to meet my eyes.

"What?"

"The odds are very long against Rosie Caldwell having a key to anything in the Grove Park Inn, let alone room 341. I suppose that he could have given it to her and asked her to meet him there. But either way, he, whoever he is, had the key. A passkey. Which narrows down the roster of possible suspects considerably. Who was at that reception who also had a key?"

"Impossible."

"What?"

Loftis was focused now. In fact, he was sitting up much straighter in his chair, and his face had taken on not just its usual primness but something more than that. There was a harshness in his eyes, and his jaw was clenched. "Impossible. What you say happened is impossible."

"Why? It's almost the only thing that is possible."

"It's impossible unless it was someone like Conrad Stoneman, and I don't believe that he could . . ."

"I don't believe it either. Not him and not you."

"What did you say?"

I shrugged. "I don't like either you or Connie Stoneman for this. It was one of the guests at Aycock's reception. She was drawn to somebody fancy because he looked like he could pay for it. You look like you could pay for it, Ben, but you're not the type."

"It's *Benjamin*, you degenerate, low-life son of a . . ." I'd hit him hard, straight in his morals, but even so, he couldn't quite bring himself to finish the phrase.

I shrugged again. "It has to be one of the guests who was there that night. You can cuss me if you want to, and I suppose there are a few other ways it could have gone, but the longer I look at this, the more it plays the way I've described it."

He reached out with his right hand, carefully manicured and sporting a nice gold pinky ring, to wave a pale finger in my face. "What you say is impossible because the men who were there that night are not, I say *not*, the sort of men who would enter a hotel room with a young woman intending to engage in sexual intercourse with her, and most certainly not with the intent of offering payment for the act. The men who were there that night are not only extraordinarily successful men of the city and the region, they are also Christian gentlemen of impeccable moral character." He slapped the arm of his chair very hard for emphasis, intending, I suppose, to intimidate me.

I couldn't help myself. I laughed out loud. "Good God almighty, Loftis, what world do you live in? Just because a man wears satin drawers and flaunts a Bible doesn't mean he can't imagine a warm woman in the middle of the night. And if he is successful, he's likely used to having his way, and by that, I mean buying his way. Paying for his toys, including an occasional party girl if she's willing."

"You are a heathen wretch, Robbins. A woman is not a toy. A woman is a sacred vessel of God's making, and the men who were there that night were either happily engaged in the sacrament of marriage or were looking for a potential mate, not the rank sweat of a seamy bed."

I was impressed, sort of. "Shakespeare, Loftis, not bad. And you were close; the line is actually 'the rank sweat of an *enseamed* bed.' Hamlet to his mother. But here's the thing, you sanctimonious little . . ." It was my turn to lean forward and stare straight into his eyes. "That's exactly what the man who killed Rosie Caldwell was after, and the evidence suggests he came within a cat's whisker of getting all the rank sweat he could stand. And he was the one who lost his . . . nerve . . . at the last moment, not her." I paused to let that sink in. "Come on, Loftis, some of those jokers who threw their cash money into the punch bowl that night might be rich churchgoers, but they're still human, and they still want it when it's there for the taking."

There was a long pause. I let him rest, for I was asking him to digest a lot, including several mouthfuls he didn't want to chew or swallow. He was looking wrinkled again, as well as deep in thought. He ran his hand nervously through his thinning hair. "I know just about everybody who was at that reception that night," he said softly. "The men and the women. I'm not joking when I say they are the pillars of our society. And it just seems incredible to me that any one of them would . . . act like you're describing."

"Try thinking about it this way," I offered. "Connie Stoneman told me that you sometimes ask him to invite young society women, *debutantes* I believe he called them, to events at the inn. As a way of dressing up a party, giving it a little more . . . spark or energy."

"Vivacity," he said absently.

"Exactly. So imagine for a moment that Rosalind Caldwell really was a debutante. Imagine that her parents lived in the nicest part of town and that she was often seen at the country club dances with the most promising young men. Then, would it make sense to you that one of your pillars of society might want to slip into a hotel room with her late at night?"

He took his glasses off and laid them on the desk in front of him, stared back at me balefully with his naked eyes. "You mean if she was of the same class, the same rank in society?"

I nodded encouragingly.

"If she was one of us?"

I kept nodding, trying to keep a sympathetic, understanding look on my face even though I wanted to slap him.

He grimaced. "You don't understand at all, Robbins. If she was of the same class, the same background, the same upbringing, then she never would have gone into that room herself, now, would she? Never would have lowered herself to that sort of animal behavior. And money never, ever would have been involved."

The thought crossed my mind that if he was right—and I didn't buy it for a second—then the people he was talking about, of the proper background and upbringing, would die out in two generations because they'd never take off their evening attire long enough to reproduce. I thought it, but didn't say it. What I did say was this: "Who was at the reception that night, Loftis, who also had a key to that room?" I didn't say it particularly nicely.

Before he replied, he slowly sat up even straighter, made a show of polishing his glasses with the handkerchief from his breast pocket, and pulled his immaculate suit jacket even tighter, straighter over his thin frame. He glanced at me condescendingly and then stared past my eyes and just over my shoulder as he said coldly, "No one who concerns you."

Only later would I suspect just who he might have had in mind.

INTERLUDE

THE MAN CLIMBS OUT OF THE BACK SEAT OF THE ROADster. Standing beside the open door of the car in the scant moonlight, he reaches back inside for his trousers. The old silver buckle his grandfather gave him is caught under the seat, and, after a moment's frustration, he slides the leather belt from the belt loops to free his trousers. Standing in his socks on the cold ground, he balances on first one foot and then the other to pull the pants up over his pale legs.

Waste, he thinks to himself, what an utter goddamn waste.

What he says out loud is slightly different. "You are an utter waste of a human being."

He is speaking to the woman still sprawled across the back seat of the automobile. She sits up slowly and scoots to the open door. As he backs away from her, he bends over to pick up his suit jacket from the dew-soaked grass. He is reassured to feel the weight of his father's little secret in the jacket pocket.

She, too, stands on the cold ground now and mutters something in reply.

"What did you say?" he asks.

"I said, where's my other shoe . . . ?" Calling him by name.

"Don't say my name," he snarls at her. "I told you before: I don't ever want to hear my name come out of that nasty mouth of yours."

"Oh, shut up. Here it is." She has found the shoe wedged under the back of the front seat and bends to slip it on her foot. She bends again, frees the buckle from the springs under the back seat, and hands him his belt.

"It didn't work any better than last time, honey," she says. "I did everything you asked and then some, but that little pup dog of yours ain't barkin' tonight."

"You . . . filthy . . ."

"Filthy is what you wanted and filthy was what you got, but it didn't do no good, now did it? And this time you're paying for it." She turns to search the back seat of the roadster for her underwear.

She is bent over in the car door, and the sight of the thin fabric of her dress pulled tight over her ass is too much for him. He grasps the silver buckle and lets the fine leather belt dangle before swinging it hard. The sound of leather striking her flesh in the stillness is vicious.

"I will not pay you," he grunts, "for what you failed to deliver." Swings the belt again.

She twists to face him, snarls his name like a curse, and spits on the cold ground. She steps toward him in the roadside gravel to fight back. No rich son of a bitch is going to use a belt on me, she thinks.

She is ready to claw his eyes and take what he owes her. But she didn't count on the derringer. And even when she glimpses it in his hand, she can't imagine that he knows how to use it.

PART II

CHAPTER EIGHTEEN

THAT EVENING AT DINNER, WHEN I SAT DOWN AND UNfolded my napkin, Michael brought me the usual china coffee pot; cups and saucers were already on the table. Brought the pot without even asking. I assume my face alone conveyed that I needed the wine secreted within. When he returned with the basket of wheat rolls a few minutes later, he asked, while barely moving his lips, "How did it go with Loftis?"

"You already know about that little interview?" I asked.

He nodded. "Of course."

I shook my head. "Not sure," I murmured. "I tried to make a dent in his thinking about that night, but I'm not sure I made much progress."

Michael nodded. "Some things the boss man doesn't like to think about."

I met his eyes. "Or can't afford to."

Michael stared down at me for a long moment. "Steak" was all he said.

"Steak?"

"You need some red meat to keep your spirits up. Put some fight back in your . . ." He nodded suggestively. "Steak."

I smiled. "Medium, like last time?"

"Medium to medium-rare. Better cut tonight."

My smile turned into a grin, a toothy grin. "So be it."

Bites of the thick bread with butter chased with sips of the wine: that alone was enough to ease the wrinkles out of my forehead, loosen some of the knots in my shoulders and neck, start me breathing again.

I'd come later to the dinner table that night, and the sun had already set behind the western mountains on the far side of the river. The light was smoky blue, and an evening mist was rising off the golf course. So taken was I by the vista that I barely even noticed the maître d' approaching my table with someone in tow. When I did glance back at him, he only nodded, stepped aside, and then suddenly Ella Loving eased into the second chair at my table.

She set her standard beaded purse on the windowsill, looked across at me, and reached up to her matching hat. "May I?" she asked, looking directly at me under the brim. I nodded, and she pulled a hatpin—a long, very sharp hatpin—out of the elaborate arrangement on her head and then lifted it free. It too went onto the windowsill over the purse.

"I told the maître d' that I was meeting you for dinner," she said. "I hope you don't mind."

"Do you like steak?" I asked.

"I don't eat meat . . . Well, at least not that kind." She smiled as she said it, and the effect was electric.

To this day, I couldn't tell you what she was wearing while we sat at that table, although, later, as we talked into the night, I registered that it was a blue chiffon sheath—I suppose that's what you would call it—that glimmered as she moved. I couldn't have told you as we sat there and the great windows beside us went dark, because she had this trick of drawing your gaze directly into her face—her mouth and eyes—and holding it there for as long as she willed it.

I poured some "coffee" into her china cup, and she was delighted to discover that it was dark and strong but not coffee. "You do get special service, don't you?" she whispered. When Michael returned with my steak, he smiled at her but only briefly, as if he recognized her but didn't quite approve of her at my table. "The usual?" he asked her, and she nodded, looking demurely down at the tablecloth.

"What are you doing here, Miss Loving?" I asked after a bit. "I don't mind the company, but it's not what I expected."

"Not what you ordered . . . ?" Again, that barely suggestive twist of her lips, and another spark zipped almost audibly up my arm.

"Stop that," I muttered.

She raised her eyebrows as if to say, "Stop what?"

"Whatever you're doing with your mouth, your whole face actually, that makes me . . ."

"Twitch," she said suggestively.

I nodded. "Twitch. Close enough."

"Most men like that feeling." Her eyes over the rim of her cup.

"You're doing it again."

She set her cup down lightly in its saucer and laughed, and I was reminded once more of distant chimes. You couldn't help smiling when you heard it.

"What am I doing here . . . at your table, with you?"

I nodded, tore a roll in half, and buttered a piece for each of us.

She shrugged. "I got stood up, and I'm hungry."

"Stood up? That's hard to believe."

She smiled as she chewed, then swallowed. "Actually, what happened is that when my date appeared in the lobby, already late for our appointment, his wife was hanging on his arm, looking very much like a ball and chain."

I couldn't help myself. I laughed out loud at the look of complete and utter innocence on her face. "I assume, Miss Loving, that you can't perform the . . . what to call it . . . services you offer if the man's wife is present."

Her lips twitched, but this time it was more out of honest humor than seduction. "Oh, I can *perform*—I like that word by the way—quite well under those circumstances, but neither of them looked up to the challenge." This time, she broke the bread and buttered a piece for me. "He looked like an animal in a trap, actually."

"What is it, exactly, you do, Miss Loving, for the trapped animals of the world?"

She shook her head and directed my gaze with just her eyes. Michael was threading his way through the tables in our direction. And then, suddenly, he was there and setting two plates down on the table. My steak, steaming hot on the plate, with some grilled potatoes and green beans; her plate filled with salad except for a small serving of the beans. "Thank you, Michael," I said, while she looked up and smiled.

"Careful, Stephen," he said, or at least I think he said, it was done so quickly and quietly.

"Careful of what?" I asked, almost as quietly, but he was already gone.

"Careful of me," she said. "He's warning you against me."

"Why? What is it that—?"

"Call me Ella. Just Ella, and I'll tell you." Another twitch of those lips, but this time perhaps a little sad as well as humorous.

"Why are you so dangerous, Ella?"

A significant pause, while I carved two bites of steak and forked the first into my mouth. It didn't cause an electric shock the way her face had earlier, but it was still sinfully good. She poured dressing onto her salad from a small pitcher and took a healthy bite of the greens. We both chewed.

"Do you like words?" she asked after a moment. And then, before I could answer. "I love words. Words fascinate me. So, I'll give you some to think about." And then, after a pause for effect. "Coquette . . . temptress . . . minx." She was watching my face closely to see how I would react. I swallowed the second bite of that delicious steak and focused on her face in turn, almost as if we each stared into a mirror. "Flirt. Jade. Tart. Hussy . . . Tramp."

I shook my head; *tramp* was a wrong note. Something out of tune.

But she wasn't done. "Chippie. Doxy. Floozy. Slut." Her face was hardening despite her efforts to hold it perfectly still. Her eyes were narrowing.

"Stop," I whispered. "Courtesan," I said, barely above a whisper. "I would choose *courtesan*."

Her face softened again, her mouth relaxed into a smile. And she laughed. "*Courtesan*, then. That's what I am. That's why I'm dangerous."

We both paid attention to our food for the time it took to cut, select, chew a few bites. I let what she'd said settle inside my mind. Of course I'd suspected it, even knew it on some deeper level, and she was subtle enough to give me time to think, all the while watching me surreptitiously to see how the flitting words and images inside my mind might change me in relation to her. Was I turning into an enemy, a client, a friend? "How in the world do you get away with it?" I asked finally.

"It?"

"How do you get away with who you are and what you do? Right here in the midst of Benjamin Loftis's own personal garden of earthly purity. Let me see. No children, no animals of any kind, no loud or intrusive behavior, no unseemly conversation in the lobby . . . hell, no writing except in the writing rooms."

"Are you suggesting I'm an animal?" She was smiling, and she had that glint in her eyes again, so that it was hard to say if she was joking or flirting, or both.

I leaned forward to whisper, "Hell yes, that's exactly what I'm saying."

She took a bite of her salad and, while she chewed, began to carefully, precisely cut the green beans on her plate up into very small bites. Swallowed, shrugged, and said, "I don't object to *animal*. And neither, I suspect, do you."

I had to laugh. "Oh, I'm not objecting. I'm just curious as to how in God's name you get away with . . . ?"

"Plying my trade?"

I nodded. "Sure, call it that."

This time the pause was longer. She was thinking, I could tell. I glanced toward the kitchen where I saw Michael watching us. He raised his eyebrows to ask if we needed anything. I pointed to the china coffee pot, now empty, to suggest more wine. He rolled his eyes and shook his head. Feigned disgust, disappointment, but in a moment brought an identical pot to replace the first. This time, he made eye contact with her rather than me. "Careful, Ella," he murmured before taking the first pot away.

She laughed, and the bells seemed closer, the laughter more natural. "Now, he's warning me," she said. "What makes you so—"

She was going to say *dangerous*, but I interrupted her. "Topic for later," I said. "How in God's name do you ply your trade here of all places, Ella Loving? Can you make yourself invisible?"

CHAPTER NINETEEN

"*INVISIBLE* IS A GOOD WORD," SHE SAID AFTER A MOMENT.

"How do you mean? I saw you the first time I . . . saw you. Sitting at the very next table with the *Wall Street Journal* man."

She smiled. "You saw me because I wanted you to see me. I never would have looked up otherwise, never would have let you see my eyes."

She had me there. It was a curious trick she had of either hiding or exposing her face and especially her eyes.

I was chewing the last bite of steak, and I noticed that almost without appearing to eat, she had devoured every morsel of food on her plate, including the last drop of the salad dressing. "Let's walk up to the Palm Court," I suggested. "Sit for a bit while you explain how it all works. Have you got time to just sit and talk?"

She nodded. "It seems this is my night off."

LOOKING BACK, I THINK ELLA DELIBERATELY SHOWED ME what she was talking about between the dining room and the Palm Court. Had you seen us in passing, you might well have noticed me, especially the scar on my face, and perhaps caught a glimpse of a woman as well, but I don't know that you would have registered that we were together or that we even knew each other. She walked perhaps a foot or so to my left and behind me. I knew she was there, but she did nothing, absolutely nothing to suggest that we even knew each other, rather that we happened to be walking in the same direction at the same time.

When we came to the elevator, she hung back just enough so that I was forced to enter first, stifling any chivalrous inclination I might have, and even let another man—younger and in a hurry—enter between us. She might have smiled at him but didn't acknowledge me, and once inside the small space, she moved such that he was situated between us, brushing against his arm without looking up, sending a clear if subtle signal that she was alone. She also moved so that she was directly behind the elevator operator, so that he didn't have anything like a clear view of her. She was not the sexiest thing in his elevator that night, or if she was, he missed it.

When we got off on the third floor, she stepped out first, but not because I let her, suggesting that I was not somehow with her or even aware of her. She was a woman returning to her own room, looking forward to some privacy. It was only when the elevator doors closed behind us and she had the chance to glance up and down the third-floor foyer and step into the Palm Court—which was empty except for a man sitting alone smoking a cigarette at the far end—that she turned to me and smiled that impish grin of hers.

"You're right, invisible *is* a good word," I said ruefully. "I didn't even know you were there."

"Sure you did," she replied. "You knew because you're a watcher. You pay attention and you let yourself blend into the background just like I do, but nobody else would have noticed me."

"And they sure as hell wouldn't have put the two of us together."

She stepped to my side and actually reached out and tucked her hand behind my elbow, touching me for the first time. "Where would you like to sit?" she asked.

We settled across from each other under one of the potted

palms, even inched our chairs a bit closer so that we could talk comfortably without being overly loud. I brought the battered old flask out of my coat pocket and showed it to Ella. "If needed," I said.

She smiled and said, "Let's play another word game. I'll say a word, one word, and then you describe to me—in detail—what you think when you hear that word. You ready?"

I nodded, intrigued.

"Whore."

Images flashed across the surface of my mind. So quick and so vibrant that I unscrewed the top from my flask and took a swig of brandy. I leaned forward and handed Ella the flask. "Dirty," I said. "In the dark except for flashes of skin. Do anything. Cheap. Grunting. Quick, over and done with. Money. *Cash* money." I paused, wondering how much of what I said was colored by the needle-like thoughts of Rosie Caldwell. "Dangerous," I added.

Ella was staring at my face, intent, almost as if she'd hypnotized me. "That's good," she said. "That's what people think whoring is if they're capable of thinking about it at all. Now, can you imagine that here?" She waved her hand to indicate what was all about us, the grand and glorious Grove Park Inn.

I glanced up and around, following her gesture. The Palm Court was empty and beyond that, serene. Halfway down, one of the room doors opened on oiled hinges and a couple—so obviously a bored and very married couple—came out and locked their door behind them. On the floors above, stretching up to the ceiling, there was quiet conversation, another door opening and closing, footsteps muted by thick carpet, the ghost of quiet laughter.

I shook my head. "I've been a hotel man off and on for most of my life, and I can't imagine sex here at all, let alone anything that makes the bed springs creak or the headboard bang into the wall. For God's sake, this place is so clean, they wash the nickels, dimes, and quarters behind the front desk every night so they'll be pristine in the morning."

She laughed quietly and let herself have a sip from the flask. "Most of the time," she said, "it's like sex in a tomb here. But you wanted to know how I get away with it. I get away with it because most people can't see what they haven't been told is there. Most people only see what they expect to see, hear what they expect to hear, and their minds will explain away everything else."

I nodded. "It's especially true if the contrast between what's assumed and what's real is a mile wide, like it is here."

She nodded and took another tiny sip from the flask before handing it back to me. "Especially here. What did you say earlier? 'No loud or intrusive behavior, no unseemly conversation, no gambling'?"

"No cursing, no grunting or groaning. Hell, no laughing." I took my own gulp from the flask and handed it back to Ella. The liquor stung the back of my throat quite nicely. "Did you know," I asked her, "that there's no alcohol in the inn? Benjamin Loftis told me so himself."

This time, she laughed right out, so loud I'm sure that someone on the balconies above could have heard her. The chimes in her laughter were bells now, close by, pealing. When her laughter died away, she raised the flask and murmured, "Here's to Benjamin Loftis and his own brand of prohibition." She took another dainty sip and handed the flask back to me.

"To Mr. Loftis." I took a swallow of my own and discovered that it was the last. The flask was empty.

We stared at each other for more than a moment, and again I had that odd feeling that we were both gazing into a mirror. Her eyes were unusually hot, sleepy perhaps. "The French have a phrase that I like," she whispered, "even more than courtesan. They call a woman like me *une fille de joie*." She said it as if the phrase, and the language, came naturally to her. "'A woman of pleasure.' It suits me, don't you think?"

"How did you learn French?" I asked, intrigued by the lilt in her voice.

"I spoke it as a child, in New Orleans." She glanced up and around, breaking the stream between our eyes. She seemed to gather herself, and then, suddenly, she was standing, carefully replacing the elaborate hat on her tousled hair. The long, sharp hatpin.

"I'll walk you out," I think I said.

There was a slight shake of the head and a bare smile. "No, no," she replied. "This is the part where I disappear."

CHAPTER TWENTY

I MUST HAVE DREAMED THAT NIGHT, THOUGH IT'S HARD now to recall the details. It seems to me that both were there, the two women. The ghost of Anna Ulmann, who had come increasingly to haunt my deeper thoughts, and the present specter of Ella Loving. *Anna* and *Ella*, two names that seemed almost to merge in the dark singsong of my dreams, and two figures who somehow danced together in time to a music I couldn't quite hear. Or, if I heard, couldn't quite recall the next morning.

The morning when Brody Mitchell called me at the inn to ask if I wanted to go see a second corpse.

He picked me up in a plain sedan so as not to draw attention to the two of us at the crime scene. He needn't have bothered. When we arrived at the isolated spot along Beaverdam Road, a sheriff's department cruiser sat parked strategically in a gravel pull-off to block the view from the road, an ambulance parked behind it. The uniformed deputy and the ambulance driver leaned against the hood of the ambulance, casually chatting while sharing a smoke. The deputy straightened when he saw Brody get out of the car, crushed his cigarette butt against the back bumper of the cruiser, and tossed it into the weeds.

Brody and I glanced at each other, both thinking about the deputy corrupting the crime scene. Hard to tell his butt from one that had gotten dropped or tossed during the incident, whatever the incident turned out to be. While Brody cussed at the deputy, I walked around the front of the cruiser and was brought up short by the sight of the body.

She was lying on her left side in roadside gravel and mud, curled into a hideous parody of the fetal position. Her hair—dyed, not very expertly, red—was tossed around her head. Her floral print dress had ridden up over one hip, the right hip, so that the pitifully pale skin of her flank and thigh was exposed in the thin morning sunlight. One shoe, her left, was on her foot, but the other foot was bare. Her right shoe had somehow been scraped off her foot as she struggled to save herself in the dirt and gravel.

I knelt down beside her, whoever she was, careful not to disturb anything. I was behind her, and the inevitable pool of black congealed blood was mostly in front of her, as if cradled within her bent legs and arms. The iron smell of her blood was brutally strong when I bent over her. Her lipstick, a thick bright red, was smeared over most of her cheeks and chin, and a thin stream of dried spit and blood had cascaded from her mouth as she died. In addition, a nasty brown bruise on her right cheek, the side of her face closest to me, made it all too clear she'd been struck hard. Perhaps, unlike Rosalind Caldwell, she had tried to scream, and someone had shut her up.

I rocked back on my heels and leaned to one side to look at her back and legs. She wasn't wearing any underwear, and I knew we'd have to search in the roadside weeds. What struck me then was the saddest sign of all: her buttock was marked by long savage bruises made by a belt perhaps or something similar. Whipped, I thought, presumably when she was still alive.

I could sense Brody standing beside me. I discovered that I was holding my breath and had to cough before I could speak. "We need to find her underwear and her pocketbook," I said finally. "Plus anything else."

"I'll set those two to looking," he said. He'd lit a cigarette; I could smell the smoke.

"Tell them not to touch anything they find," I muttered. And then, "Okay with you if I turn her over?"

"Sure," he said. "Ain't nobody coming way out here to take any crime scene photos. This ain't the Grove Park Inn."

She'd been dead at least since the middle of the night, and her body had stiffened in place, so I used her knees to slowly pry her loose from the dark puddle and roll her onto her back. When I did, her left arm stayed more or less in place, glued down in the congealed blood. Her right came up and over with her body. What I saw made my head swim. There was one wound, most probably a gunshot wound, low in her abdomen, almost in her groin, and another high at the base of her neck, roughly at her collarbone. I let her slowly sink back into place as I'd found her and stood up.

It took a long moment for the dizziness to pass—from having squatted on my heels that long and from what I'd seen. A shadow fell over the corpse, and I could smell cigarette smoke again. Brody.

"It's the same pattern," I grunted. "One shot high and one low. We're going to need an autopsy," I added after I caught my breath. "Will Mitch approve it?"

"Doubt it. He won't like nothing that complicates things at this point."

"Shit on him."

"Sure. But whether he approves don't matter. I been counterfeiting his signature since he was in high school."

A LIGHT DRIZZLE BEGAN TO FALL AS THE FOUR OF US walked slowly up and down that lonely stretch of Beaverdam Road, searching through the weeds on either side of the pavement. When the drizzle turned into a cold drenching rain, we all paused to help the ambulance driver pry the body out of the gravel and lay her on her back on the stretcher so we could lift her into the back of the ambulance. Brody had to yell at the driver to be heard over the rain pounding on the roof of the ambulance to take the body to the county morgue and to warn the coroner that an autopsy request was coming later in the day.

As he and the driver were hollering at each other, I turned back one last time to the spot where the body had lain. The eerie pool of black blood was beginning to soften and dissolve in the hard rain. Something that looked like a piece of paper was being hammered into the gravel just beside the blood. It had been hidden under her body before. I bent to grab it before it, too, either dissolved or was blown away in the increasingly strong breeze. When I straightened, the paper clutched in my fist to shield it from the rain, I had a sudden instinct that I knew what it was.

Brody and I sat in his roadster while we waited for the rain to at least subside, and I handed him what I'd found under the woman's body. The paper was folded in half and melted into a damp mash by the rain, so that only half of Grover Cleveland's head was vaguely visible, but the number twenty was clearly printed in the corner. "Another goddamn twenty," Brody muttered, and laid the bill out on the dash of the car so that it could begin to dry.

I nodded. "And I'll bet you another twenty that when the coroner digs the bullets out of this woman, they'll match the ones in Rosalind Caldwell."

Brody sighed. I could tell he wanted to light another cigarette.

"Crack your window," I said, "and fire one up."

He nodded gratefully and did exactly that. After the first long draw, his one eye blinking at the smoke, he said, "Where does that leave us?"

"You know perfectly well where it leaves us. If things match up, and my gut says they will, then whoever killed Rosie Caldwell isn't done. He's using prostitutes for sex or at least women he thinks of as prostitutes, and when it doesn't work out the way he hopes it will, he kills them. Out of anger, frustration, shame . . . who knows? But something about the experience pushes him over the edge."

"Why the money? You said he threw the Caldwell girl's twenty down as he was leaving. Why the hell do that if she was already dead or at least well on the way? Wait, and why pay her if they never did the deed in the first place?"

"I don't know, Brody." I nodded with my head toward where we'd found the new corpse in the gravel. "But I'm betting he did the same thing here. Threw the money down after he shot her, and somehow, before she died, she rolled over on her side and it ended up under her body. It would fit the pattern."

We both sat for a long, still moment, listening to the rain hammer the roof of the auto. "Did you see where her cheek was bruised?" I finally asked. "And where he'd whipped her back and her butt?"

"Saw her butt but not her face," Brody replied. "What do you think?"

"Means he's getting more frustrated, maybe. As time passes, he can't stop thinking about it, wants it more and more, is afraid he can't have it."

"Impotent," Brody offered.

"Maybe," I agreed. "See what the coroner says about this woman, see if she'd had intercourse. And if not, maybe the more he wants it, the angrier he is when he can't have it. And the more violent the reaction when everything falls apart."

"Will he give up? Just stop trying?"

I shook my head. "Doubt it. Worse case, he starts to like the killing. Like it even more than what he wanted in the first place."

"We've got to catch this sick bastard," Brody muttered.

I shrugged. "Somebody does. And one thing's for sure . . ."

"What?"

"The poor guy your brother's got locked up ain't the one. What're you going to do about that?"

CHAPTER TWENTY-ONE

AFTER THE RAIN SLOWED TO A DRIZZLE, BRODY SENT the uniformed deputy on his way, so that just the two of us were left. The sun was beginning to burn through the clouds, and the air was taking on an almost crystalline quality as we scoured the weeds up and down the side of Beaverdam Road. We finally found her pocketbook almost twenty feet up in a pasture on the other side of the road where someone—presumably the killer—had thrown it. We never found her underwear.

A crushed envelope in the purse along with several other slips of paper suggested the dead woman was named Viola Martin, and that her address was on Starnes Street. In her billfold were three one-dollar bills and a five, folded small. A lipstick, a compact, and a wadded-up copy of a Wassermann test for Viola Louise Martin, result positive. Which meant she might have given her killer syphilis had things gone far enough.

By the time Brody dropped me off at the inn at noon, the sun was fully out and the day was hot for mid-October, hot and muggy. We agreed to talk by phone as soon as Brody knew something from the coroner. I sloshed into the lobby, sweaty and rain-soaked, my muddy shoes squeaking with every step. As I passed the reception desk, James, the man who had checked me in on the very first evening, motioned me over and handed me an envelope, which appeared to be from Loftis himself. Probably dismissed me, I thought, and tracked mud toward the elevator. I was wrong.

I tore open the thick cream-colored envelope while simultaneously stripping off my soaked clothes and tossing them at the dirty-clothes basket that came with my room. Rather than a pink slip, it was an invitation.

Benjamin N. Loftis—Manager

GROVE PARK INN

Sunset Mountain—Asheville, North Carolina

Dear Mr. Robbins,

It occurred to me that yesterday's discussion of your findings ended on a sour note, perhaps, in part, because of my surprise and dismay at the conclusions you reached about those who were in attendance at the reception for Madison Aycock. Many of these individuals are my own friends, and I am personally acquainted with all of them. If you knew them as I know them—patrons of the arts and letters, supporters of all good and fine causes—you would realize that you are mistaken about their possible involvement in the unfortunate incident that occurred later that night; you would also see why I was upset and disoriented by your speculations.

So that you might see for yourself what caliber of people these are, I'd like to invite you to my home for a dinner party tomorrow evening, where many of the very same individuals will be in attendance. This event is to celebrate the engagement of our friend Madison Aycock and Miss Beatrice Avery, daughter of the rector of First Presbyterian Church.

I'm confident that the evening's festivities will be an education for you personally and serve to allay your suspicions. In that way, it will also serve to further your investigations by clearing your mind.

Please plan to arrive by 6:00 for light refreshment, followed by dinner at 7:00. You need merely to instruct the taxi driver that your destination is Overlook Castle. If you would like to bring a guest, please inform the front desk clerk by midday tomorrow so that we may prepare accordingly.

Sincerely,

Benjamin L.

I THREW THE INVITATION FROM BENJAMIN L. ALONG WITH its torn envelope on the bed while I ran a hot bath. The reality of the rain-soaked scene beside Beaverdam Road, with the poor, disheveled body of Viola Martin up against Benjamin Loftis and his Overlook Castle was almost too much to digest. Once I had sunk down into the tub and let the horror of the morning drain out of me, I tried to make sense of Loftis's note—not just the invitation but what lay behind the invitation. What was he really saying? So aggravating were these ruminations that I climbed back up out of the tub—even though my body was screaming for warmth and relaxation—and stood dripping beside the bed to reread his careful, precise handwriting.

My own friends . . . patrons . . . of all good and fine causes . . . mistaken . . . upset and disoriented . . . clear your mind . .. Overlook Castle . . . A castle, for God's sake! *Prepare accordingly.*

I threw the embossed sheet of stationery back onto the bed in disgust and climbed into the tub for the second time. The water had begun to cool, so I twisted the hot water knob savagely.

I'll prepare accordingly, I thought, to see which of your fine friends, patrons of the arts and letters, will kill a woman he can't screw and then casually throw money at her while she's dying. Oh, I'll prepare all right—to look behind the mask of silk and satin and see if there's a flame of stunted desire burning inside one of your Boy Scouts. And the gun . . . Who's carrying a little two-shot piece in his pocket, just for emergencies or for women who might talk after the fact?

And so, my thoughts ran on, even though I ever so slowly tried to ease the fury in my gut and breathe deep some sense of quiet, watchful determination rather than red-hot anger. If Loftis wanted me to see for myself, then I would do just that. I'd pay the kind of attention seldom seen in Overlook Castle. I'd see just whose nicely manicured hands hid folded claws and whose finely tailored trousers covered a nasty little secret.

Later, as I was drying off, I wrapped that Grove Park Inn towel around my waist and sat on the side of the bed to read Loftis's note yet one more time, seeking the motivations behind it. I knew full well that Stephen Robbins was not the sort of man Loftis would choose to entertain at his castle, even if I did come with a recommendation from someone high up at the Bureau of Investigation. I wasn't a patron of the arts and letters, nor was I a supporter of fine causes. Hell, I was a patron of creeks and rivers and a supporter of mountainsides too steep for human habitation. A runaway boy who was still running, even as a man. I read on to the last sentence: *If you would like to bring a guest, please inform the front desk clerk by midday tomorrow so that we may prepare accordingly.*

Just who in the world did Benjamin Loftis imagine I might invite as my guest?

I WENT FOR A LONG WALK AROUND THE GOLF COURSE THAT afternoon and tried not to think about the cold bodies of Rosie Caldwell and Viola Martin, tried not to think about what circumstances might have brought them to the lonely places where they'd died. I stuck to the graveled paths designed to guide the golfers and their caddies from one hole to the next, ignoring the sometimes pointed stares of both—stares that suggested I was on hallowed ground without the necessary equipment to worship the eighteen holes.

As I walked, I tried not to think at all, mainly because I trusted the depths of my mind more than the surface. Believed in my instincts more than my analytical powers. I figured that by the time I'd circled the whole manicured plot of ground two or three times, patterns would emerge that I'd been too distracted to notice before. On my last circuit, a nicely dressed gentleman wearing knickers—actual, honest-to-God knickers—emerged from the clubhouse and inquired as to who the hell I was.

I told him. He didn't believe me. I fished Loftis's original letter of introduction out of my billfold and handed him that. He studied it and then glanced up at my battered, scarred face. I think my face might have been more convincing than the letter.

He seemed to relax a bit then as he refolded the paper and handed it back to me. The smile on his face went from fake to genuine. Almost friendly. "You searching for a murderer out here on the golf course, Mr. Robbins?"

I returned his smile. "Maybe," I said. "Maybe I am."

WHEN I GOT BACK TO THE LOBBY, IT WAS ALMOST four o'clock. I went by the front desk to check for messages, hoping Brody Mitchell might have called. Turns out he had but didn't leave any details, only asked that I call him back at the sheriff's office. I stepped away from the desk and used one of the lobby phones, so that my end of the conversation wouldn't be quite so public.

I had to talk to the switchboard operator plus another deputy before someone on that end could track down Brody and bring him to the phone. He'd spent most of his day at the coroner's office, nagging the county coroner to do at least a preliminary examination of the Martin woman. Finally, by midafternoon—right before the coroner himself left to play golf—Brody got what we needed. Yes, there were two bullet wounds. Yes, the bullets themselves came from a small-caliber handgun, probably .22 caliber or less, like the bullets that had killed Rosie Caldwell.

The Martin woman had been struck at least twice on the right side of her face, probably by a fist. The coroner had pointed out the peculiar bruises left by the knuckles of the person who hit her.

"Sex?" I whispered into the mouthpiece of the phone, trying not to draw attention to myself. "What about sex?"

"Readily apparent previous vaginal penetration, but nothing in the hours before she died."

"In other words . . . ?"

"In other words, she didn't have vaginal sex with the man who shot her. Almost word for word what the coroner said. We'll get more later, when he's done the autopsy."

"What about the—"

"The bruises on her back and buttocks were probably caused by being struck with a belt. Presumably leather."

There was a long pause. The large ornate lobby clock behind me struck the half hour. "It's our guy, Brody. You know it is."

"Sure," he said. "Tell that to my brother."

When I hung up, I realized that I was starving, so I drug myself back to room 340 to change clothes for dinner. I also realized that I'd already suspected everything Brody had told me. The only surprise might have been just how experienced our Viola apparently was, which went, of course, with her positive Wassermann test. What did that mean, if anything?

On the way through the lobby, I saw a young stylishly dressed woman sitting quietly to one side, her head down, as she was apparently reading a book she held in her lap. I eased through the various grouping of chairs and tables to approach her, and it was only when she glanced up briefly that I was certain. I sat down across from her. She was wearing a blue so dark it was almost black.

"Ella?" I said.

"Mr. Robbins."

"I need to ask you something."

She glanced up for real then, closed her book and gave me a long look at her eyes. "Yes?"

"Are you free tomorrow evening, Miss Loving?"

The faint smile I'd learned to look for flickered across her lips. "I'm never *free*, Mr. Robbins, you know that."

"I mean . . ."

"I know what you mean. Are you asking if I'm available?"

"Are you? Available?"

Her gaze shifted over my shoulder for a moment, and she seemed to make eye contact with someone standing behind me. When I began to shift in my chair, she murmured, "Don't turn around, Stephen. It's my date for this evening, and I don't want you to scare him off."

"He'll think we're negotiating," I said.

"We are, aren't we?" Again, that ironic flicker of a smile like a passing ray of sunlight across a flower.

"I'm not requesting the honor of your company in your professional capacity. I want to invite you to attend a dinner party at Overlook Castle as my companion. My . . . guest."

"That's different. I haven't been called that before." She looked over my shoulder again and rose from her chair almost effortlessly, as if floating to her feet. "Let me think about it. Appearing in a place like that . . . uninvited . . . can be dangerous for somebody like me." She nodded to the evening's prospect and stepped around the coffee table that separated our two chairs, beginning her dance in his direction. "Where will you be in a few hours, say around nine or ten?"

"In my room. 340."

"I know the number," she said and was gone.

AFTER DINNER, I FOLLOWED MICHAEL'S DIRECTIONS down into the basement, where I found an employee setting pins at the bowling alley, a country man from Haywood County, who was glad to sell me a jar of apple brandy made "up home," as he put it. I carried my jar up to 340 and secreted it away inside the fancy chifforobe that stood in the corner. That with a couple of clean glasses from room service and I thought I was ready to receive my guest, not as a working woman but as an ally.

CHAPTER TWENTY-TWO

THE KNOCK ON THE DOOR CAME JUST AFTER NINE, FIRM but quiet, meant to be heard within but not in the court and certainly not in the adjoining rooms. When I opened the door, Ella slipped past me quickly, easily, close enough that I caught a hint of her perfume but without any actual contact. She went straight to the mirror above the chest of drawers and leaned over the chest itself to examine her face. From behind her, I could tell that one cheek, her left, was flushed a bit.

"Why don't you wash your face?" I suggested. "Kick your shoes off, and I'll pour you a drink."

She turned and started to offer up a truly coquettish smile but then thought better of it. "What are you drinking?" she asked.

"Brandy. Homemade."

She pursed her lips, almost as if tasting it. Nodded and reached up to pull the long hatpin and then set her hat, something ornate in a lighter shade of blue, on the chest with the pin. Slipped between me and the end of the bed into the bathroom. The door closed, and a moment later the commode flushed. I could hear water running while I poured a solid bite of the brandy into each of the two glasses.

When she came back out a moment later, her face was different, more than just clean or fresh. Bare, I thought, and . . . younger. I handed her a glass and nodded at one of my two chairs. She eased down into the chair and, with an ironic grin, literally kicked her shoes off. It was unexpectedly childlike, not seductive. She sipped from the glass and sighed.

I collapsed into the other chair where I'd been sitting earlier while I waited. I took a solid mouthful of the brandy and savored it before I spoke. "Are you alright?" I asked her and pointed to my own cheek.

She groaned and took a second sip. "My date for the evening, some young man from Georgia, didn't turn out to be such a peach."

"Was he named Son-of-a-Bitch?"

She laughed. A real laugh with the bells in it. "He was. Roland Son-of-a-Bitch, actually. And he thought it would be fun if he slapped me around a bit as part of our playtime."

"Want me to find him and break his nose?"

"Would you? That would be so kind." She paused for a sip. "But the truth is, you don't need to. See that hatpin over there? I keep it handy for when I'm with somebody like him. Usually a puncture or two will stop that sort of thing before it really gets started. I stabbed his hand with it. Twice. And asked him how it would feel in his eye."

"Did he pay you?" I'm not sure why I asked it, except that somehow, I was feeling protective all of a sudden. Older than she and . . . brotherly.

"They pay first, Stephen. They always pay first, before anything else."

She let me think about that for a moment and watched my face over the rim of her glass. "Are you interested?" she whispered finally. "On another night, when I'm not so tired, you might find me worth the investment."

"Oh, I'm interested," I said. "Very. But not in that way. I'm interested in what you see and what you think. I'm interested in your eyes and your intuition and your mind."

She lowered the glass and let me see her bare face. "That's funny. Most men don't notice that I have any of those, except the eyes maybe. Some men like my eyes. Women too."

"I'm interested in what you see with those eyes of yours, not how alluring you can make them."

"You're hurting my pride. A Methodist minister I had a transaction with not long ago said my talents were biblical."

"I'm sure they are. But I'm after something deeper. What you think. What your instincts tell you when you're surrounded by a room full of men and women."

"So that's why you want to take me to Loftis's castle on top of the mountain? You want me to spy on the people there?"

I had the vague sense that she was disappointed somehow, and I wondered if I really had hurt her feelings. "That and I like you. Find you endlessly entertaining."

"Why? Obviously, it's not for the usual reasons."

"Partly for the usual reasons, but mostly because I think you're the smartest damn person in any room. Man or woman."

"I almost believe you," she said after a moment. "Mainly because I've thought the same about you once or twice. But you need to understand something. I make my living doing what I do, and whether you appreciate it or not, I'm very, very good at it." She sat up and leaned forward, every inch of her emphasizing what she was saying. "And the Grove Park Inn, along with the Battery Park and the Roosevelt and a few other high-dollar establishments where men from out of town—*wealthy* men from out of town—tend to stay are where I'm most at home and most in demand. And if even one of the country club types who are likely to be there tomorrow night recognizes me, or even suspects me for what I am, then they tell Loftis, and I'm back on the street. Do you understand what that means?"

She took a deep breath and held out her glass. I reached out and poured more brandy for her from the jar.

"Are you saying no?" I asked her.

"I'm saying it's a big risk you're asking me to take. And why me?

Sure, I keep my eyes open when I walk across a room. I have to. But I've got the feeling there's something you're not telling me."

So, I told her about Viola Martin, all of it. Including what Brody Mitchell had said when I returned his call.

"You think it's the same gun? You're sure?"

"Same type, probably the same small caliber. We'll know for sure by tomorrow when Brody gets a chance to compare the bullets with a magnifying glass."

"He hit her?"

"Whipped her with his belt at some point and hit her in the face, probably with his fist and probably twice."

"Which side of her face?" She reached up to touch her own.

"Right, which means . . ."

"He's probably left-handed."

I nodded.

"Tell them to check her fingernails," she offered quietly. "She must have fought back, and that's why he hit her with his fist. She may have scratched him." Ella leaned back in her chair and took a meditative sip of her brandy. I watched her face as she thought. On the one hand, it was quiet, passive, almost like a mask, but a mask with a storm of thought brewing behind it. "Tell me again, Stephen, why you think it's one of Loftis's crowd. One of the country club types."

I circled back to Rosalind Caldwell and gave her the short version of what I'd told Loftis himself. She met him at the reception, was drawn to his style, his class, his money. Agreed to meet later, skipped her ride home. Was ready and willing to do whatever he wanted. Love nest, something went wrong, no penetration. Shot her and threw money at her as he left.

"Makes sense," she said after a bit. "Somewhere down in here . . ." She placed her hand on her own stomach. "It rings true. And you told Loftis all this? How did he react?"

I opened the top drawer of the chest and handed her the

invitation to Overlook Castle.

She read, surprisingly quickly, and then again, more slowly from the beginning. "'If you would like to bring a guest, please inform . . .'" She mocked the formal tone of the note out loud. Threw the invitation on the coffee table and leaned her head to one side to stare at me. Speculatively. Raised her glass and, when she realized it was empty, sat it on the table. "Damn you, Stephen," she said. "I'll go with you. But only on one condition . . ."

"Name it."

"You must call me by my real name and introduce me to any and every one we meet by that name." She stood and slipped on her shoes. Then stepped to the chest and, after running her fingers through her hair a few times, used the dagger-like pin to fasten her hat on. She was, I knew, preparing to disappear.

I stood as well, suddenly not wanting her to leave. "What *is* your real name?" I asked.

"Esther Lovenier," she replied, again with the same French lilt as *une fille de joie*.

"It's lovely," I whispered. And after a moment, "Can I pick you up tomorrow evening, Esther? I'll hire a cab."

She hesitated, and it struck me how hard this was for her. To surrender anything private, anything personal, was almost painful. Finally, she nodded. "I'll write down the address for you," she said.

CHAPTER TWENTY-THREE

NOTHING ABOUT ELLA LOVING, OR ESTHER LOVENIER for that matter, looked like Anna Ulmann.

Nothing in the way she spoke reminded me of Anna's voice, except perhaps the humor that lurked there.

Her clothes, her personal accessories did not remind me of those I associated with Anna. Except perhaps during the dozen or so instances when the Anna I first met set out to make herself especially attractive, especially enticing.

Hell, even Ella's perfume was something far too exotic and spicy to recall the soap-and-vanilla smell of Anna's hair and skin.

And yet . . . and yet, there was something. Like an echo of one woman in the other. Something like the refrain of a tune heard long ago at a country crossroads that resurfaced in Ella's presence. One woman reflected and recalled the other. In a harsh, physical sense, one woman rekindled the other. Although Anna's grace was largely unstudied, unconscious even, and Ella's was practiced to perfection, the grace was there in each. Two verses of the same song.

SINCE THE SHATTERING EVENTS IN NEW YORK, WHEN I had discovered the woman I thought of as *my* Anna at the Anderson Gallery in the arms of her well-heeled patron, I had set about to forget her. To consciously erase her from my memory along with the glimpse of her exposed flesh and his grasping fingers, along with the sound of her moans mixed with his audible grunts of desire.

Not long after, I had fallen into the refuge of Lucy Paul, returned with her to North Carolina, where we married, and she died giving birth to Luke. Each step along the way, I meant to forget Anna Ulmann. I meant to forget the penetrating pain she had caused me, and I meant to leave every emotional vestige of her behind me—not just for my sake, but also for the sake of my dead wife. Out of respect and loyalty for Lucy, out of my love for my son, I had been determined to walk on, beyond the reach of Anna Ulmann.

And yet, here she was. When Ella Loving breathed, it seemed to me that Anna breathed. When she spoke, she reminded me that Anna spoke. When she turned from the waist and glanced over her shoulder, there was the ghost of Anna.

The question, though, was this: In recalling Anna Ulmann, did Ella redeem her? Or did she merely release her to haunt me?

CHAPTER TWENTY-FOUR

Overlook.

How many separate and related meanings are associated with that word? A high place that allows you to see far, a perch from which you may peer down your nose at the rest of humanity. A commanding position from which to regard the world. Or in a different sense, a failure to notice something. Whether an accidental failure or an intentional one. A deliberate ignorance of something right in front of your face, especially if that something is beneath you somehow—as when the rich man manages to *overlook* the bum starving on the corner.

Castle.

Given the opportunity, who builds for himself—or herself—a castle? Or if you do choose the grand expense and imposing construction of a large house from which you might look down at the world, what would possess you to call it a castle? Biltmore, the Vanderbilt estate southwest of town, was merely a house, but Overlook was a castle. If you were Benjamin Loftis, what pressing needs would those two words—*overlook* and *castle*—satisfy inside you?

All these thoughts surged back and forth through my mind during the taxi ride across town to the address Ella had given me, which turned out to be a small house on a side street in a fancy neighborhood named Montford. The house itself might even have been called a cottage, as it was nestled to the side and behind a much more significant edifice. Later, I would learn that

Ella, rather Esther, owned the edifice as well and rented it to a large family.

I never made it to the door of the cottage because the moment I was out of the taxi in the drive, Esther Lovenier rose from a swing partially concealed beneath a tree at the edge of her yard and stepped out to meet me.

I've said before that to watch Ella Loving move through the crowded lobby of Grove's inn was a fascinating experience because she could manipulate how she was seen and if she was seen at all. She could be a hot-blooded cat on the prowl if you were her mark, and she wanted you to experience a sudden rush of blood to your head or some other part of your body. Or she could—a moment later—blend into the background of people, chatter, furniture so that she was barely there at all . . . and gone before you even noticed her.

But the woman who met me on the sidewalk at 29½ Pearson Drive was not Ella Loving. Her twin, perhaps, if you looked closely, but it couldn't have been the woman herself. Rather, a demure, somewhat breathless young woman, closer to thirty than forty, was dressed quite tastefully, even expensively, in a wine-colored dress that managed to draw a subtle attention to itself without saying anything at all about the body beneath. Dark brown shoes and belt to match a leather purse. Cream-colored gloves. A stylish brown leather jacket against the chill. It was late evening, almost dark, when this woman who was not Ella Loving emerged from the shadows.

Then she spoke, and it was, despite the costume change, her voice and her laugh. "I believe you are my escort for the evening," she said, as I held the door of the taxi for her.

"Yes, Esther, I am. Please, call me Stephen." And then, after we were safely in the taxi, "Teach me to say *Lovenier* the way you say it."

OVERLOOK CASTLE TURNED OUT TO BE EVERYTHING the two words implied. First of all, it was set on a high promontory that overlooked the wooded expanse on the other side of Sunset Mountain. And second, when the taxi dropped us off at the head of the wide circular drive at the rear of the castle, we were welcomed by a handsome, well-dressed young man, a doorman, I suppose, who waved us into what we were told was the reception hall.

The room itself was narrow near the doorway but wide at the far end to support three large windows that faced west, where the sky was still fiery from the distant sunset. A second handsome, well-dressed young man—bookend to the first—took our coats away down a left-hand hallway after explaining that they would be safely stowed in the first guest bedroom and that he could fetch them at a moment's notice. What struck me almost at once about the two handsome young men is that Esther Lovenier had no noticeable effect on either. Ella Loving could have slain both with a glance and stepped blithely over their bodies, but Esther chose to cling to my arm and walk with her head slightly down and away from any prying eye. She was there, I realized, but in an entirely different way than any version of Ella I had experienced.

Two stairways flanked the reception hall, one to each side, both of which served as galleries for what I guessed were Loftis and Grove family photographs, framed and displayed. There was a small crowd of people in the reception hall, shedding coats, wraps, even a fur or two, calling out to each other in a way that clearly said they knew each other, had expected to see each other, mutually admired each other.

We turned to our right and passed under the staircase into what we came to understand was the living room. The space had the same, high-ceilinged grandeur as the reception hall, only with more space, more light, more quiet style. Just inside the door, Esther and I fell into a kind of informal line waiting to be greeted by Loftis and his wife. When our turn came, Loftis made a point of introducing said wife, a rather dowdy woman who seemed the perfect prim and proper complement for Loftis himself. In turn, he named me, without bothering to say who or what I was. I offered my companion. "Esther Lovenier, visiting from New Orleans." Loftis wrinkled his brow and glanced at me, as if to ask how in hell I knew such a stylish young woman from New Orleans.

Esther herself all but curtsied to the Loftises, mostly, I thought, as a way of obscuring her face and also disarming any suspicions they might have about her. We moved on into the large room, free from immediate social obligations. I secured a cup of punch for each of us from a table beside the ornate fireplace, and we circulated through the crowd. Nodding and smiling, sipping from our crystal cups. Each of us, in our own way, recording what was going on in that large space. The sound of a piano from a distant room, the clink of glasses, and the tidal wash of people, almost all of whom knew each other but didn't know us.

In the midst of it all, I saw Madison Aycock on the other side of the room, surrounded by a group of men, mostly older, holding court on some subject or other. I remembered that this whole event was to celebrate his engagement to the preacher's daughter, but I didn't spy her anywhere. Was she to be produced from offstage at the appropriate moment? I felt a subtle pressure on my arm and leaned toward Ella, whom I kept reminding myself to call Esther.

"I can feel the flask in your jacket pocket," she whispered. "What's in it?"

"Pure white liquor from Madison County," I whispered in reply.

"Lightning?"

I nodded and smiled as if replying to someone, anyone who might have spoken to us.

"I'm going to need it," she murmured, "to get through this." Then, as she had my attention, she nodded to the curved stairwell immediately across from the fireplace. Loftis himself had ascended two or three steps so that we might see him clearly above the mob of guests.

"Dear friends," he began. "We are gathered here this evening for the most delightful of occasions. My young protégé, Madison Aycock . . ."

Smattering of applause and appreciative laughter.

"Madison plans to announce something quite special this evening. And in anticipation of that announcement, I want to first recognize our other hosts for this little gathering. First, his father, Judge Bishop Aycock . . ." Loftis paused for the general acclamation of the old gent who was standing at the foot of the stairs below Loftis. The judge looked like a badger, old and ornery, with thick side whiskers from a previous generation. "And also, our dear friend, the minister of First Presbyterian Church, Reverend Doctor Avery, who will pronounce our blessing when we adjourn to the library for dinner." He paused for more admiration, this time for a bird that looked like he could use a square meal.

A scarecrow, I thought.

"And now, here is my young friend, Madison Aycock."

Aycock climbed up a few steps to stand beside Loftis, and in the general spasm of happiness and celebration, Esther managed to slip the flask out of my jacket, unscrew the top, and introduce a dollop of liquor into her punch cup and mine.

"Praise the Lord," she whispered as she slipped the flask back into my pocket.

Then ensued something that I struggle to believe actually happened, so strange did I find it. "Friend" Madison, of the tennis court tan and eternal, white-toothed smile, made a little speech. It went something like this.

"Ladies and gents," he started. Not gentlemen, gents. "I want you to know that in a few minutes, I'm going to announce something that will happily change the course of my life and, perhaps, the life of this fine community. I'm going to speak of commitment and virtue, love and marriage. But before I enter unto that sacred ground, I want to tell you a bit about what I believe."

I could feel Esther's grip on my elbow tighten. "Not that," she muttered for my benefit. "Anything but what you believe."

"I have been called a man's man," Madison told us. "The real McCoy, the true son of a distinguished father. Most of you probably think of me as the epitome of sophistication. And yet, despite the fact that I live in passionate pursuit of athletic and professional success, I am first, last, and always a Christian gentleman. I tell you tonight, ladies and gents, that I believe in something my friend, the Great Commoner, William Jennings Bryan, calls muscular Christianity."

A surprised but approving round of applause.

"Muscular . . . Christianity." Madison repeated himself in reply to the applause, bearing down on each word in turn, as if they were bloated with meaning. "I believe that a true man, a real man, loves his celestial Jesus just as much as he loves his terrestrial girl—both, I say *both*—the object of his sacred affection."

Applause broke out, real spontaneous applause. I glanced at Esther, who at the same instance, perhaps on the same impulse, met my eyes. Her face was perfectly still, perfectly composed, but her eyes shone with sly humor at Aycock and his Christian muscles.

"And in that spirit, the one true and Holy Spirit of our Lord and Savior, I want to invite Miss Beatrice Avery to join me here on the staircase."

Beatrice walked in through an opening from the far end of the living room, advancing slowly to yet another round of applause, blushing at all the attention. She also climbed the stairs to stand on the landing beside her Madison, who beamed at her. She was dressed beautifully but properly for the occasion, her dress barely revealing her ankles, and again you could see the ornate gold cross suspended around her neck.

Madison, holding her hand and smiling out at the crowd, now almost filling the room, raised his other arm for silence. You could see the successful politician in the man. He was the person just about every other man in the room wanted to be at that moment, the center of that well-heeled universe. "Ladies and gents, this"—and by *this*, he apparently meant the woman beside him—"this is what I've been saving myself for. This is the altar upon which I hope to present myself, pure and unsullied." He grasped Beatrice's arm and turned her slightly by way of presenting her to us, as we stared up at this show from below.

You can imagine. He didn't kneel before her, but he did remove a small box from his jacket pocket and place a ring on her left hand. She blushed an even deeper shade of pink and nodded as she choked back what appeared to be a genuine, spontaneous sob. He kissed her chaste, tear-stained cheek. More applause rang out, and that was that. They tripped lightly down the half-dozen stairs from the landing to the living room proper and began to collect the hearty congratulations of the assembled multitude.

As the crowd surged naturally forward toward the young couple, I half-turned toward Esther and leaned in a bit. "You buy all that?" I asked her. "All that purity and chastity, muscular Jesus?"

She shook her head almost imperceptibly. Whispered, "Him, not at all, or he wouldn't make such a show of it. Her, I'm not so sure. Maybe she's simple-minded." And then, after a moment, "I'm going to wander around a bit, visit the ladies' room, powder my nose. Who are we again?"

"I'm a friend of the Loftis family from New York, and you're my fond acquaintance visiting from . . . ?"

"New Orleans." She finished the sentence and then asked, "Just how fond of you am I?"

I started to answer, but she'd already slipped away.

CHAPTER TWENTY-FIVE

I DRIFTED OFF IN THE OPPOSITE DIRECTION, TOWARD THE door Beatrice the betrothed had entered from, curious to see what waited beyond.

What waited were tables set for dinner, crowded into a room lined with bookshelves. I counted tables and estimated chairs and figured that, just as the invitation suggested, Loftis planned to feed his guests, perhaps fifty people all told. Miniature cards with carefully scribed names sat at each place setting, alongside what appeared to be champagne flutes as well as wine glasses. Apparently, even though there was supposedly no alcohol at Loftis's inn, there might be for a private engagement party at Loftis's castle. After a moment's search, I found my own name—although somebody had misspelled it *Steven*—and beside me, a card listing Esther Lovenier. We'd been seated at what looked like the back of the room, in a corner farthest from the main table. When, after a moment, I turned back toward the passageway to the living room, I found Aycock's father, the judge, staring at me.

Our eyes met as I walked casually back in his direction, and he nodded to me. "You Robbins?" he growled. Again, there was the impression of a badger in evening dress, huffing at me.

I nodded. "You the father of the groom?" I smiled when I said it, being polite.

Another nod. "I'm Judge Bishop Aycock, Superior Court."

I didn't have anything to say to that, being neither a judge nor a bishop. I intended to ease by the old goat, but he had planted himself firmly in the middle of the doorway and wasn't budging.

"You and I need to have some private conversation," he said finally. "Perhaps you'll join me for a cigar after dessert."

"Glad to," I said. "Although I didn't bring anything to smoke."

"I can set you up," he said and reached up to punch my chest lightly with his fist. "It won't take me long to say what I have to say."

BACK IN THE LIVING ROOM, THE CROWD OF GUESTS flowed slowly around the large space, as different individuals, couples, and groups made their way to Madison Aycock and Beatrice Avery to congratulate them. I still didn't see Esther, so I grabbed a second cup of the punch and let myself be swept along, chatting aimlessly with several people, all of whom were in awe of the castle and all of whom inquired—once I'd given up my name—about what I "did." Meaning what was my profession or, on another, deeper level, why was I there.

I tried "acquaintance of Loftis's from New York," on the assumption that it would be enough to satisfy, but one matronly type went a question further and asked me, "Just what is it that you do in New York, Mr. Robbins?"

I thought of my friend, Jack Durand, the man so highly placed that he didn't have to surrender his name. I told the inquisitive lady that I worked for the Bureau of Investigation and really couldn't be more specific than that. Her eyebrows shot up, for now I was a man of mystery.

When the natural flow of the crowd brought me around to the guests of honor, I stepped forward to do my duty. As I did, I happened to glance up and into the curved stairwell behind the couple, and there, on the landing where they had performed the engagement ritual ten minutes before, was Esther standing quietly in the shadows to one side, observing the scene below. I raised my eyebrows and nodded toward Madison and Beatrice. She shook her head and raised a finger to her lips. Meaning that I should let her be, let her keep watching.

Then I stepped up to the glowing couple, and the room seemed to brighten a bit, just from the heat and excitement that radiated from the two of them. Beatrice first. The pieces of the girl—for it was hard to call her a woman—had been carefully assembled for her big night. Her hair and makeup were impressive, perfect even. If most of the women there were dressed quite nicely, she was dressed as if for a ball, a princess at a ball. Her gown was a pale pink that matched her face when she blushed, as she did a lot that evening. She still had a perfect white glove on her right hand even though she'd removed the matching one from her left for the ring. The ring was big enough to choke a mule.

"Miss Avery, you look lovely this evening. Congratulations on your—"

Madison Aycock cut me off. "You remember him, honey. Stephen Robbins from the Grove Park Inn. He's here to . . . well, I suppose I'm not supposed to say why he's here. But he's our friend. Fine man, fine man." Aycock had me by the hand by then and was pumping my arm up and down with some of that muscular Christianity he was bragging about earlier. I glanced back at Beatrice Avery for a brief moment and was struck by the absolute triumph in her crystalline blue eyes. And then Aycock pulled me past her and directly to him.

As always, there was the smooth, tanned skin, the impossibly white teeth, the blistering enthusiasm, and, up close, the reminder of how big he was. Taller than me and broader through the shoulders. "We need to talk, Robbins . . . Stephen. Can I call you Stephen? Get to know each other. Let's have a cigar after dinner. Stroll around the grounds. Have a chat, man to man."

I nodded and agreed and was swept past. That's two cigars and two talks, I thought to myself, and wondered just what in the hell all these conversations were supposed to be about.

DINNER WAS UNEVENTFUL EXCEPT FOR ONE, NO, TWO things. The first is that we were seated with the parents of the bride and several of their family members, plus another couple who were prominent members of the Presbyterian Church. The whole meal took on a solemn, even somber tone at our table. There were flares of laughter and high tides of talk all around us, but after the Reverend Doctor Avery hauled himself to his feet like a crane to pronounce the blessing, a pronouncement that went on and on, we had a quiet time of it.

Nobody drank. Oh, the reverend toasted the bride and groom with something like a tablespoon of champagne when the waitress offered the bottle. His wife, mother of the bride, perhaps a teaspoon. The rest of us about the same, following the stern lead of Reverend and Mrs. Reverend. At one point, Esther slipped first her water glass and then mine beneath the table and managed to turn water into clear corn from the flask without batting an eye and without me even feeling her hand in my pocket. Thus, we survived what would have otherwise been an interminable meal.

The second remarkable thing about that dinner—eaten in the castle library of all places—was that Esther was not Ella. Even though she managed to doctor our water with all the dexterity of her counterpart, Esther gave no outward sign that she was anything but a deferential and devout young lady who paid attention to my needs and regarded the table with quiet respect. When the reverend asked both of us about our lives as Christians, Esther insisted I go first. I admitted to having been raised up as a solid-rock Baptist in the shouting and immersing line, which caused little surprise. Apparently, I looked like I'd been shouted at and immersed. Esther then confessed she'd been raised as a Catholic in New Orleans, which elicited no little shock and a good deal of sympathy from the Presbyterians. But she was recovering from that experience, she murmured, and hoped to hear the good reverend deliver one of his famous sermons on her next visit to Asheville. Everyone smiled and nodded, and Mrs. Reverend suggested that Esther should take counsel with their own daughter, Beatrice the betrothed, who taught the young women's Sunday School at their church.

All this sober, humorless conversation, and Esther managed to fit perfectly into place, while I must have looked and sounded like a convict recently released.

When we finally stood up from this dinner, Esther and I stepped back against the bookshelves that lined the walls, fitting ourselves into the corner of the room and letting the crowd slowly disperse.

"That might just be the most boring hour I have spent since I left the convent," Esther muttered.

I glanced at her. "Convent?"

"I'm joking. But I was raised a good Catholic girl, trained to keep my morals up and my skirt down. Why do you think they sat us—meaning you—with the churchgoers?"

"The whole point was for me to see just how utterly impossible it is for anyone in this room to have paid the Caldwell girl for sex and then shot her," I whispered.

"Well, nobody at our table has ever had sex in their entire lives, let alone paid for it." She smiled sweetly out at the room as she said this.

I nodded. "Precisely. Look, I'm supposed to have a few words with Judge Aycock and then talk man-to-man with his son before we can escape this place, so . . ."

She squeezed my arm. “I’ll be fine,” she assured me. “I’m going to take them up on their suggestion and see if I can spend a few minutes with Saint Beatrice. Learn how to be a Sunday School teacher.” And then she was gone.

CHAPTER TWENTY-SIX

IT DIDN'T TAKE ME LONG TO FIND THE JUDGE, MAINLY because the judge was looking for me. When Esther faded away into the crowd, I worked my way through the tables toward the doorway into the living room, and there he was, at almost exactly the same place he'd ambushed me before dinner. I had the strange sensation that he'd trapped me somehow, that I couldn't escape without dealing with him, and nothing that happened after suggested otherwise.

"Robbins," he called to me gruffly as I approached him, almost in a "hail fellow, well-met" sort of way, as if we were two gents who actually knew and liked each other. I nodded and smiled in turn, not trusting his tone for a second.

He motioned toward the far wall, and when I turned, I realized there was a door between the bookshelves—a door that led the two of us to a sort of porch beside the circular drive where the taxi had let us out earlier in the evening.

The judge produced two cigars from his inside jacket pocket and handed one to me. They were long and dark and looked expensive. They'd already been trimmed on one end, ready to go.

The judge was ready as well. He had a silver lighter in his hand almost before I'd stuck the stogie between my teeth to wet it with my tongue. He lit his first and then held the lighter up so I could set fire to mine. Most men would have just handed over the lighter, but not the judge. He casually let me see how expensive it was but kept it firmly in his own fist.

I thought there would be a few pleasantries first. "Warm night" or "wonderful meal," but Judge Bishop Aycock didn't waste any time with pleasantries.

"You're the Robbins who killed the sheriff down in Madison County, aren't you?" This he more or less growled around the stem of the cigar as he puffed away to get it burning evenly.

"I was there when the shot was fired. His name was Roy Robbins."

"Weren't you related? Brothers or something?"

"Cousins."

"I followed it in the newspaper at the time. Colleague of mine presided over your trial, and frankly I'm surprised there wasn't a conviction." He was jabbing at me, testing me.

"Sure," I said evenly. "We were known enemies, and it was my shotgun put him down."

He huffed. Only word I can think of for the sound he made . . . huffed, the way an angry bear does. And then, after a moment, "Listen, Robbins, I am good friends with Benjamin Loftis, close enough so that he told me why he invited you here tonight. Someplace you obviously don't belong if you grasp my meaning."

I started to reply, but he shook his head brusquely.

"You just listen, young man. Benjamin tells me that you've developed this cockamamie theory that someone who was at my son's campaign reception might have killed that Caldwell girl. You're probably not capable of understanding just how cockeyed that is. Somebody like you, smart maybe, but with barely a scrap of education to your name and no culture to speak of, wouldn't understand the difference between the kind of people who were there that night—hell, the kind of people who are here tonight—and the bastard that killed that girl." He paused to catch his breath and take a pull on the cigar.

"Must have," I said.

"What?"

"You said my cockamamie theory was that someone who was there *might* have killed Rosalind Caldwell. I'll call your bet and raise. I'd say that someone who was there *must* have done it."

This got him stirred up. He had to cough out a mouthful of smoke before he could rejoin, and you could tell he was irritated. "I take that personal, Robbins, whatever the hell your first name is. Sheriff Mitchell has a suspect locked away downtown for that crime, and I happen to know that he and the district attorney intend to indict him on Monday. This is over, and you need to understand that this is over. Whatever little game you're playing, acting like some sort of secret operative or whatever the hell you style yourself to be, the case is solved, and your presence is no longer required."

"I don't work for you."

"Everybody in this town works for me," he grunted. He took a pause, during which he must have realized he'd taken a step or two over the line. "And besides, I will instruct Loftis to dismiss you as soon as the indictment is a matter of record. We wouldn't want him wasting his money on a detective when the case is closed, now would we?"

I grinned back at the old codger. "I kind of like it here," I said to him. "Estates and castles and such. Might hang around even if I'm unemployed."

He stepped closer to me and jabbed me in the chest with the forefinger of his free hand. Not a Mitch Mitchell punch below the belt, but more than a gentle tap. "You hang around after you're no longer needed, Robbins, and I'll find a way to make you regret it. And I'm just the man who can do it. You understand me, son?"

"Oh, I understand you," I said.

"Good. Make goddamn sure you do." And then he turned on his heel and more or less shuffled back through the door into the house, closing it behind him. After a moment, when I tried the knob, it turned, but the door wouldn't budge. It was locked.

I stood there in the cold autumn air, nonplussed, and then started to laugh. The old man had grumped and growled and gnashed his teeth and then made a perfect exit. *Well, the hell with him*, I thought to myself, and enjoyed thinking it so much, said it out loud. Twice.

I walked on a gravel path toward the drive. To my left was a whole new part of Loftis's castle under construction, something that would eventually be several stories high by the looks of it. Mounds of large square-cut quarry stone blocked out the light of the moon. Whatever problems Loftis was having filling up Grove's inn apparently hadn't interrupted his castle-building. When I reached the circular drive, I turned to my right, aiming for the formal entrance all us guests had used earlier. It was a cool evening, but I was enjoying the cigar too much to hurry.

As I approached the door, full now of the light and sound of people departing, who should appear but the guest of honor, the golden boy himself striding straight at me as if aimed and fired. He strode up purposely with a cigar of his own ready to light. "Just the man I'm looking for," he said. "I was hoping you hadn't already left."

"I've been having some heart-to-heart with your old man," I said, "and he locked me out of the house."

Aycock laughed while working with his own fancy lighter, a twin to the one his father carried, to get his stogie up and running. "You have no idea how many times he's done that to me. Mostly when he didn't like something I'd said or done."

"In this case, he was just threatening me."

Aycock paused to slip the lighter back in his pocket, took the cigar out of his mouth and struck a pose. "'Everybody in this town works for me, young man,'" he intoned in a pitch-perfect impression of the judge.

I had to laugh. "Actually, he did say that," I admitted. "Among other things."

"Well . . ." Aycock shrugged. "He is powerful, and he is used to having his way. Come, walk with me for a bit." He reached out and took hold of my upper arm to steer me away from the door and across the lawn. "Mrs. Loftis doesn't like cigar smoke in the house," he offered by way of explanation.

"Just for a few minutes," I said. "My companion is still inside, and I hate to make her wait." I shrugged his hand off my arm. I'd had enough of the Aycock touch for one night.

"Understood, understood. I just wanted to tell you that I've been recruited by some of my father's friends to run for governor in a few years. I'm not sure I want the job, but they seem to think I'd be good at it. Everybody I talk to says that you are a very influential man up in Madison County, and I'd love to have you as part of my team, if you know what I mean."

"If by influential, you mean infamous."

He chuckled. "Oh, I know you've hit some bumps in the road. The judge told me you had a run-in with the sheriff up there a few years back and that you've done a little detective work now and then, but that's the kind of thing real men understand and appreciate. Not just cocktails and golf clubs. How about we stay in touch, the two of us, and in the spring, maybe you'd take me around and introduce me to people up there. Your good word would carry a lot of weight up in them hollers."

It suddenly struck me that Mr. Madison Aycock, esquire, might have hit the champagne and the wine a little too hard while celebrating his engagement. "You mean the hillbilly vote?" I asked him, trying to keep the sarcasm out of my voice.

"Exactly. The damn hillbilly vote. I'm glad we understand each other. You'd be willing to help me out, wouldn't you? There might just be a job in it for you, after the election, I mean."

"I'll think about that," I said and leaned over to crush out the last inch of my cigar in the pathway gravel.

"Excellent. I knew you were a good man, the first time I saw you in the lobby of the inn. Only the finest circulate through that establishment . . . what I like about it, in fact."

I had turned back toward the entrance of the castle, assuming he'd follow, which he did. "Congratulations," I offered, intending to keep him moving. "On your engagement, I mean. Miss Avery seems like a fine young woman."

"Cold, cold," he muttered, and at first, I thought he was talking about the October air. "She is a fine young woman, lots of connections, but cold as an icicle, if you know what I mean." He was almost slurring his words.

"Perhaps she's saving herself the same way you are," I suggested. We were almost to the door. "For the altar of matrimony." Somehow, I managed to say all this with a straight face.

"That's right," he seemingly brightened at the thought. "That will be a hell of a wedding night, don't you know."

We were at the steps, and I turned to shake his hand, mentally preparing myself for having my arm nearly wrung off. Once he had hold of me, he leaned in close enough for me to smell the alcohol and cigar smoke. "Don't forget about what I said," he murmured. "About helping with the campaign and all."

"Oh, I understand," I returned. Which was almost exactly what I'd said to his father.

CHAPTER TWENTY-SEVEN

"WOMEN SEE EMOTIONS."

This in the taxi on the way back to 29½ Pearson Drive. Esther Lovenier and I were leaning close in the back, whispering such that the driver couldn't hear what we were saying. It was dark in the back of the cab, and other than the murmur of our voices, almost silent.

"Men see and hear thoughts, or at least think they do." A slight shrug of her shoulders. "Women see and hear emotions."

"What's the difference?"

She poked me hard in the ribs. "Don't be dense. Thoughts are on the surface. It's the words that come out of your mouth. Emotions are what lies underneath the thoughts, what gives the words color and shape."

"Are you going to tell me what you saw at the castle? What emotions?"

"Tomorrow. I'm tired, and I need to think. Buy me lunch tomorrow downtown, and I'll tell you what I think I saw. Heard. Felt."

And that was it. That was all. When the cab pulled up at the foot of the driveway, she leaned closer for the briefest moment in the dark and kissed my jaw beside my eye. "Battery Park Hotel at noon. I have a date in the afternoon, but we can have lunch first."

FROM THAT DARK, SHADY STREET IN MONTFORD BACK across town in the cab, I was distracted by what she'd said, but even more by what she was. In the cab, tired and distracted, she was real somehow. Esther Lovenier had faded into Ella Loving almost as if the two women had merged into one. I placed my left hand on the ancient, cracked leather of the seat beside me, feeling for the leftover heat of her body, and it was there, faint but telling. Luminescent but fading. She was real, and this aspect of her, the Esther of her, reminded me yet again of Anna Ulmann. This part of her was less studied, less self-conscious. Not as graceful, not as seductive, not as feral as Ella Loving, and yet more appealing somehow. More human.

Questions, questions. Of the two women—Ella Loving versus Esther Lovenier—who would show up at lunch tomorrow?

Who was she? Esther? Ella? Anna? I was tired, and I was confused, and I decided I was thinking like a woman. Beneath reason, behind reason, feeling my way in the dark.

THE NEXT MORNING, I CALLED THE SHERIFF'S OFFICE and asked for Brody Mitchell. Was told brusquely what day of the week it was and why the hell did I think the deputies worked on Sunday. And before I could leave a message, the line went dead.

NOON AT THE BATTERY PARK HOTEL. A PLACE I'D heard of often enough but never visited. I waited in the lobby, a sort of miniature version of the Palm Court at Grove Park, pretending to read the Sunday paper. And when she arrived, a few minutes past high noon, I had to smile, for in the light of this day, it was crystal clear who she was. I was having lunch with Ella Loving.

Even though I prided myself on seeing without being seen, she was halfway across the lobby and walking in my direction before I noticed her. But when I did notice her, it was as if the air around us suddenly hummed. I was reminded of the first mention I'd ever heard of her name, when the old geezer running the Grove Park elevator named the sexiest woman he'd ever given a ride to. Noon and she was in full flower, I suppose you might say, dressed all in red, with her typical matching shoes and hat.

Then she was standing beside my chair, looking down at me and smiling. "I was looking for a Mr. Robbins. Might you be him?"

"Stephen," I countered. "And I was hoping to meet a Miss Loving. And if you are not her, I can't imagine who else in this brick-dust town might be." I was hoping to inspire one of her happy laughs, the sound of midday bells, or at least distant chimes.

But all I got was the twisty, ironic smile. "I'm famished, Stephen. Will you feed me?"

I stood up, and she took my arm, as she did from time to time when I least expected it.

As we walked into the hotel dining room, I glanced down at the side of her face, some fifteen or twenty inches away. "I thought you had a date this afternoon," I offered. "Aren't you afraid I'll scare him off?"

She shrugged. "His train isn't due in until one-thirty, and he shouldn't arrive on the scene till closer to two. I don't think you can scare him off long-distance. Besides, being seen with a stylish woman might do you some good. Stir up some interest in the local girls."

"Last thing I need," I muttered, "is interest from the local girls. I want to finish what I came here for and go home to Hot Springs." We were following the maître d' by this point.

"How many people live in Hot Springs?" she whispered. "Twenty or thirty?"

"Enough," I whispered back. "My best friend, his wife. My son."

She stopped dead in her tracks, which meant I stopped as well, tethered. "You never mentioned a son."

"Luke," I said. "He's three."

We were in motion again. And then, after I asked for a more private table, we were seated against the back wall, near the kitchen.

The waitress was not Michael Joyner, with his magic coffee-wine pot and his occult insights into the kitchen. Rather, she was friendly but bored and could tell us little about the menu except that it was all good, very good. This with a sleepy nod of her head.

Ella ordered a fancy salad and hot tea. I ordered a plate full of every vegetable they could offer and a piece of cornbread, plus coffee.

"Cornbread," Ella muttered. "You are homesick."

Once the food was on the table, I asked her what she heard and saw at Loftis's castle. "You first," she said. "It will help me put my thoughts together."

I told her about the two Aycocks, father and son, how one went out of his way to threaten me and then lock me out of the party, while the other just laughed it off and invited me to help him collect the "hillbilly vote."

And then, after a bite or two of food, added what Aycock Junior had said about Beatrice Avery being cold. Frigid.

Ella's eyes glittered when I said this, and she had to cover her mouth so that she could laugh. "I don't doubt he thinks that. After spending a little time with the girl, I'd say that she's so wrought up that it would take somebody a lot smarter than Aycock to get her clothes off. How's your food?"

"Except for the cornbread, lousy. Your turn."

She stared past my shoulder for a moment, and her eyes lost their focus. It was unusual in her, someone who was so intensely present. She was remembering, I realized, sifting through her impressions from the previous night, and then, just as suddenly, she was back. And she was whispering. "It might interest you to know that I saw three good country club men there at the castle who have paid me for an evening's entertainment."

"Entertainment?"

She shrugged. "Sex. Two of them because they claimed their wives were no longer interested, as if they had to justify it somehow—to me, of all people. And one cheerful gent, a bit older, who asked me to tie him up."

"Does that cost extra?"

That got a smile out of her. "No, but untying him after does. Otherwise, he'd still be in that hotel room."

"Did any of them recognize you?"

She shook her head, almost impatiently. "Of course not. Even as Esther, I didn't get close to any of them. But I did get close to the women. In the upstairs hallway, waiting outside the bathroom, standing casually on the stairs looking at the family photos. Listening all the while. And what I heard was that the jury is out on Mr. Madison Aycock."

"What do you mean, the jury's out?"

"That the women who were there were almost evenly split over whether Beatrice Avery, with that big shiny cross hung around her neck, has scored a major victory by getting herself engaged to the boy and will someday end up in the governor's mansion, or whether she's tied herself to . . ."

"To what?"

"To a relentless little prick who will do anything for power and money."

"Jesus."

She nodded and then, as the waitress had wandered by, asked for more hot water and another tea bag. I asked for another piece of cornbread and some butter this time.

The water, steaming, plus my bread and butter, came more quickly than expected, and as soon as the waitress was gone, I asked the obvious question. "Which is it, do you think? Governor or prick?"

In reply, she looked up from her tea, straight into my face, giving me full access to her eyes. "Both, Stephen. Don't be a child. With men like that, it's always both."

"You think the father is driving the son? Pushing him to succeed on . . . what? A bigger stage?"

She shrugged and then nodded. "I don't understand fathers and sons. That's for you."

"My father died when I was a boy, and I ran away from home not long after. But from what I've seen, most fathers, ambitious fathers, can't help themselves. They push the sons to be and do what they couldn't. Take the whole family enterprise to the next level."

After I said this, I looked up from spreading butter on my cornbread and caught her watching me. "Who raised you?" she murmured.

"After I was fourteen, I raised myself."

She nodded, paused, and then nodded again. "Interesting," was all she said.

There was a full stop in the conversation. We both were thinking our thoughts and sipping the coffee and tea to give our hands something to do.

"One more thing about the Aycocks," Ella said after a moment. "Apparently, Madison's mother killed herself a few years back. Despair, loneliness, hard to say, but she took poison, and the two women I heard replaying it pretty much blamed the judge."

This time, when our eyes met, there was a bleakness, an emptiness, and I again had the odd but distinct feeling that I was staring into a mirror. Seeing some version of myself inside the wavering image in front of me.

"Who in Loftis's crowd, at that dinner last night, could have done it?" I muttered.

"Killed the Caldwell girl?"

I nodded.

"I don't know, but I'll tell you this. Half the men there probably have enough fire in their bellies to pay somebody like me to put out for them. Half the men there could have been in that hotel room with her that night if circumstances favored it."

"Half?"

She smiled ruefully, ironically. "Trust me, Stephen. Half."

"So the question, then, is really who among the half could have shot her when it didn't go as planned."

She seemed to nod, even though her head barely moved and her face not at all. "Ask yourself who has the most hatred coiled up in his gut" is what she said next. "Or who has the most to lose if he's found out."

I chewed the last bit of cornbread slowly, savoring the rough texture with the sweet butter. Thinking about what she'd said. "You know what I just realized?" I offered after a moment.

She raised her eyebrows.

"I think about that woman's lonely, abandoned body out in the mud on the side of Beaverdam Road, and I remember just how nasty and cold this world can be. But then, when you really stop to consider, you see that the life inside Loftis's reception, the country club people and their sweet little engagement party, is just as nasty and just as cold. Only difference is it has a castle wrapped around it."

A few minutes later, she took the last sip of her tea, dabbed at her lips with the napkin, and asked me how she looked.

I considered, searching for the right words. "Exquisite," I finally said, "but sad."

She deliberately recomposed her face.

"Less sad," I replied.

"Good. I'm meeting my date in the lobby in a few minutes. Sit here and finish your coffee, so you won't terrify him. And Stephen?"

"Hmm?"

She was standing now, beside the little table where we'd sat for lunch. Standing and looking down at me. Her lips parted as if to speak, but she hesitated. I got the feeling that I was watching her change her mind. "Where will you be later?" she finally asked. "Tonight, after your supper?"

"Back at the inn," I said. "I'm going downtown this afternoon, but I should be back at the inn by dark."

"I might see you there," she offered. "At that room of yours." And then she did an odd, uncharacteristic thing. She laid her gloved hand on my shoulder, an almost affectionate gesture. "I'm worried about you," she whispered. "You look like death."

CHAPTER TWENTY-EIGHT

When I found Brody Mitchell, he was standing out in front of the Buncombe County courthouse with about a hundred other people, mostly men, jostling to get close to a makeshift podium that had been set up on the broad sidewalk near the side entrance that led to the sheriff's department. Brody was leaning against the monument to the Confederate dead, waiting for whatever was coming from the podium.

When I walked up, he nodded and smiled through the smoke from his Camel. "You're right on time," he said. "Mitch is supposed to make an announcement in a few minutes, and the crowd is getting restless."

"What's he going to announce?"

"Don't know for sure, as I'm on the outs these days. Since I started hanging around with you, I'm not so much in favor with brother Mitch. What I think he's going to say, though, is that they've solved the case. Made the world safe for the citizens of our fair city."

"Bullshit."

Brody nodded and grinned. "Of course it is. But the city fathers have been after Mitch to put an end to this for days. He's starting to feel the pressure, plus he's up for reelection in November and doesn't want to give up his badge and his bulletproof car."

"Did you try talking to him about the woman we found out in Beaverdam?"

He shrugged and stubbed out his cigarette on the side of the monument. "You know, I did. Just yesterday at his house out in Black Mountain. But he wasn't doing much listening and finally told me to shut up and grow up. Had a few choice things to say about you as well."

Just at that moment, the high sheriff himself came out through the side door of the courthouse and stepped up to the podium. The crowd pressed forward. Flashbulbs began to pop, and pocket notebooks came out. I realized that a good portion of the crowd were reporters and photographers from various newspapers, enough to represent a wide swath of the region.

"Murder sells, don't it?" I remarked to Brody, who nodded.

"This kind does," he muttered.

"Think we'll see Viola Martin in the newspapers?" I asked.

Brody shook his head impatiently. "Not if Mitch has anything to say about it. He'll hush it up. Besides, the side of a dark country road is a different matter from the high and mighty Grove Park."

Mitch himself looked downright presentable. His dark blue suit was pressed, and somebody had convinced him to put on a clean white shirt for the occasion. Even his tie looked like it had been knotted by human hands. He took his hat off and set it on the podium and then smoothed his hair back for the photogs. He held his arms up for silence.

"Ladies and gentlemen of the press. I am pleased to come before you this afternoon with good news. We have had a breakthrough in the case. I can't give you all the details at this time because I need to consult with the district attorney and his office to confirm our arrangements for prosecution of the murderer.

"But what I can tell you is that we have released one of the two suspects we were holding in the Rosalind Caldwell case, as we no longer have any interest in him."

"Which one?" a reporter shouted. "Which one did you turn loose?"

Mitch once again held up his arm for silence, fully aware that the pose would look good on the front of the evening edition. "We have released Roscoe Taylor, of Haw Creek, who was one of our two primary suspects. Mr. Taylor and his wife have asked that you respect his privacy, as all he wants is to return home to his family. He will not be making a statement."

"That means you think the colored boy done it!" shouted one of the men in the crowd, lean and angry, obviously not a reporter.

Mitch ignored him but did pause to let the hornet's nest buzz work its way back and forth through the crowd. "That's all we have for you at the moment," he called out. "I'm asking all of you in the press to refrain from making any further speculation on this matter until noon tomorrow, when I promise you to release the full facts of our investigation along with our plans for indictment and prosecution."

"Can we print what you've already told us? Solved the case, released Taylor?"

Mitch nodded dramatically. "Yes. Just that and nothing more until tomorrow. Remember, I said noon!" And with that, he slapped his hat back on his head, turned, and disappeared back through the doors into the department.

"What the hell's he up to?" I asked Brody. "'We've solved it, but we can't tell you.'"

Brody shrugged and nodded toward the doors where Mitch had disappeared inside. "I figure he's settled on the colored man as his best bet."

"That's ridiculous."

Another shrug. "Of course it is, but my guess is that Mitch thinks he's got enough to go forward, and that little show he just put on is making the high and mighty around here awfully happy."

I sighed. I didn't like it, any of it. I knew that the smart money would tell me to just walk away and let George Moore—whoever he was—get torn to pieces in the sawmill that was Southern justice at its worst. I remembered how the judge had threatened me the night before, told me that if I hung around after I was no longer wanted, he'd find a way to make me pay. But then, I'd spent my own days and nights in the Buncombe County jail, and I didn't favor getting sent home by a judge who looked like a badger.

"What do you want to do?" Brody asked.

"Let me try to talk to Mitch," I said. "Just for the smoking hell of it."

YOU COULD HEAR MITCHELL LAUGHING FROM DOWN THE hall. A deep, echoing "haw, haw, haw" that sounded like something you'd hear in a swamp on a dark night. When Brody and I eased into the office, the same office where the honorable sheriff had sucker punched me last week, Mitch and the hired goon from New York were standing around his desk with two other deputies, and all four were hoisting glasses, toasting their success with a jar of confiscated moonshine.

Brody stepped aside, and I stepped forward.

To Mitch's credit, he was the first one who noticed me, and when he did, he snorted a mouthful of shine all over the desk and one or two of the other men. "What the hell are you doing here?" He coughed. "We're in the middle of a high-level strategy meeting, you little . . ."

Thankfully, both the desk plus six hundred pounds of idiot law enforcement were between me and Mitch, so I had a chance to say a few things while he was working to get at me.

"I'm trying to keep you from making a bad mistake, Mitch. There's been another prostitute murdered since you locked up your suspect. Another murder with the same weapon, same rationale, same twenty-dollar bill. That poor bastard you got upstairs couldn't have . . ." And that's as far as I got. Mine were all valid points, carefully selected, expressed in a simple English that even Mitch could understand.

But that's not what our dialogue sounded like, because Mitch was squealing and cussing at the desk, at the other men in his way, at his brother, and at me. In his hurry to express himself, he came over the desk rather than around it.

I backed up as he careened toward me, but I missed the open door and backed into the wall beside it instead. Before I could edge sideways and out into the hall, Mitch slammed into me belly first, which was the way Mitch slammed into almost anything, and then his hog face was all but grinding into mine. The stench of hard twist chewing tobacco, rank sweat, and raw alcohol almost put me down, and his words didn't help either. "Listen, you snaggle-toothed little shit . . ." He was whispering for some odd reason, maybe thinking that no one else in the room could hear him. "I don't care who killed that girl in that goddamn hotel room, and I don't care who killed that tired old whore on the side of the road that you and Brody are so mired up about. All I care about is getting this nightmare over with. And if you get in the way or otherwise muddy the goddamn water, I will put you in jail for obfuscating a law officer, and I will keep you there. In fact . . ."

He stepped back. I knew what was coming but didn't have time to get my hands up before he hit me so hard right under my breastbone that my eyes went dark and every stitch of air I owned went moaning out of my gaping mouth. "In fact," I think I heard him say over the sound of my own groaning, "I think we'll just lock your sorry ass up right now and hold you for cause."

I WASN'T IN THE CELL ON THE THIRD FLOOR FOR LONG, three hours maybe, before Brody showed up with a ring of jailhouse keys and let me out. Long enough for my lungs to remember how to breathe and for my back to stop aching where I'd caught a nightstick across my kidneys on the way upstairs. When I finally began to feel like I might live, I sat up on the bunk and scrubbed Mitch's stink off my face using my own spit and the tail of my shirt.

Only three hours or so, but it was long enough to bring flooding back the long days and frigid nights I'd spent in the basement of the old jail, waiting to be tried for murder and knowing full well that the odds were long against me. My skin, my bones, my mind recoiled at just how much I hated being locked up, cut off, buried alive. I remembered just how much . . .

How much I needed to go home.

Brody showed up as soon as things quieted down and they switched off the lights in the cell block. He led me quietly down a back stairway and out a mysterious door into the darkest of dark alleys. When I tried to thank him, he just shook his head and pointed me toward a distant corner, barely lit by a flickering gas streetlight.

CHAPTER TWENTY-NINE

"YOU ALL RIGHT, STEPHEN?" THIS FROM MICHAEL AT dinner. "Look like a conscript in hell."

I followed his lead, barely moving my mouth to whisper a reply. "Feel like hell." I turned to stare out the window beside my table so no one in the dining room could read my lips. "Tried to talk sense to Mitch Mitchell this afternoon and got beat on pretty good. Beat on and locked up."

"Talk sense about George Moore?"

I nodded.

"The kind of sense that says he never could have killed that woman?"

I nodded again. Then glanced back up at Michael's broad brown face. Met his eyes.

"I'm going to send a little something up to your room after dinner. Bottle of something that might help ease the evening along."

I smiled. "Thank you, Michael. It's a very old and troubled world, isn't it?"

MICHAEL'S BOTTLE DIDN'T HAVE A LABEL ON IT, BUT IT was the sort of medicine that they made up in Kentucky before prohibition. Bourbon whiskey, dark and almost spicy.

Plus it arrived at room 340 at just about the same time as my nurse, who was dressed all in red and was also spicy, like the bourbon. I pulled off my jacket, slowly, painfully, and kicked off my shoes. She drew out that long hatpin and tossed her elegant hat on the dresser. Kept her shadowed eyes on my face while she removed her own shoes, more slowly and carefully so as not to scuff.

"You look worse than you did at lunch," she said. "What the hell happened?"

WITH THE HELP OF THE BOURBON, I TOLD HER ABOUT the afternoon. With the help of the bourbon, she kept asking questions. Questions that went further back than the Grove Park Inn and the murder of Rosalind Caldwell. I told her that too. Damn near my entire life story starting with the death of my father, the whole woven in threads and strands of loss. Especially that of Anna in New York, followed by what happened on Ellis Island. So many ghosts, grieved only by the wind.

I do seem to recall that she said at one point, "At least your son is alive." Meaning Luke. Then she whispered, "Unlike mine."

"What do you mean, unlike yours?" I asked, but she only shook her head, refusing to answer.

When I was done, when I'd brought the story up to the death of Lucy, I had talked myself into a dark corner. She got up and poured more bourbon for both of us.

"That's a long, sad tale, Stephen Robbins, I grant you. But it's been three years since your wife died. Why haven't you found somebody else?"

There was a long pause, while I struggled with how to explain. "Sometimes, I think there is someone, someone I need to . . . contact."

"A real person made of flesh and blood? Not some ghost that hovers over you while you sleep? I bet you talk in your sleep."

"Yes."

"Yes, what? That you talk in your sleep?"

"No. I mean *yes*, she is a real person. As real as you." I reached across and pressed on her knee with my fingertip. "If she were here, you could touch her."

"Nobody is as real as me, Stephen."

I grinned at her, the liquor glowing in my gut. "She might be."

"Well, then, why in the hell don't you go after her? Send for her. Bring her here. Hell, marry her if that's what it takes." Ella crossed her ankles on the coffee table. "You can be aggravating as hell sometimes." She took a sip from her tumbler and laughed.

I nodded. The bourbon was stronger than the wine that Michael normally sent me. So strong that it hit me down low. Hot in the throat and warm beneath. "I don't think I work anymore," I said.

"What do you mean, 'work'? You're always working, some days even harder than I do."

"Not what I mean." I nodded down at my lap. "Below the belt. I'm not sure I'm alive anymore." I could feel the hot flush of blood in my neck and face as the truth came out.

She slowly arched her eyebrows, her cat eyes as wide open as I'd ever seen them. "How long has it been, Stephen, since you had a woman? Tell the truth."

I counted back in my mind to the days and nights in Hot Springs around the time that Lucy and I married. There had been a few months when I was recovered from Ellis Island and she wasn't yet so big with Luke that it became uncomfortable. A few, mostly happy months.

"How long, Stephen?"

"Almost four years."

"Jesus, Mary, and Joseph." She let her bare feet slip to the floor and sat up. "Are you lying to me?"

I shook my head and held up four fingers.

"And you don't think your cock works?"

I was still shaking my head.

"*When the pecker don't peck and the rooster won't crow,*"

she sang softly.

"Something like that. I think it's dead."

She shook her head slowly and then nodded toward the bedroom. "Come into my examination room," she said quietly. "And let Dr. Loving consider your case."

"I'm not sure . . ."

"No, you aren't sure, damn it, of anything. That's the problem, isn't it? But honey, I'm the resurrection woman. I can be sure enough for the both of us."

In the bedroom, she made me take off all my worn and soiled clothes, including my briefs, wash with a cloth soaked in warm water, and prop myself up with pillows against the headboard. I was sore both front and back from the beating I'd taken at the jail, but between the bourbon and what came next, I soon forgot about that. She extinguished all the lights except for the lamp glow through the sitting room doorway.

Then, while she hummed to herself, she took off most of her clothes.

But that's not right. It's not how you and I take off clothes. She took hers off like the bourbon in her hand and the jazz in her head were together stripping her down to skin. As if her own hands had little to do with it. Down to some barely there red items that flitted and gleamed like flame against her alabaster skin. Items that were there and then gone.

She had a body like a young, feral cat. Mostly thin and wiry but rich with possibility.

Watching her dance, you could hear what she heard, the narcotic pounding in her blood rising through her body. Her thighs, her hips, belly, breasts—even her neck, her shuttered eyes, her face were all in motion. She was humming under her breath and then the humming became half moaning, crooning. I could feel sweat beading all over my body.

I took one more sip of the bourbon—my throat was

suddenly as dry as road dust—before she sat both our glasses on the side table and floated onto the bed to commence her examination.

I will tell you that she did some things with her fingers and her tongue and her teeth and her nipples and her sex for which there are no words raw enough to describe. Neither you nor I know a language that thoroughly lascivious. I would tell you to use your imagination, but you could not imagine some of the things she did.

She ripped the pity out of me and bit it in half with her teeth. She darted her cat's rough tongue inside my mind and rifled through any inhibitions that were left—and shamed them, shredded them.

She used my body the way a half-drunk musician uses an instrument to the breaking point and beyond. By the end, she even had me convinced I was leading the dance. That I was riding her like the witch she was rather than the other way around.

And when she was done, she left me washed up on a midnight beach with no more awareness than if I'd been struck deaf and dumb by the forked lightning of her thighs, her hands, her throat. Expended, wasted, and possibly . . . healed.

THE NEXT MORNING, WHEN I SLOWLY—AND I DO MEAN slowly—came back to life and rolled over in the tangled sheets, she was sitting in the bedroom chair fully dressed, even down to her jewelry.

"Can you breathe?" she asked me.

"No."

"I have completed my examination, and there's nothing wrong with you."

"Jesus."

"I know. Not so bad for an old man with too many scars."

She paused to consider. "No, that's not quite right. 'Old,' I mean. I have decided you are a young man hiding inside an old man's scars. You need to stop paying attention to the scars and listen to that drum inside you. Which, by the way, offers up a pretty fine beat."

Her words alone caused my cock to stir. "Maybe you're right," I admitted.

"I'm always right, Stephen. At least when it comes to things like this. I'm the doctor in matters like this." She stood up, preparing to leave, even while I was still sprawled across the bed. "But if you want any more of this medicine, you're either going to have to marry it or pay for it."

"I've got some time . . . this afternoon. Get married?"

She paused before answering, but not for long. "Nope. I'd make you miserable, and besides that, since the operation was a success, it's time you got in touch with whatever her name is."

"Anna."

She nodded, smiled. "Her."

I took an experimental sip of the warm bourbon still sitting on the side table, just to dampen my tongue. It tasted about how you'd expect at seven o'clock in the morning, but at least it was wet. "Pay for it, did you say?"

"You can't afford it." She was grinning now too.

"How much?"

She told me, by the hour and by the night, including a menu of favors so wonderfully graphic that I won't repeat them here.

"You're joking. There's no way in . . ."

"Are you saying I'm not worth it?" She was teasing, but then again, she wasn't.

I grinned my foolish grin. "Obviously, you're worth it, but who has that kind of money?"

"Oh, you'd be surprised. Many of the men—and a few of the

women—who stay in this cave, as you like to call it."

She stood to go, and I sat up on the bed, more or less. "If you ever need a friend," I offered, the words out of my mouth before the thought was fully formed.

She lifted her chin to regard my scarred, beaten, hungover self. "I don't need anybody, Stephen," she said, suddenly serious. "Not anymore. Not like you need your Anna." She walked to the door, and then turned, smiled, fully herself again. "Besides, who would be friends with somebody like me?"

CHAPTER THIRTY

NOON.

I'm not even sure why I bothered to go back downtown, especially considering that as far as I knew, Mitch Mitchell thought I was three floors up, locked safely away in a corner cell.

But somehow, I thought it was the end of the story. The last chapter in my little sojourn in Asheville, North Carolina, searching for the murderer of Rosalind Caldwell. Thought I might as well blend into the audience and see what the real actors, the people with the power, had to say. So, I found an inconspicuous spot in a copse of trees a half block away from where Mitch had made his teaser announcement the day before. Blended into the shade, cool even at noon, and waited. Seeing without being seen.

Or so I thought. A minute or so before straight-up noon, who should stroll by on the sidewalk in front of me but Madison Aycock himself, the golden boy, the hope of good white men everywhere. Impeccably dressed as usual, looking like he'd just sprung fully formed from the teeming mind of some advertising executive, the perfect young man on the make. I couldn't help myself; I cleared my throat just loudly enough for him to hear me.

He glanced up and noticed me leaning against the trunk of a sycamore. Saluted me with two fingers to his hat brim. Then paused, seemed to consider for a moment, and without regard for his perfectly polished shoes, stepped into the trees to join me. He didn't offer his hand to shake, perhaps because I had my own arms crossed firmly over my chest. "I'm glad to see you, Robbins," he said loudly, firmly, full of good fellowship. "I'd heard that you already left town, and I wanted a chance to say goodbye."

"Still here," I said softly. "Like a bad penny." I wondered if he'd remember some of what he'd said to me up at Loftis's castle, about the hillbilly vote and his icy fiancée.

He chuckled. "Well, I'm glad. Glad I caught you before you left. Men like us have to stick together, you know?" He was jingling what sounded like a ring of keys in his pocket, too loud for just spare change.

"What made you think I was leaving?"

He shrugged. "Mr. Loftis called you in to solve his little murder, and from what I hear, Sheriff Mitchell has finally gotten that all squared away." He turned and pointed toward the podium. The same podium as the day before, set up by two courthouse employees in roughly the same place. "Perhaps you helped him solve the case?"

I shook my head. "The sheriff and I don't exactly agree on—" But before I could say what we didn't agree on, Mitch himself came striding confidently out of the building, accompanied by a smaller man, dressed in a trim dark brown suit. Dry hair lay combed back over a high forehead, a thin, pale, intelligent face, and wire-rimmed glasses. He looked vaguely familiar. "That the DA?" I asked Aycock.

"Sure is. Sam Adler. Doesn't look like much just standing there, but he's hell in front of a jury."

The name Adler finished the thought for me, sent a little shiver up my spine.

"Once he gets you in the courtroom, you don't walk away," Aycock added.

I did, I thought, but didn't quite say. I walked away.

And then Mitch started his spiel, rocking back and forth on his heels, gesturing grandly for the cameras, and telling us all that it was finished. They were confident they had their man, George Moore, and that our fine prosecutor, Mr. Samuel Adler, was confident of the case. Everyone, everyone could sleep safe in their beds at night and walk the streets and drive the roads of Buncombe County knowing that law and order reigned supreme.

Mitch stepped back—even though you got the sense that he really didn't want to—and Adler stepped up to the mic, adjusting the height down to his level. "Ladies and gentlemen, I would just like to say that it is a mark of civilization when we can band together to stamp out the violence in our midst, and in this case, Sheriff Mitchell and his peerless deputies have worked night and day to—"

"You got that boy up there on the third floor, sheriff?" This shouted from up front, close to the podium. "Sitting pretty, is he?" Only one voice, but the crowd, you could tell, was starting to hum. "Leave the door unlocked tonight, sheriff, and we'll take care of him for you!"

Mitch pointed, and several of his peerless deputies shoved their way into the mass of reporters and photographers to drag the man who was yelling and shaking his fist out of the crowd.

Adler tried again. "The sheriff and his men have taken great care to guarantee that they got the right man and that we can now proceed with a mercifully swift trial. Are there any questions?"

"Not merciful for him," I remarked to Aycock.

"Who?"

"For George Moore. Not so merciful for him."

"He deserves what he gets. If the jury convicts him, and I think we both know it will, he deserves what he gets." Aycock turned away from the spectacle in front of the sheriff's department to face me. He was jingling the keys in his pocket again, restless maybe, or even nervous. "I just remembered. Didn't you once stand trial for murder?"

"Twice," I said. "Once down in Marshall, and once right over there in the old courthouse."

"And you were acquitted? Both times?" You could tell it surprised him a little, maybe just the thought that anyone could walk away from a jury, not once but twice.

I gave him my best mysterious grin. "Both times. And your Mr. Samuel Adler prosecuted me the second time."

Aycock chuckled. "You might be the luckiest son of a bitch in North Carolina." He reached out to clap me on the shoulder. "Well, George Moore won't be so lucky."

"What makes you think he'll even stand trial, Aycock?"

"What do you mean? And call me Madison, since we've become friends."

"What makes you think that he'll even live to stand trial, Madison? That he won't somehow mysteriously hang himself in his cell while under the watchful eye of the sheriff? Or that Mitch won't look the other way while the local bedsheet boys come to drag him out of his cell? What sort of fairy-tale world do you live in?"

You would have thought I'd punched him in the gut, Mitch Mitchell style. He took both hands out of his pockets for the first time and used one stiff finger to poke me in the chest. "I'll tell you why Moore will stand trial," he said, looking down at me in more ways than one. "He'll stand trial because this is the twentieth century, that's why, and this is a civilized community. The stalwart men of this county, my father among them, would never allow anything to happen to that boy in the jail. Never. Our reputation is at stake."

"Moore's no boy," I countered, feeling the blood rising. "He's a grown man like you. Mitch should move him to another location. This afternoon, before nightfall. Probably to another state. And you know it."

"I know nothing of the kind. That bo—man is going to stand trial right here in Asheville, and then the world will know that we are a modern city on the make. Fair, upright, and honest. The kind of place where anyone can take a safe, restful vacation. The kind of place where any modern family would want to live."

The amazing thing was, he believed it, every word of it. "Five'll get you ten," I said, "that if George Moore does stand trial, it'll be over in two days."

CHAPTER THIRTY-ONE

MADISON AYCOCK AND I TURNED AND WALKED UP THE street, away from the spectacle of the sheriff and the DA preaching to the crowd of reporters and posing for the photographers. Seemed to me that there was still a vicious undercurrent in the edges of the crowd, back away from the bright lights of noonday sun and flashing light bulbs. Something that smacked of the Klan and prisoners dragged out of cells at midnight.

I was at loose ends. It did feel like I was done with Asheville, North Carolina, even though my erstwhile employer, Benjamin Loftis, hadn't cut me loose quite yet. Walking beside me, Aycock was equally quiet, thoughtful even, although you don't associate deep thoughts with a man like him. As we came up to Pack Square, he paused beside a new Packard roadster, all beautiful, glossy metal and shining chrome.

Aycock stopped beside the driver's door and finally pulled the ring of keys that he had been playing with from his pocket. I had a dull flashback to the cabinet of keys behind the registration desk at the Grove Park, but that seemed far away now, as if in another time and place. I started to turn away and walk on without speaking to the handsome young brute in front of me, but he reached out to grasp my hand. "I'll take that bet, Robbins," he said, and smiled.

"What bet?"

"You offered me five against ten that the prisoner will be railroaded at trial. I say he stands trial fair and square, and this whole thing disappears into the history books."

He wasn't pumping my arm up and down the way he did when he shook hands in public, but his grip was strong enough that I couldn't pull away without an effort. "Why do you think that? Given all the long history of this sort of thing, why would you think *fair and square* is the way of the world?"

"Because it has to be. It just has to be. The Grove Park Inn needs it. The city needs it. Hell, the whole region needs it. Reputation, tourism, prosperity. You know the drill, you used to work in the hotel trade, for God's sake."

"What the hell are you selling, Aycock? You don't give a shit about the Grove Park Inn."

"Myself. That's what I'm selling. And don't you for one minute think otherwise. Everybody is selling something. My father taught me that a long time ago. And one day before long, I'm going to be selling Madison Bishop Craig Aycock to the entire state, and trust me, the state will love every minute of it."

I stood by and watched as he drove away. What had he said? *Madison Bishop Craig Aycock.* Church and state, family pride and prestige, old money breeding new money.

And who was I to argue with all of that? Stephen Baird Robbins, hill born and runaway, failure at love and life, rarely two bills in my wallet to rub up against each other.

It felt to me just then that I'd done all I could to slow down the awful machine that was Asheville power and influence, grinding its way to a solution and an execution, with salty old Mitch Mitchell as its puppet. It felt like I couldn't really name the killer any more than I could save the poor man upstairs in the jail who was going to take his place in the electric chair. There were too many brick walls without doors, too many dark rooms without windows.

Or even if I could put my hand on the real killer, there wasn't a single soul in this lopsided town who would believe me. Even Brody Mitchell couldn't afford to listen to me after the past few days. Prince and I had been right when Loftis first approached us in Hot Springs. He might have claimed that he wanted *the* killer instead of *a* killer, and he might have even meant it at the time. But the truth was that he had way too much at stake in this game—too many hotel rooms, too many guests, too many meals cooked and served. Any old killer would do so long as he fit the equation, so long as he fulfilled the bloodthirsty expectations of all those who consumed the newspapers hot off the press, ink still wet on the page.

What they had with George Moore fed their gut-deep fear and hope that this would all come down to a young white girl, naked in a pool of blood, murdered by a desperate Black man over his unholy desire to use her body for his pleasure. I hadn't yet heard the words *attempted rape*, even out of Mitch's tobacco-spattered mouth, but it was only a matter of time. The reporters would find a way to slip those words into the evening edition, and thousands of readers would gulp them down knowingly, leeringly.

What had Aycock said? Everybody was selling something. And the newspapers knew exactly what sold and what didn't. Sex and death, Black skin on white, naked limbs in a pool of blood.

What had I been selling? To Loftis and the guests at his castle? Me, Stephen Baird Robbins? I'd been selling my eyes and ears, my heart and mind. That's what I'd been selling, all to people who disliked or even hated me.

It was time to go home.

CHAPTER THIRTY-TWO

TURNS OUT THAT MR. BENJAMIN LOFTIS WAS LOOKING for me just as surely as I was looking for him.

When I walked into the lobby that evening—almost supper time—I was given a note from the great man himself, asking me to stop by his office as soon as was convenient. Given the darkening sky and the mood I was in, I decided it was convenient right then, a few minutes before five o'clock.

The outer door to his elegant suite of rooms was standing open, as it had been before when I'd visited him there, and, as before, Mrs. Rice—the stout, stern middle-aged lady—was guarding the inner sanctum. Only this time, she was in the middle of donning her hat and coat, preparatory to leaving.

"Calling it a day?" I asked her from the open doorway, friendly enough.

She turned to regard me but didn't answer until her coat was buttoned and her hat set firmly down over her gray hair. "This office usually closes precisely at five," she said, "so that Mr. Loftis can go home to his family and enjoy the evening."

I held up the note I'd been given at the reception desk. "I was summoned," I offered. "Appear as soon as possible."

"I will see if he is willing to invest a few moments of his time in conversation with you. Although, as I said—"

"I know. Five o'clock and the lights go out."

She rapped quietly on the inner door, opened it just enough to inquire as to whether I was worth a few minutes of the great man's time, and apparently got the green light. She opened the door further and then stepped out of my way. Went steadfastly to the outer door, left, and closed it behind her. For a brief moment, it felt like I'd been trapped inside with Loftis, but the moment passed, and I walked into this office.

This time, he didn't get up to greet me, only gave a nod and a smile from behind his desk. A smile that was open and genuine. It was a smile, I thought, that reflected his relief.

"Mr. Robbins, Mr. Robbins, please sit down. It's been a long and interesting day, and here at the end, I thought we might chat for a few minutes."

"Mr. Loftis." I adopted his tone. I sat in the chair across from him, his immaculate desk between us.

He didn't bother to come around to my side of the desk as he had the first time we'd met in his office. "I understand that you were downtown today when Sheriff Mitchell made his announcement."

I didn't ask how he knew that, though I did wonder.

"Well, then you know that he and his deputies have finally solved the case, and that they have the murderer under lock and key. It disturbs me, of course, that the man was one of my own employees, and I've already begun the process of having all our staff here at the Grove Park fingerprinted, so that in the future, if anything happens, we'll have the evidence at our . . . well, at our fingertips. Do you know about fingerprints, Robbins?"

"You forget who recommended me to you in the first place," I offered.

"Of course, of course. My contact at the Bureau of Investigation." Oddly enough, Loftis hadn't stopped smiling this whole time, as if he was somehow holding the winning hand and couldn't keep a straight face. But then, of course, he thought he was holding the winning hand. His problems were almost over. "Well then, you understand that your services are no longer required in solving the murder of Rosalind Caldwell. I believe the phrase you people use is 'case closed.'"

I nodded again. Loftis smiling and me nodding. But then, for some perverse reason, I thought I should say something about the truth. Just for the sheer, unmitigated hell of it. "You do know, don't you, that the man Mitch has locked up on the third floor is no more guilty of that murder than you or me?"

That did it. That killed the smile. Or rather didn't kill it, only damped it down for a long, painful moment. "On the contrary, Robbins. I know nothing of the kind. No, wait. Let me finish. I heard you out before, with your crazy theories about one of the guests at our reception, but the time for that sort of speculation is over. It troubles me to have to say what I'm about to say, Robbins, but who do you expect me to trust? You or Sheriff Mitchell? Mr. Mitchell is an officer of the court, three-times elected sheriff of Buncombe County, and a man fully embedded in and accepted by our community."

"Embedded he may be, but you would no more invite Mitch to your castle than you would Attila the Hun," I countered. "He'd spit in the flowerpot, or worse."

"Perhaps . . . perhaps. But he is one of us. You, on the other hand, are not. You're a mere . . ."

"Hillbilly?" I suggested. "Redneck?"

"A brute," he said definitively. "A man who has stood trial for murder."

"Twice," I said. "You forgot *lout*, by the way. But enough is enough. I assume you called me in to fire me."

A pause. Seems I had spoken his line in our little drama. But then his smile was back. "Rather, let us say that I invited you in to declare an end to our agreement. Words matter, don't they, Mr. Robbins? Please stay the night, of course, and enjoy your dinner. Rest yourself after your labors. And if you would, tomorrow, when you check out, leave an itemized list of your expenses along with the entire amount that we owe you at the front desk, and I'll mail you a check in the next day's mail."

Now it was my turn to smile at him. I had a brief moment of wondering just how much he knew, even who he might be protecting. But I didn't care enough to push. He was, after all, himself through and through, undisturbed by the world, and he'd managed to turn *take your lunch bucket and go* into *rest yourself after your labors.* Whatever it was that I was selling—mind, heart, soul—the deal was over and the contract concluded.

I stood up and extended my hand across the broad expanse of his immaculate desk. I wanted to force him to touch me, simply because I knew he wouldn't like it very much. "It's been an education," I said. "Working for you."

"Of course," he replied, his grip like picking up a dead fish. "Of course."

CHAPTER THIRTY-THREE

TURNS OUT THAT I DID GO IN TO DINNER THAT NIGHT. I hadn't eaten since that morning, and that meal had consisted only of a fried pie and a cup of scalding coffee from a vendor behind the courthouse. I was too hungry and tired and cold to care much anymore—about how this little simmering drama was playing itself out.

I suspect Michael recognized the signs, could see the fatigue etched in my face. When he first approached me at the usual table, I could tell he was studying me.

"Would something to eat and drink help?" he asked after a moment.

"Food" was about all I had it in me to say in reply. "Hot."

"And drink?"

"Strong."

He nodded with a grim smile and turned on his heel.

A bowl of thick, steaming beef stew, with several biscuits to crumble into it. And a coffee pot not unlike the coffee pot he had brought me the very first night I had eaten there—in the dining room of the glorious Grove Park Inn. A coffee pot full of a rich red wine that tasted like hot sun and good earth. Michael refilled the bowl not once but twice, and when I was done with the stew and the biscuits and the wine, I felt as though I might live.

"I'm leaving in the morning," I said to Michael finally, as I was giving my face a tired swipe with the linen napkin. "Might be the last time I'll see you."

"Did you resign?" he asked. As always, quiet and reserved in his formal role.

"Fired. Dismissed. Sent packing."

"Do you recall the bowling alley?" he asked. Meaning the spot in the basement where we'd met after hours days before.

I nodded. "I remember."

"Ten o'clock" was all he said.

THE FOOD AND EVEN THE WINE HAD REVIVED ME ENOUGH so that I didn't go back to my empty room to pack as I had imagined I would. When I emerged from the dining room into the lobby, it was already a quarter of eight, and I felt restless on top of the fatigue. Fidgety, on edge in a way that made no sense, and I thought a walk down along the golf course might take some of that edge off. Then, after meeting Michael to say goodbye, I could stumble back to my room to sleep, just sleep. With not a single dream to haunt me.

The moon that night was almost full, and the golf course did not appear at all as it did during the day, when it was burnished in sunshine and full of people smacking a little ball back and forth across the links. Rather, it had a haunted, abandoned quality, as if the world were suddenly emptied of people and left to moonlight and moon shadow. Stars glimmering through the increasingly bare trees, and all that light glittering like diamonds in the dew-wet grass.

I stuck more or less to the paths as I walked, just to keep my shoes dry, but even so, the wide expanses of ghostly landscape had a wild and feral aspect, and the air was sharp with impending winter. Old fall was returning, it seemed to say, and the season demanded its full recompense. Human experience meant little when the earth began to tilt on its long axis and winter appeared on the horizon. Experience meant little in the face of the changing season, and what we called wisdom even less.

I was footsore and leg-tired when I made my way back to Grove's inn that night. Tired of my own racing thoughts and respectful of what I'd seen and felt out under the moonlight. I paused in the lobby to warm myself beside one of the fireplaces, letting my eyes adjust to the light and burning away some of the haunting chill from the night air. By my old Elgin, it was a quarter of ten, almost time to meet Michael, and so for a moment, I let myself luxuriate in the radiant heat from the blaze.

As I stood there, a voice brought me back to reality, a voice that I recognized instantly.

"Stephen?" It was Ella Loving.

I turned. She was seated in one of the rocking chairs that faced the fireplace, and in my moonstruck state, I had walked right past her when I came in. "Miss Loving," I said to her. "I hope that . . ." I wasn't sure what came next. What did I hope? For her happiness, her success, her wealth?

"You've been out walking," she said, a statement rather than a question. "You're not afraid of the dark?"

I had to smile. "No, the dark and I are long acquainted."

"Me too," she said with a rueful smile. And for just a moment, I caught a glimpse of Esther Lovenier, the woman inside Ella Loving.

"I'm leaving in the morning," I said simply. "I expect I won't see you again."

She nodded. "I'm used to that. Prefer it, actually. But you'll miss me."

"Of course. But you won't miss me."

She paused, and there was again just a hint of the real woman who lived within. "You'd be surprised," she said. "Perhaps you mean more to me than you know." In looking up at me, she let me see her face clearly in the firelight for a long moment. Her full face, unadorned, shorn of pretense. And then it was gone. She looked down to adjust her gloves and her purse and then floated to her feet. "I'm sorry," she said as she stood. "I have a date. I'm meeting him in the parking lot."

"I'll walk you to the door," I offered. Or rather more than offered. Insisted. "And don't worry, I'll be careful not to frighten him away."

"Thank you" was all she said. So, I would never know if she meant *thank you for escorting me across the lobby* or *thank you for not frightening my customer.*

And in a trice, we were at the broad front doors of the inn. Ella patted my arm without looking up to meet my eyes, meaning that it was as far as I should go, and then she slipped out the double doors and was gone. I stared after her through the glass and saw something that should have surprised me but didn't. Should have disappointed me but couldn't. The world outside was too dark for disappointment.

I watched her open the passenger-side door and get into Madison Aycock's automobile. Then I watched it drive away.

CHAPTER THIRTY-FOUR

"THE BOY IN THAT PICTURE IS MY NEPHEW, MY SISTER'S CHILD."

"Looks to be a handsome young man. In fact, looks a lot like his uncle."

By instinct, Michael and I had returned to the storage closet where we had sat together before. Once there, we claimed the same chairs, and unlike the previous time, Michael had brought a glass fruit jar half full of the wine that he sometimes managed to serve me at dinner. Down in the bowels of the earth where we sat, the wine in its jar looked almost black in the dim light. He'd poured us each a tot into what were probably the same mugs we'd used before, still stained with moonshine, no doubt.

When we'd each had a deep, rich sip and each exhaled in appreciation, he'd handed me the photograph of the good-looking, young Negro man.

"Turn it over," Michael said after I'd stared at it for a moment.

On the back, scribed in childish block letters was "For Uncle MIKE From GEORGIE."

I looked up to smile at the man I'd only ever known as Michael. "You're Uncle Mike," I said, all I could think of to say. And then: "No. No, Michael, no."

He nodded somberly. "And even though Georgie might look like a man in that photo, might look like a man if you saw him walking down the street, he has the mind of—" His voice broke, and he looked down at his hands, at the mug in his hands, to regain his composure. "He has the mind of a child. Ten years old, maybe. On a good day."

I studied the image in the photograph, the image of a young man. Then turned the photo over to study the writing on the back, the careful block lettering of a schoolchild.

"I'm sorry," I murmured.

"I came back here from Detroit to help my sister take care of him. Once he turned mannish in his body, he was more than she could really handle by herself."

I stared into his face and nodded. Quiet. Letting him talk.

"I thought I was doing him a favor by getting him a job here at the inn. Didn't let anybody in the management know he was my nephew, which, as it turns out, was a good thing."

"A good thing because they didn't fire you when they arrested him?"

"Yes," he said, and paused to clear his throat. "I can tell you've put it together. He's the George Moore they've got locked up in Mitchell's jail, intending to try him and kill him for the murder of that girl."

"Jesus Lord," I muttered. "Is there any . . . ?" Meaning to say *is there any way he could have done it?* But stopping myself because it made no sense.

"No, there isn't. You should know that I asked myself the same question you almost asked me. Day and night, I asked it. I thought that maybe he'd somehow gotten his hands on a pistol, treated it almost like a child does a toy. That maybe he'd done something horrible without really understanding. Because he wouldn't understand, you see. I was horrified that it could somehow be true."

"But it wasn't?"

He shook his head slowly, thoughtfully. "I even thought that maybe the girl saw Georgie and . . . and . . ."

"Wanted him. Desired him."

"Sure. Because he's every bit of a good-looking man, a sweet man, even. And some girls, women, they are drawn to . . . you know what I'm trying to say."

"I know. Nothing wrong with it, Michael. My wife has . . . had dark skin."

"Well, I thought that. And the night it happened, Georgie got off work—he stokes the furnaces down here in the basement—he got off work and for some reason he could never explain, he came up to the first floor looking for me. Wanted to tell me something that had happened to him, something somebody had said. But here's the thing, Stephen. He was not supposed to come up out of the basement, one of Loftis's rules. The men who work the furnaces, dirty and covered in coal dust, are not supposed to ever be seen by the guests. And the night manager . . ."

"Evening manager or night?"

"Evening manager, I guess."

"Stoneman."

"Yeah, that Stoneman saw him wandering around in the lobby, asking people where the dining room was because he needed to tell somebody something. He couldn't say who except for *uncle, uncle*, and he didn't know what he wanted to say. Stoneman sent him on out of there, threatened to fire him, and told him to take his Black ass on home. The poor boy was home at his mother's house long before that girl was killed." Michael was growling. The anger was boiling up out of him now, choking him. He'd been sad before but was angry now at the thought of Conrad Stoneman.

"It's the worst thing that could possibly happen," I said. "I grant you. And Stoneman is an ass. A stupid ass at that."

"Doesn't matter. You know that. I've seen the look in your eyes. You know what the world is made of."

"Let me see his picture again." I don't know why I asked. Part of my mind was already screaming that I couldn't do anything about this. I couldn't fix this. The president of the United States and all his generals couldn't fix this.

Michael handed me the photo and took a gulp of his wine. Slugged like it was water.

I stared at the young man's face, Georgie's face. It was open and sincere, friendly and disarming. But also simple, like that of a little boy who has never seen pain, never understood what cruel things were being done around him, being said about him, even to him.

I took a long drink of my own wine but couldn't savor it. Couldn't even taste it for what hung in the air between Michael Joyner and me. The knowledge that was passing back and forth between us. "He'll never understand what's happening to him, will he? Up there in the jail, I mean?"

"No. He won't. It started out as a blessing, Stephen, but the good God knows it's turned into a curse. He'll help them convict him by agreeing to whatever words they put in his mouth. They'll tell some tale, show a picture of the girl, and ask him if he thinks she's pretty, and he'll nod and smile and agree. He won't know how to say no, and so he'll end up saying yes."

My glass was empty. I didn't know what to do with it, so I set it carefully on the floor to keep myself from flinging it against the stone walls. Walls that now more than ever felt like a cave, like the rock-strewn bowels of the earth. I reached over and grasped Michael's arm. "I don't know what to do," I said.

"There's nothing you can do," he said, placing his broad hand over mine. "I just wanted somebody to know."

INTERLUDE

SHE ALMOST PASSES OUT WHILE HE IS GETTING DRESSED. Time slows. The room swims around her and becomes strange, dark, different, even though it is her own. Her own cottage, her own spare bedroom, and yet strange to her.

Her own blood. She is sprawled in a puddle of blood on carpet worn so thin that the hard, cold planks beneath hurt the side of her head, the arm trapped under her, her hip.

It is this pain that pulls her again from the dark, fast river she has fallen into. The pain and the bastard talking to himself as he bends to tie his shoes and straightens to pull on his suit jacket. She opens her eyes so that she can watch him in the ghastly radiance of the one lamp he'd asked her to light.

He has shot her in the belly. She burps soundlessly from the pressure, but oh, dear Christ, it hurts. If she were able to speak, she would shout the bastard's name . . . loudly, defiantly. She knows his name, of course, even though he refused to tell it to her.

And if not speak, scream. Stephen would want her to scream, would plead with her to scream. But he isn't here, Stephen, and try as she might, she can't draw the necessary air into her lungs. The bullet burns inside her belly.

Still talking, muttering to himself, he pulls the billfold out of his pants pocket and begins searching through its contents.

Who is he talking to? Her, she realizes, he's talking to her.

"Whore," he keeps saying over and over. "Bitch. Slut." But mostly just the one tired, groaning syllable. *Whore.*

Her arm where it is trapped beneath her aches so, is soaking in the warm blood coursing. Can't I at least die on my back? she wonders vaguely. Like I lived . . . The thought brings a weak smile to her crusted lips. The way I lived. She eases over onto her back, straightens her arm.

Oh, Mary, Mother of Jesus, how it hurts.

He finds what he is looking for and steps out of the lamplight toward her. Careful of the blood, she thinks, you bastard.

He leans over and drops something deliberately on her face. Paper, it feels like, fluttering down onto her lips. "Now die, slut," he says hoarsely. "Just . . . goddamn you . . . die."

Then he's gone, out of her light, out of her room. Tiptoeing ludicrously to the door and leaving it open. With the door open, the cold breeze revives her enough. Just enough in the icy air . . .

What does she have left? Lying there on the floor, in her own stark spare room. The bedroom she'd hoped would be her son's someday. What does she have?

Nothing.

She has nothing except the blood. So, with what raw breath she has left, she rolls over again, onto her other side. And breathing carefully, using the arm that was trapped under her, she dips her forefinger in her own thickening blood and begins slowly, laboriously, to write. Using her left hand to scribe letters in the thin light, on the thin carpet.

She thinks that Stephen might read what she writes and understand . . . if he weren't already gone. Thank God he is gone. But no matter. Letters . . . She makes three and part of a fourth before she gasps . . . and then faints.

Chokes slowly to death.

PART III

CHAPTER THIRTY-FIVE

I WAS LEAVING ASHEVILLE AS I HAD COME, DRESSED IN the same suit of clothes, and carrying my old leather valise along with the carpet bag. Most of the clothes in the valise were dirty now but still the same. The carpet bag was weighted down with the disassembled Parker ten-gauge wrapped in a shirt, never fired.

I knew I was leaving as a failure. Sure, I'd written out a personal bill for Benjamin Loftis that morning, charging him for every penny I could even remotely justify. And I was sure I'd get paid, having been on the scene when the things that troubled him were resolved. But the murder—the murders rather—remained unsolved. The truth buried somewhere under a mound of granite boulders.

I felt as if I had been running headlong into the boulders of Grove's inn for the past week and bouncing off without making a dent in the monumental self-certainty of the place. Not just the inn but the whole society it represented—polished, rich, assured. And once inside the high, holy places of that society, the inn and the castle, it felt as if I'd visited the underworld, the cave of the dead. Dramatic, I know, and I'm not so much given to the drama, but after my week there, I was hungry for light, for morning, and for home.

I bought my ticket from a sleepy agent in the grand old train station down by the river and stood on the platform, waiting as the northbound Norfolk & Southern eased into place, the engine wreathed in steam and smoke. I remembered my half-waking dreams from the night before . . . the train and the river would take me home.

As I stared absently at the passenger car doors, waiting for them to open, a small grimy boy came striding down the platform, hawking an armload of newsprint. "Murder, murder! Read all about it!" he was shouting. "Only a nickel, read all about it!" The people waiting to board the northbound mostly just ignored him. Apparently murder just wasn't that interesting anymore. Not worth a nickel. But the kid with his high, screeching voice reminded me of myself at his age, trying to somehow make my way in the world. So I gave him a dime, told him to keep the change, and folded his sheaf of newsprint under my arm when I bent to pick up my bags and board the train.

When I threw my two bags onto a seat on the train, the folded newspaper fluttered to the aisle floor, opening to the front page. I glimpsed a photograph of a driveway under trees, leading to what might be a cottage, and the image whispered to me. A place, it said, some place I recognized. But my eyes were tired, and my brain even more so.

I threw the paper onto the carpet bag and collapsed on the seat opposite, intending to put my feet up and lower my hat brim over my eyes. But my eyes were waking to the image, and my brain was whispering back. *Pearson*, my mind was muttering, *Pearson Drive*. What was Pearson Drive, and why did I care? *29½*. There was a number also, that mattered. 29½ was . . . Esther Lovenier's address. She had written it on a piece of paper for me after I'd talked her into spying on the castle people, Loftis's people.

My stomach lurched. My head was shaking as if to refuse this. I could hear myself muttering the profanities I usually saved for pain or loss. But I sat up and opened the newspaper to read.

The body of an Asheville woman . . . There it was, the address. *29½ Pearson Drive . . . Shot with a small-caliber pistol . . .*

Discovered in the early hours of the morning . . . after a barking dog alerted . . . Police believe . . . Searching for anyone who saw or heard . . . And there, the ink bleeding into the cheap rag of the paper. *Tentatively identified . . . Miss Esther or Ella Lovenier.*

I wadded the single sheet up and threw it on the seat. Violently against the backrest, so that it fell against the valise and bounced back into my lap. Then I was standing. Why, I wasn't sure, but standing, the paper again clutched in my right fist.

"She was my friend," I could hear myself saying to no one in particular. "She was my friend, and they can't even get her name right in this goddamn rag in this goddamn town."

People were staring. Afraid of the madman. A mother was sending her son to find the conductor. I shook my fist full of paper at her and at everyone, anyone who would look up. "She was the best thing about this damn town. The most . . ."

"Sir, I'm going to have to ask you to sit down."

"Beautiful. The most interesting, most intelligent in this . . ."

The conductor had me by the arm, pulling at me, and I jerked my arm out of his hand. "Leave it," I warned him. Shook the fist with the newsprint in his face. "This woman was my friend, and I'll be damned if some two-bit piece of . . . like you is going to . . ."

"Sir, I need you to leave the train until you can get a grip on yourself."

His face, straining, red, lined with broken blood vessels, was inches away from mine, stinking of stale coffee and garlic, and I could feel myself coiling to strike him. I was breathing heavily, everything about me was heavy, and slowly, slowly I remembered where I was, who I was.

"I'm going to have to ask you to—"

I shoved the wadded-up newsprint into my pocket and bent over to pick up my bags. My throat was too tight for speech, and tears formed in my eyes. But I found I could walk, walk and carry the bags.

"You can take the midmorning train," he whispered to me. "Your ticket is good for the . . ."

A few breathless and angry minutes, and I was standing again on the platform. The northbound toward home—the river and the train—was flowing away from me. Leaving me stranded on the platform, silently cursing.

The chill air of a fall morning was just enough to bring me back to myself. Back to some sense of where I was. I was no less stricken, but I was breathing, conscious of taking slow, deep breaths. People were no longer staring at me as if I might erupt at any moment.

She was my friend. Those words kept echoing inside my mind. My friend. And what did that mean, what did one do, where did one go, when your friend—young, vibrant, alive—was suddenly ripped out of the scene? One of the last things Ella Loving had said to me the morning after in room 340 was to ask, "Who would be friends with somebody like me?" Who indeed?

"Somebody like me would be friends with somebody like you," I whispered. The thoughts cascaded. In my country, friendship outweighs almost everything else. It is more important than money or gain or politics or law. Friendship is its own law, makes its own time, keeps its own place. I didn't have many friends, I knew that. I was too rough, too dark, too hard on myself, even if easy on others. Prince was my friend, Prince and Dora. Jack Durand, the nameless man, he was my friend. And Luke, my son. There it was, perhaps the entire list.

But she had been my friend. Ever so briefly, but still. Whether she went by Ella or Esther, Loving or Lovenier, what did that matter? And one thing I did know in this glittering, spinning world is that nobody, and I mean nobody, brought harm to one of my friends.

When I walked out the front door of the train station onto Depot Street, intending to hail a taxi, an unmarked sheriff's car

I thought I recognized pulled up to the curb just in front of me. I turned and started down the sidewalk, thinking that the last thing I had any stomach for was a sheriff.

But the driver tapped on the horn to summon me. When I bent to look inside the driver's side window, there was Brody Mitchell, with a lit Camel hanging out of one side of his mouth. He held up a fistful of newsprint. "You seen this?" he asked.

I nodded.

"We got work to do."

"I'm ready," I said. And then after a moment, "To bring the fire."

CHAPTER THIRTY-SIX

THE COTTAGE AT THE END OF THE AVENUE, 29½ PEARSON Drive.

Brody parked on the street in front of number 30, and we walked up the driveway under the trees. The ambulance had already come and gone in the wee hours, removing the body to the morgue at the hospital.

The Asheville city police had also come and gone, as well as the reporter who'd ginned up the blaring newsprint—*Murder! Murder! Read All About It.* All that was left was one bored beat cop in uniform sitting on the front porch to keep the curious away. He'd taken off both his shoes and had his right leg crossed over his left so that he could massage one sore, tired foot. "Can't go in, boys," he growled at Brody and me, or at least it would have been a growl if he hadn't been up all night. "Murder scene."

Brody hauled his badge out of his jacket pocket and let him study it for a few seconds. He nodded to Brody and then at me. "Who's Scar Face?" he asked. Brody extended his arm to hold me back as I was already taking a step forward. "He's with me," Brody offered. "Special investigator."

The beat cop shrugged and nodded toward the front door. "Help yourself," he muttered, still massaging his toes. "Watch your step, though."

IT WAS A SMALL PLACE FOR SOMEONE AS MYSTERIOUS AND complex as she had been. A small sitting room in front that felt seldom used. A small kitchen with a kettle on the stove and meticulously clean dishes in the drainer. A bathroom with a large clawfoot bathtub and rich, thick towels on the rack. The lavender smell of soap, lots of soap, and several candles. Her bedroom, her private place, it felt to me, where no one went but her. A bookshelf all along one wall, crowded with books of many shapes, sizes, all of which looked to have been read. A closet that was itself as large as a small room, all those clothes hanging empty now. Lifeless without her flowing form to animate them.

And then a second bedroom. Perhaps the room she'd intended for her son. Obviously, the room where she'd died. As we stood in the doorway, Brody shook a cigarette out of a half-crushed pack. I shook my head. "Why don't you take that outside?" I asked.

He looked quizzical.

"Go suck on that nail in your hand and let me have a few minutes." I could hear the nasty edge in my voice, for which I was sorry. None of this was his fault. "I knew her, Brody. Not well, but well enough."

He nodded and slipped back down the short hallway to the outer door. I could hear him speak to the beat cop on the porch.

I stood a moment longer, just stood, trying to slow the hammering of my heart. There was a light switch beside the door, and I pushed the brass button to turn on the overhead light, sudden and bright after the half dark in the house. It was simple enough, this room. Directly in front of me was the double bed with a simple, scarred headboard of cheap pine. To the left was a chest of drawers, with a middle drawer pulled partway out and clothes—her clothes, the clothes I'd last seen her in—neatly folded and laid across the drawer. To the right, an old overstuffed chair beside the one window and a standing lamp, with the shade knocked slightly crooked.

It was a room not often used, a spare room. And it struck me that whoever had killed her had been allowed only this far. Into this spare, shockingly empty room. Not into her own bedroom, her own sanctuary, but here.

And just here, at my feet, between me and the end of the bed, was the pool of her congealed blood. Black now. And the single detail that I would never forget. When they had removed her body, they had lifted her—no, peeled her—up out of the coagulated blood, and the outline of where she had last lain was still there . . . preserved. It was at this moment, staring down at the place where she wasn't, that it all came back to me in searing detail. The night she'd spent with me when she'd resurrected my body and pinched my soul back to life. When she'd danced naked in front of me, then over me, and then into me.

Her narrow hips, her flat belly, the breasts full if small. Her legs like those of some graceful animal. Her teeth, her tongue, her lips. Her face, her eyes. The feral, knowing light in her darkening eyes. Everything about her a revelation.

All of it came back and flashed through me like a sudden flood of sensory emotion, of knowing, and of desire. I had known her, Ella and Esther. And she me. My body twitched at the memory of her. The presence of her scorched into me by her absence.

I pulled a breath deep into my lungs. I could sense Brody coming back down the hall; he'd given me my moment alone and was returning. He stepped through the door to stand beside me. "You all right?" he asked quietly. And I nodded, all I could do. "What's that?" he said and pointed to what might be lines, drawn with blood on the carpet, beside the pool.

I crouched down and stared. Something or someone—the bastard who'd killed her?—had used a stick, a pencil, a finger to draw something, some hieroglyphic on the carpet using her blood.

Brody leaned over and gestured. "Numbers maybe?" The first figure did look vaguely like a loosely scribed "3."

"Not numbers," I muttered. "Look at the second pattern.

And the third. They're letters."

He put one hand on my back to steady himself and then bent closer, so that his perspective more closely matched mine. "*M . . . A . . .* maybe a *D . . . MAD* and then something else. A number one or an exclamation point? You think he wrote it, using her blood? After she was dead?"

We were both about to topple forward. I put one hand down to steady myself . . . straight into the puddle of clotted blood. I cursed under my breath. "Help me up." All four fingers and my thumb were coated, and the spots where they'd sunk in were smeared, bleared, and . . . permanent. The iron stink rose from where I'd disturbed the rotting blood.

Brody pulled me to my feet. "Look!" I pointed. "It was written when the blood was fresh. She was still alive, and the blood was fresh."

"You think . . . ?"

"She wrote it herself. Saying something. Telling us something." Telling *me* something, I thought. She knew I'd come.

Brody handed me his handkerchief for my hand. "Telling us the killer was mad? Furious? Crazy?"

I shook my head. "The fourth mark is a letter too, Brody."

"*M . . . A . . . D . . . I . . .*"

"It's a name," I said, "and it's meant for me."

CHAPTER THIRTY-SEVEN

"It's impossible."

"It's more than possible. It's the answer. Hell, he was there that night at the reception at the Grove Park. He leaves to take his preacher's daughter home and then comes back later to meet the Caldwell girl. He—"

"He's running for governor is what he is."

"So what? When did that make somebody pure and sweet? He told me himself that his fiancée, what's her name . . . Beatrice. Beatrice is frigid. So what does he do? He goes looking for it in places that won't affect who he is or what he has."

We were sitting in the lunchroom in the basement of the Jackson Building, just a block from the courthouse and the sheriff's office. My friend LaVada, who'd waited on me last week, was working—you got the feeling she was always working—but something about Brody and me caused her to keep her distance. She brought our ham and eggs along with the scalding coffee, but the look on our faces and the tone of our voices didn't invite her to hang around to chat.

"I buy all that," Brody muttered. "I can buy the idea that he's a young buck full of himself and he needs to find a way to get a piece of ass now and then just to satisfy his sense of how important he is, but why in God's name would he . . . ?" He paused to lower his voice. "Why in God's name would he risk everything by shooting the women? He's got the inside lane to fame and fortune. Why would he take chances he doesn't need to?"

He had me there, but only for a moment. "You remember that neither Rosie Caldwell nor the woman we found out beside the road . . ."

"Viola Martin."

"Yeah. Neither Rosie nor Viola had actually had intercourse. Remember?"

He nodded. "Keep your voice down."

"And you and I both decided that maybe, just maybe, he's impotent. Can't get it up when it matters. Wants it so bad he can taste it, but at the very last minute, he wilts like a posy."

"Like a what?"

"A flower. And it's maddening to him. He's supposed to be the young bull with the whole world lying there just waiting for him, and yet, when there's a naked woman right in front of him, all but begging for it, the candle melts in his hand."

"You boys want pie?"

We'd been so intent on the wilting flower and the melting candle that LaVada had walked right up to our table without either one of us bothering to notice. She had the metal coffee pot in hand and was already pouring.

"Pie for breakfast?" Brody asked.

"Yes," I said, "apple."

Brody shrugged and looked at me. "Is it . . . ?"

I nodded. "Delicious."

"Okay. Me too, then."

LaVada leaned over and whispered. "Unless you want everybody in here to know who you're referring to, talk a little softer. You're only a block from the damn courthouse."

I grunted and Brody nodded. LaVada patted my shoulder and went for pie.

"So, if he can't do the deed, who does he blame?"

"The woman?"

"Hell yes, the woman. If you're somebody like him, who can do anything and do it well. Looks like, hell, a movie star on the tennis court or the golf course, but at the end of the day, there's only one thing that really matters. Down in the pit of your stomach matters, it has to be . . ."

We paused as LaVada set two generous slices of pie down in front of us. "Better," she whispered before she turned away.

"Humiliating. I get it. And with his ego . . ."

"Exactly," I whispered. "And hell, it's happened to every man who ever lived."

"Yeah, but every man who ever lived doesn't shoot the poor woman who's down on her knees in front of him."

"I know, I know. But the way I figure it, this is the one thing he can't abide, the one thing that for whatever reason, he can't lose at." I paused to take a bite of the pie. It wasn't hot, but it was as good as I remembered.

"And the woman knows he failed," Brody said after a moment. "The woman in front of him is the one person on earth who knows who he is and what he is."

"Exactly. If he wasn't famous, or at least as famous as it comes in this town, then it wouldn't matter. That's another reason why Aycock makes sense for this."

There was a long pause while we both took a bite or two of pie, blew on the hot coffee and sipped at it. A long pause before Brody gave voice to what he must have been thinking all along. "He's untouchable. You know that, don't you? It doesn't matter if he did it or not."

CHAPTER THIRTY-EIGHT

"IT MATTERS TO ME."

We were standing on the sidewalk in front of the Jackson Building, having paid LaVada for breakfast and pie. This time, I'd left a five-dollar bill under the pie plate, figuring she'd had to put up with way too much aggravation out of Brody and me.

"What are you talking about?" Brody asked.

"You said it didn't matter if Madison Aycock killed those three women. You said he's untouchable."

Brody nodded. "He *is* untouchable, at least to people like you and me."

"It matters to me that he killed them." I glanced down at the cracked concrete of the sidewalk, sighed, and looked up at the gray sky, a cold winter sky. "Especially the last one. Ella. She was personal."

"What the hell are you saying, Steve?"

"She was my friend, Brody."

"She was a whore. Nothing more."

I regarded his tired, bloodshot eye. "Ease up, Brody. Don't ever say that again." Something in my voice broke through to him.

"Jesus," he muttered. "I didn't know you felt *that* way." Now it was his turn to stare at the sidewalk. Then, "Listen to me, Steve. I don't know why you care so much. From what I hear, Loftis cut you loose . . . terminated your contract, whatever you call it. Hell, you were on the train headed home a few hours ago, and now you're ready to go headhunting. Forget it."

"I can't forget it. Not now."

"Forget it and forget her. Why don't I take you down to the station? I bet you can catch the next train home, probably use the same ticket."

"Are you trying to protect Aycock too, Brody? 'Cause if you are . . ."

"I don't give a shit about Aycock. I'm trying to protect you."

I put my head back and laughed. At him, at me. At the whole cross-wired, absurd world.

"You're a damn nutjob," Brody said, trying not to laugh himself. "But you need to listen. I'm your friend too, and the last thing on earth you need to do in this town is go after Aycock, or anybody else from his crowd."

I could hear the echoes of Ella Loving's voice in my mind. "Who would be friends with somebody like me?" I said to him.

"I'm your damn friend. If I wasn't, you'd still be in jail instead of about to get on a train and go home."

"My ticket will be good in the morning," I offered. "Why don't you show me where the Aycocks live?"

THE HOUSE AT THE HEAD OF RUTLEDGE AVENUE, A WIDE, tree-shaded thoroughfare that turned off Charlotte Street and ran halfway up the mountain in the general direction of the Grove Park Inn and Loftis's castle. We drove past it twice, once fast and the second time more slowly. The house itself was built out of dark brick with a slate roof surrounded by stands of tall rhododendron so that it looked heavy and hidden away, even in the blaring light of midday.

On the second pass, Madison's roadster actually passed us, horn blaring, as we idled along, and turned sharply up into the gravel driveway. I instinctively looked down and away as the car sped past just in case the future governor happened to glance my way, but you got the feeling that if Madison was driving, everything around him was just part of the scenery.

"What do you have in mind?" Brody asked when we were back on Charlotte Street, headed toward downtown.

"You sure you want to know?"

He shook his head and grinned his lopsided grin. "Not really. But at least I can stop you from doing anything truly stupid."

"Drop me off downtown at some flophouse, some place where I can rent a room for the night. I'll pay cash and no names involved. Get a few hours' sleep, maybe grab something to eat later. Then I'm going to come back up late tonight—midnight or after—and visit with our friend Madison, the untouchable. Maybe touch him a little bit. Then, in the morning, I'm going to get on the train and go home. Out of your town and out of your life, so you don't have to worry anymore about what I'm up to."

He nodded slowly. "Fair enough," he said. Then after a moment, "I'll be your driver. Too far to walk, and you don't want to be taking a cab."

"And that way you can make sure I get on the train in the morning?"

He smiled. "Exactly."

CHAPTER THIRTY-NINE

IT WAS A DARK NIGHT, THE BLUE-BLACK SKY RIVEN WITH wind-borne clouds that obscured and then revealed the full moon. Everything was shadows and strange, muted sounds.

When Brody pulled up at the top of Rutledge Avenue, it was well past midnight. We sat for a moment, and he let the car idle. "Well, I guess this is it," I said quietly. "Thanks for the ride. Hell, thanks for everything." I reached for the door handle.

He shook his head roughly. "Nah. Not so fast. I'm going with you." He made as if to grab my arm but then thought better of it.

"Bad idea," I muttered. "Every way you look at it, it's no good." I paused, but he didn't reply. "If you're going along to keep me from doing harm to some of these Aycocks—cocks and Aycocks—you're not going to be able to stop me, Brody, and if you get in the way, it's more blood on the ground." I paused again but still nothing. "But on the other hand, if you're going along to lend a helping hand, render justice to some of these Cocks, then that's not good either. I'm a nobody in this town, less than a nobody. But you're somebody, part of the pattern, the system, and if you pull a trigger in that house or take a swing at a damn judge or lawyer or governor, then it's your life all to hell."

"Fuck you, I'm going in." He was so fiercely earnest that I almost laughed.

"I appreciate the sentiment. How about this? You cut the engine, sit here, and have a smoke. Enjoy the night air. Have a look at the moon and think about some broad you'd like to get your hands on. That overcoat I threw in the back seat is wrapped around a Parker ten-gauge. I aim to leave the coat but take the gun, just in case I need a little force. The Parker is loud as hell. If you hear something sounds like a bomb went off, come on in and arrest me. If a car comes along, turns up the drive, then lay down on the horn, so I'll know company's on the way. Otherwise, give some thought to that broad I mentioned earlier, and stay the hell out of that house."

He shrugged. "I'm married to her," he said. "Five years and I still like to get my hands on her."

I reached over and gripped his shoulder hard. "You don't know how lucky you are," I offered. "Let's keep it that way."

I got out and slammed the car door, pulled the ten-gauge out of the overcoat, and broke it open to insert a couple of shells from my jacket pocket. It was ready now to do whatever God and the devil required. I walked around to the driver's side window and reached through to shake Brody's hand. "This won't take long" is what I told him. "Even so, if I'm not back in an hour, go on home. Burn my old overcoat and live your life."

EVEN ON THE OUTSIDE, THE AYCOCK HOUSE SEEMED TO be made all of shadows. I walked up to the driveway, listening as I did to the odd whinny of a screech owl from further up the mountain. Haunting. At the top of the drive, I could make out a garage attached to the house with two doors for cars, both closed. In front of the garage, parked carelessly across the width of the drive, was Madison Aycock's fancy Packard, the car I'd seen Ella getting into outside the Grove Park the night before.

The back seat door was open, left open presumably by Madison or a friend of Madison. I walked over, as quietly as possible in the loose gravel. With the small pencil flashlight I'd learned to carry on night hikes like this, I glanced in at the back seat, wondering if Viola Martin's underwear—which we'd never found—

were buried somewhere under that elegant leather seat. I left the car door standing open just as I'd found it and turned toward the front door. A half dozen stone steps and I was standing before the door itself. Dark wood with ornate, hand-forged hinges and doorknob.

I paused to pull out a pair of thin leather gloves I'd bought that day just for the occasion. The knob turned easily in my hand, and when I pushed, the door swung in with little pressure. Not only had Aycock forgotten to close his car door, he didn't bother with locks either. Maybe he was drunk. Maybe he just didn't care.

I eased down the hallway directly in front of me toward a broad set of stairs. Dark paneling, wooden floors with what felt like thick carpets. Dark rooms to either side. A library perhaps, a dining room, and over everything a patina of darkness. Only the white paint on the ceiling gave off any sense of luster and a shape to the space I was moving through.

My right foot was on the first step, assuming that the bedrooms were above and that it was way past bedtime, even for someone like Aycock. Then I heard something behind the stairs toward the back of the house. The shattering of glass, dropped on a hard floor perhaps, and some muted cursing. I eased around the left side of the stairs, and when I did could see light through an open doorway. I crept up to the doorway with the Parker held down beside my leg where it would not be so obvious.

The room was lit by a single lamp, and in the shadows cast with that yellow glow, I could see comfortable furniture and what looked like a bar against the far wall. Some sort of library or den. And with his back to me was the tall, broad-shouldered form of the man I wanted. The great white hope, the next governor.

I stepped into the open doorway. He was busy at the bar and didn't hear me. At his feet, I could see the shards of a bottle that had landed hard on the wood floor. He was in his shirtsleeves, and from his movements, it appeared he'd gone on to a second bottle and was busy building himself a strong one.

"Having a drink?" I said to his back.

He turned with the glass in his hand. He seemed puzzled to know who had spoken, so I took a step forward and then another one, so he could get a better look at me.

"Robbins?" he said, still not quite sure. And then, "Stephen Robbins, the redneck detective?" His voice was slurred, slightly so, but enough to suggest that it wasn't his first drink of the night.

I took my hat off and tossed it on the closest chair. "I thought you and I might have some words," I said. "About the women you've killed."

That staggered him a bit, and I could see the hand with the glass shaking, but he was big and he was strong and he was the next governor. He glanced over to one side, toward a telephone sitting on a table.

I raised the shotgun and let the double barrels rest on the back of an overstuffed leather chair where he could see them clearly. "Just the two of us," I said, "man to man."

He cleared his throat. "I was just having a nightcap," he said. "Care to join me?"

I nodded. "Sure. But move nice and slow. I'd hate for you to throw a tumbler at me and the ten-gauge go off."

He smiled or at least tried to. "Do some damage?"

"From here, it would tear you in half."

There was a long pause while he worked to get his breathing back to something like normal. "What are you drinking?" I finally asked him to give him something else to think about.

"Bourbon. The judge is a bourbon man, and it's the only decent liquor he keeps."

"Pour me a tot in one of those fancy glasses, then. Maybe a splash of water. There you go. Now, just leave it on the bar and sit down."

He left my drink on the bar and lowered himself into the closest chair, just like I'd told him, but you could tell he was thinking . . . thinking about how he was going to get the better of me, how he was going to get out of this.

I picked up the drink without taking my eyes off him and sat down in a matching chair, maybe ten feet away, far enough so that I could pull the trigger on him if he got the urge to play rough.

Once he got himself settled, he pretended to take a sip of his bourbon, but over the rim of the glass, his eyes went two places. One was the telephone again and the other was his suit jacket, which he'd draped carelessly over a barstool.

I took a real sip of my bourbon, just to feel the burn on my tongue and down my throat.

"What the hell are you doing, Robbins?" He leaned forward in his chair. "You know full, damn well you don't belong here. You're out of your hillbilly jurisdiction, if you even have a jurisdiction."

I crossed one leg over the other and used it to steady the shotgun barrel, aimed straight at him. I kept my forefinger outside the trigger guard, not quite trusting my instincts. I took another sip and then set the tumbler on the arm of my chair. I smiled grimly. "You're right. I don't have a jurisdiction. Which means I can go anywhere I like."

"Then what in the hell makes you think you can—"

The Parker was one of the fine old-style guns, with double hammers. I cocked one, which clicked nice and loud and served to interrupt him. "Madison Aycock, I hereby accuse you of the murder of Rosalind Caldwell in room 341 of Grove's inn, of the murder of Viola Louise Martin beside the road up Beaverdam, and of the murder of Esther Lovenier last night at her home in Montford. I have a feeling there are more, but those are the ones I'm aware of."

"Did you say Esther? Esther who?"

"Lovenier. It was her real name."

"Where did you learn to talk like the Clerk of Court?" He was getting a little of his attitude back. I hadn't shot him yet, and so maybe I was just there to chat.

"You forget that I've sat in the chair where you sit now. On trial for murder. On trial for my life."

"I'm not on trial, you little . . . Besides, you have no proof."

"Don't need any. This is a shotgun court."

He had to pause to think about that. "Very well, then. How much do you want?"

"How much what?"

"Money, obviously. How much do you want?"

"Shit on you, Aycock. You and your family and your kind. People like me don't do what we do for money."

He chuckled and took a drink from his glass, his hands steadier than before. "Everybody does what they do for money, Robbins. Every . . . damn . . . body. You claim you're not a whore, but each one of those women you mentioned, including your precious Ella or Evelyn or whatever, were tramps and you know it. Every single one of them was there for the money. You know that too. Problem was that they couldn't deliver the goods, couldn't do what they were paid to do."

"I believe you just confessed."

He shrugged. "So what. This isn't a court of law, and you're sure as hell not a judge."

I pulled back the other hammer on the Parker. "I'm a self-appointed judge," I said.

The hand with the heavy glass tumbler in it was shaking again. And he was back to looking around. Not at the telephone but at the suit coat.

"I do have a question, though, Aycock, before we conclude the proceedings."

He took a mouthful of the bourbon and gagged it straight down his throat. "What?" he croaked.

"Why did you kill them? You didn't go there to murder them, at least not at first. You went there to act like a big boy, fool around a little while your Presbyterian fiancée was home saying her prayers."

He nodded. "I didn't just go there to act like a big boy. I was a . . . I fucked every single one of those women. Hard. I was—"

"No, you didn't."

That's when he flung the glass at my head. Tried to brain me with it. But it's hard to throw your speedball when you've had too much to drink and you're sunk into an overstuffed chair. I just leaned a little to my right, and the tumbler flew harmlessly past.

"You failed in the clinch," I said. "Your little flower wilted in the heat."

He choked over whatever lie he was trying to say. "No, I—"

"Happens to all of us," I said.

"Hard as stone," he managed to say. "Like a—"

"But not all of us kill what we can't have."

"Damn you, I was like a lion."

"Did you say you were lying?"

"Lion. Like a lion, goddamn you to hell."

I stared at him. Unsure for a moment just what to do. But then he said the one thing that he shouldn't have.

"She was pathetic, you know."

"Who?"

"All of them really. Pathetic. But especially the last one. The cute little trick that worked the Grove Park. Acquaintance of yours, I believe. She offered to do some interesting things, but none of them worked, and in the end, what was she but a nasty piece of trash off the street?"

"Guilty," I whispered.

"Hmm?"

"Madison Aycock, I hereby declare you guilty as charged. *Rosalind Caldwell. Viola Martin. Esther Lovenier.* If I had time, I'd teach you to say their names. But it's long past midnight, and dawn is coming."

"I have all the time in the world, Robbins. Hell, I own the world, me and my kind, as you like to say."

"Not after tonight. You're a dead man."

He chuckled. "You're powerless, you little prick. You can't kill me. You can't even touch me."

"Perhaps," I shrugged. "But then men of your class and station have been known to kill themselves."

CHAPTER FORTY

I STOOD UP FROM THE DEPTHS OF MY CHAIR, HOLDING THE Parker aimed steady at Aycock's chest. For a moment, I was light-headed, dizzy from cloud and shadow and bourbon. Dizzy with the thoughts of what he had done, thoughts of what I might be about to do.

I had the impression that somewhere in the murky darkness, a hand of poker had been dealt and I was perilously close to all in. Maybe I was betting with the very heart of things as I knew them. Perhaps with my life. He must have seen me hesitate because he asked me to hand him his suit jacket.

A small detail, but it was enough, for I knew he'd wanted that jacket since the moment he realized he was in danger. I laughed at him, clear-eyed again, and with the shotgun steady, I stepped around him, set my empty glass on the bar, and picked his jacket up from the barstool where he'd slung it.

"Careful," he said. "My wallet's in there, and if you want to be paid . . ."

Holding the Parker steady on top of the barstool, I rifled through the jacket pockets. What felt like a leather wallet was in an inside pocket, and what I was looking for was in a side pocket. I let the wallet be and slipped what I wanted out and into my own belt, where it would be handy. I tossed him his jacket with his precious wallet intact.

"Aycock," I said, "you right-handed or left-handed?"

"I'm a lefty," he said. "I was hell at baseball when I was a kid."

I stepped around and in front of him, right up in his face. Feeling the threat, he started to push up out of his chair. Using my left arm, I pinned him down with the twin barrels of the shotgun against his chest. "I was hell at fighting," I muttered and slugged him with my fist on his left temple, where the bruise wouldn't matter.

He grunted and jerked but then sat back, stunned and drooling. Not out, like I'd hoped, but dazed. It was enough. I laid the shotgun on the floor and pulled the little two-shot derringer out of my belt. I wrapped his left hand around the pistol grip and raised his mostly limp arm up to his head, with my own hand wrapped around his.

At the last second, he blinked rapidly and started to struggle. Perhaps he even realized what was happening to him. I used his own hand to press the hard little gun against his temple and pull the trigger. There was a pop, so faint that I wondered if it had misfired.

But then there was blood, a surprising flow of hot blood.

I lowered his arm, now more than limp, into his lap, with the derringer still clutched in his hand.

His distorted face was half-averted, his mouth gaped open.

Time to go, I thought. You're done, time to go.

I leaned over and picked the ten-gauge up from the floor and carefully lowered the hammers.

Two more things, just two. I reached into my pants pocket and pulled out a folded and stained twenty-dollar bill that I'd brought just in case. The twenty that I'd found in the pool of Ella's blood; I dropped it in his lap.

One more thing. My hat. I almost left it but remembered at the last moment. Jammed it on my head with my bloody right hand and slipped quietly out of the house the same way I'd come in.

CHAPTER FORTY-ONE

"YOU'RE GONNA HAVE TO TALK TO MITCH."

It was noon the next day, and Brody had tracked me down at the flophouse on Hilliard Avenue. I had burned the gloves in a coal fire on the grate, washed out the sleeve of my coat and shirt, scrubbed the blood stain off my hat. I was ready. Ready to go to the train station—not to the sheriff's office.

"Why in hell would I want to do that?"

Brody tossed a fold of newsprint on the bed and lit a Camel with one twitch of a kitchen match against his thumbnail. "You seen the papers? Word is out. Aycock is dead. Mysteriously dead. The usual outrage and dismay. Mitch is furious and, hell, I don't know. Confused. I've never seen him like this. I was part of the team that went to the house when the judge called it in. Walked in on Aycock with his little pearl-handled popgun in his hand, bled out all over himself."

"Like I told you in the car. He was alive when I left him." Which was more or less true. "Must have killed himself."

"Guilt?"

I nodded. "He confessed, Brody. Told me he'd done it. Killed all three women. He was carrying around enough smoldering ash inside his soul to burn down city hall."

Brody nodded, his eye blinking rapidly. He sighed and tossed the butt into the grate, where it continued to smolder. "I don't quite believe that, but it doesn't matter. Question for you and me to consider is do you admit to ever being there."

"Will they try me for it if I do?"

Brody smiled. "Did you say try you or fry you?"

"Either one."

"Answer's yes. Try you and fry you. So I say you were never there. You were never in the house, and I was never in the driveway."

"Then, why in the red hell do I need to talk to Mitch? I'm tired of getting sucker punched by the son of a bitch, even if he is your brother."

"You need to talk to Mitch because you've got to help me convince him that Madison Pretty-Boy Aycock killed those women. And that you knew it. Hell, I knew it. So he had a reason to poke a bullet in his ear with that little derringer of his."

"Why would Mitch listen to us now when all he's done up to this point is cuss and spit?"

"He's different, I'm telling you. You'll see. I think he might've had a stroke."

AN HOUR LATER, WE WERE STANDING IN THE HALLWAY outside Mitch's office. I had nothing but bad memories of the place, and just the thought of the man brought the stink of chewing tobacco to mind. "Listen, Brody," I whispered. "Did you bring in the gun he shot himself with?"

"Of course. The old man claimed it was his, but I took it anyway. It's the thing that ties it all together, right?"

"How about the contents of his pockets?"

Brody nodded, beginning to get impatient.

"Were his keys in his pocket?"

"Sure. Why?"

"Do me a favor. Whatever happens in there with Mitch, check Aycock's keyring. See if he had a Grove Park Inn passkey."

I could actually see Brody's eye catch the scant electric light in the hallway and begin to gleam. "Rosie Caldwell?" he asked.

I reached over to rest my hand on his shoulder and nodded. "Exactly," I whispered.

A MOMENT LATER, WE WENT INTO MITCH'S OFFICE without knocking.

And he was different, just like Brody said. Before, he had been fat, and it was all the solid bulk of a boar hog, and a wild boar at that. Now, he seemed to slump in his chair, and his face sagged. Usually, when he saw me, he livened right up, and his hands turned into fists. But that morning, the morning that Madison Aycock was found dead, Mitch barely reacted at all. His eyes were deep set and bloodshot, and they didn't respond when I spoke to him.

Brody shut the door to the hallway behind us, and we both sat down in the battered, old wooden chairs in front of the desk. Brody cleared his throat, and I said good morning.

"What the hell do you two want?" Mitch managed to get the words out, and then paused. "Can't you see I'm busy?"

You're barely conscious, I thought, but didn't say. "We need to talk to you about Madison Aycock," I offered instead.

"What about him? He's dead." Another pause, and something inside of him stirred. He rolled his round head from side to side, and there was an audible creaking from his bull neck. "You come to confess?"

It was a chilling moment, and had it been the old Mitch, there would have been real threat in the words. But now, it was almost an afterthought, and not a very interesting one.

"No confession needed, Mitch," I replied. "From what I hear, your boy, Aycock, committed suicide." I could see Brody nodding out of the corner of my eye.

"The gun was in his hand, his left hand," Brody offered.

"I don't give a shit which hand." Mitch sighed. "Nobody in this town will ever believe the kid killed himself. He was going to be governor, for Christ's sake. Run the whole damn state." Mitch's words were slurred, as if he'd been drinking, but I doubted it was booze. One side of his mouth drooped slightly, and he kept trying to lick his lips as if they were numb.

"He killed those women," I said.

Mitch shrugged one shoulder. "So what? Never prove it."

"Two nights ago, I saw Ella Loving get into his car in the parking lot of the Grove Park Inn. With my own eyes, I saw it. A few hours later, she was dead. Shot with the same little pocket piece that killed Rosalind Caldwell and Viola Martin. He was guilty as sin, Mitch. Even he couldn't live with himself."

Mitch shook his head suddenly, violently, side to side. I thought he was denying what I was saying, but then I realized he was only trying to wake himself up. Trying to pay attention. "His old man," he finally managed to say.

"The judge? What about him?"

"You got to go see his old man. He's the one who wants blood for the kid. Twisting the tail of this whole damn town."

"Now? This morning?"

"Better . . . now." Mitch was fading. "Before he comes after you."

Brody and I looked at each other. I shrugged, and we stood up. Brody pulled open the door and went on out. I turned at the last moment. "Last thing, Mitch. You've got to let George Moore go. You know he's innocent."

Another shake of the head, this time less violent, more . . . confused. "Judge . . ." was all he managed to say.

CHAPTER FORTY-TWO

IT WAS EERIE TO RETRACE OUR PATH BACK UP TO AYCOCK'S house. Brody driving the same car, me riding shotgun. The day was gray and windy, and you could feel everything around you changing, shifting. Winter waiting on the tops of the high mountains, preparing to creep down the flanks of the ridges and into town.

As we drove, I studied the side of Brody's pale, unshaven face. He had driven up this street twice in the previous twelve hours, once carrying me to my secret conversation with Aycock, and the second in his official capacity as sheriff's investigator. He looked like he hadn't slept in days.

"Third time's a charm," I said to him.

To his credit, he grinned. "Bullshit," he muttered. And then: "Didn't you tell me that the old man had already threatened you?"

"I can't remember. I'm as tired as you look." Then after a moment's thought, "Yes, he did threaten me. The night of the party at the castle. Told me I was done, that Loftis was going to fire me, and to get the hell out of town."

Brody nodded and coughed. "He ain't going to be pleased to see you."

"I might be the last person on earth he wants to see. In fact, are you sure you want to be part of this little get-together?"

He glanced over at me, which wasn't easy. "They's all kinds of reasons why I want to be there. One, you need a witness in case he tries to be a hard-ass. An official witness, not some servant or beat cop. And two, when you start to get under his skin, as you no doubt will, I want to hear what he has to say. And three . . ." He pulled up to the curb at the bottom of the Aycock driveway.

"And three?"

"Three is I want to get this over and done with, so I can get you on a train back to where you came from. Mitch is coming apart at the seams, and this place is liable to turn into a sausage grinder over the next few days." He opened the car door but then paused. "And remember," he said to me. "You were never here. Unless you want to get ground up for raw meat, you were never goddamn here."

"Don't worry," I said, and then a thought occurred to me. "Who's going to be the next sheriff, Brody?"

Oddly enough, this brought another grin to his face, only this time the grin was hard, almost savage. "If you're lucky, I am," he said and opened the car door.

JUDGE BISHOP AYCOCK RECEIVED US UPSTAIRS IN HIS office. We went straight in and straight up. Neither of us even glanced past the beat cop who was standing guard to the left of the stairs, preventing the reporters in the driveway from entering the house and bothering the judge or plundering the death scene.

The old man still looked like a badger despite the morning he'd had. But now, he looked like a badger who'd been dragged out of his burrow and beaten with a stick. There were dark blue bags of skin under his almost lifeless eyes.

Still though, he was dangerous, and we both knew it. He waved for us to sit in front of his desk, which had almost nothing on it except a large blotter and a fancy ink stand. There was only one chair in front of the desk, so I dragged one over from beside a window. We sat.

As before, the judge cut to the chase. "What is this man doing here?" he asked Brody, pointing at me with the stem of the pipe he held in one hand. "This is still my home, and on this day of all days, it is not a place for ruffians."

"He's here because he was of some help to us in an investigation, an investigation that may shed some light on the death of your son."

"Nonsense. That—I hesitate to call him a man—that *thing* in the chair beside you thinks that someone in my social circle might have been involved in the death of the young woman at the Grove Park Inn."

He was exhausted, I realized, and in shock, or he never would have gone straight to the sore point.

"It's the same pistol, Judge," Brody said quietly.

"What?"

"The little derringer that we found in your son's hand this morning is the same gun that killed Rosalind Caldwell."

"Who's Rosalind Caldwell?"

"The woman who was shot at the Grove Park Inn. And, just so you know, it's also the same gun that killed Viola Martin and Ella Loving."

"Who's . . . ?" He paused, suddenly realizing that the water around him was deeper than he thought. "That's impossible. You can't know that for certain. You only took the pistol away three hours ago. You . . ."

"Four."

"What?"

"Four. We took the evidence from the scene four hours ago." Brody didn't know for certain yet, but he'd have the evidence by the end of the day.

The judge grunted and then stalled while he made a great show of filling the bowl of his pipe and lighting it. The only problem was that his hands were shaking now. Not badly, but enough so that when he hauled out that expensive silver lighter of his, the flame fluttered over the bowl of the pipe, and he almost burned himself. He puffed away for a moment, while Brody uncrossed and recrossed his legs. When he did finally speak, he'd regained some control. "That pistol you refer to belongs to me. Why am I not a suspect in these women's deaths?"

I almost laughed. Brody smiled at the thought before going on. "We have a witness that saw Ella Loving, who was killed night before last, getting into your son's automobile in the Grove Park Inn parking lot, a few hours before she was shot."

"Perhaps I was driving that car," the old goat replied.

Brody shook his head roughly. "No good, Judge. All three women were killed in what you might call . . . compromising situations. Two of the three were naked, and all three had been . . ."

"Are you suggesting that I'm too old to care about—"

"It's no damn good," Brody interrupted him. "Your son's dead. It doesn't help you or him to take the blame for something he did."

He laid the pipe down and managed, with some effort, to pull himself to his feet. He was so furious, he was sputtering. "You scoundrel, you serpent . . ." But the effort was too much, and after tottering for a moment, he collapsed back into the chair. "You don't understand," he said finally. "You just don't understand what it's like." There were actual tears now, rolling down the old man's face. And with the tears, the face itself became slightly more human. "He was my only hope. He was going to be governor, and he never, never would have taken his own life. Whatever you're implying just isn't true."

I spoke for the first time. "How did your wife die, Judge?"

"What did you say?"

"My understanding is that your wife took her own life a few years ago. Poison, I believe. The tendency toward self-slaughter runs in families."

He stared at me with his jaw hanging slack, the hand holding the pipe shaking uncontrollably. For a moment, I thought he was going to howl or bark like a dog, but he managed one last human effort. One last burst of words.

"I will find a way to hang all of this, all of this destruction around your neck," he croaked. "I warned you to leave Asheville, or I would make you pay. And you will. I will see you fry for all the deaths, the whorish women and my sainted son. I will . . ." He was winding down like a clock.

"No, you won't. You won't do anything of the kind." I was speaking very slowly and carefully because I wanted him to hear every word. "Because if you do implicate me in some way, I'll talk. I'll talk to every reporter from every newspaper in the southeast, Black as well as white. I'll paint your sainted son for what he was, and I'll do it by telling the truth, the whole truth, and nothing but the truth, so help me God."

He did howl then. The thin veil of humanity tore entirely, and he emitted a long, full-throated scream that faded finally into a hoarse, wavering cry of pure despair.

As we were walking down the driveway toward Brody's car, he paused to light a Camel and said, "You can be a cold-hearted son of a bitch at times, you know that?"

"Just following your lead," I replied.

CHAPTER FORTY-THREE

STANDING ON THE PLATFORM OF THE ASHEVILLE TRAIN station with my two bags at my feet, I didn't bother with a newspaper, having lived through the events that might consume a headline.

The first deep chill of the season. Frost on the rails that slowly melted in the scant sunlight. A convocation of crows talking to me and about me as they worked their way along the rooftops near the depot.

My belly was empty and twisted, and it occurred to me that I wanted something, anything, to put in it. Coffee. Bread. I left my bags on the platform and walked back into the station for a paper cup of black coffee and a hard roll. I wanted cream or butter or both, but there was none to be had.

Back outside, and every beat of my heart said it was time to go. Where was the goddamn train?

When it finally pulled into the siding—on time as it always was—there was smoke and swirling steam, sudden heat, and the heavy chuffing of the engine. I walked down the platform to the last passenger car before the caboose and pulled myself wearily up the iron stairs. I had the crumpled ticket from two days before, which the agent had assured me was still good. A different conductor this time from the one who'd kicked me off last time. Short, pugnacious, Irish, a man I knew from the years in Hot Springs, the years of a previous life.

"Headed home, Mr. Robbins?" he asked when he took my ticket. His voice roughened still by the brogue of his childhood.

I nodded. "Headed home."

He chuckled as he watched me set down my bags and fall into the seat. "Not much heat back here," he offered. "I'll bring you a blanket when I come back through."

I tried to smile at him. And in smiling, his name came back to me. "Thank you, Jimmy. Cold damn morning."

He leaned closer for a moment. "Cold as a well-digger's ass," he said and chuckled again.

I hadn't slept. I wondered if I would ever sleep again, or at least if I would sleep without dreaming. It wasn't clear to me in that addled moment if I'd seen those women die or only imagined their struggles and their fear. Just as it wasn't clear to me if I'd helped Madison Aycock kill himself or imagined the shot that killed him. Either way, there was blood, either way there was the last labored whimper of a fleeting life. Life intertwined with death like mist blown by a harsh wind over the river.

Was I alive?

I wanted to live, I thought. I wanted to see my son. "Luke," I whispered to myself. That was his name. Luke Edgar Robbins. I wanted to see him, and I wanted to see the river up home. I wanted to sit before a roaring hot fire and toss lies back and forth with my friend. What was his name?

Prince. Toss lies back and forth with Prince.

Jimmy McMahan brought me not one but two blankets. Instructed me to take my shoes off and prop my sock feet up on the opposite seat. Wrap one blanket around my legs and feet, and pull the other over my chest, up to my chin. "Now, that's how you sleep on a train, Mr. Robbins," he said. "Trust me, I been doin' it for years."

And then he went bowlegged on down the aisle, speaking to the three or four others in the car. Lonely travelers like me. Pilgrims.

My eyes closed of their own accord.

There was a woman also, I felt. There was Luke and there was Prince, with his wife Dora. And there was a woman. What was her name? Ella? No, not Ella. Anna. It seemed to me her name was Anna. But where in the hollow world was she? Gone, I thought. Someplace far and lost.

I suppose I slept, but the sleeping was never deep enough, never lost enough. I half slept, unable to still my mind long enough for true rest. The early morning light from the passenger car windows came and went, came and went as the northbound train snaked around the curves running up the French Broad gorge. And each time the light struck my face, I was reminded again of my own presence.

We stopped in Marshall, and though I refused to open my eyes, I could hear voices calling and the hustle of a few passengers dragging baggage as they disembarked or, in one or two instances, climbed aboard.

The next stop would be Hot Springs, and I would be home.

I could sense people around me but didn't open my eyes to see who it was. I figured my eyes just might be more frightening than my face. Reptilian. Ferocious. Haunted.

I would spare them my eyes.

Perhaps I did sleep some after that, as the northbound Norfolk & Southern engine roared downriver, trailing smoke and ash. The jostling of the last passenger car on the rig lulled me deeper into a stupor. Only a few minutes later, Jimmy McMahan's hand was on my shoulder, and he was pulling the blankets away.

"Hot Springs, Mr. Robbins," he was saying, first in a whisper and then in a melodious shout. "HOT SPRINGS . . . HOT SPRINGS, NORTH CAROLINA."

CHAPTER FORTY-FOUR

WITHIN A FEW DAYS, IT FELT LIKE I WAS ALMOST BACK again—in body if not in soul. Luke was there, and together, we fell into an easy rhythm. He was as thrilled to see me as I him. And here was my old dog, King James. Luke and I took him for short walks on the edge of town, the King tiring even before Luke.

Prince and Dora were there as well. And yes, Prince and I built roaring fires on the hearth at Rutland. Poured out liberal doses of whiskey and swapped lies. After a few days of settling, I was able to tell him the Asheville story: Madison Aycock and the three women he'd intended to take to bed and sent to the afterlife instead.

"They're in heaven," Prince offered. "I suspect all three of them are singing now."

And so on to the end of the story, where I had returned the favor and sent the future governor, Madison Aycock, out of this slant world and on to . . .

"Hell," Prince finished my thought. "In this case, I'd say hell. Old Scratch was just waiting on that boy with his claws like carving knives, sharp as sin."

Prince was interested in the fate of Michael Joyner and his nephew, George Moore. Was Moore still in jail? Would he go free now, after all that had happened? I confessed that I didn't know, but that Brody Mitchell would spring the young man if anyone on earth could.

And then came the telegrams.

S ROBBINS, HOT SPRINGS
MA had GPI key in his pocket[.]
Viola Martin underwear in his car[.]
Mitch in hospital[.] Nothing from Judge[.]
BRODY MITCHELL, Acting Sheriff Bunc Co

I sent a reply the same day and asked about George Moore. The next morning brought a cryptic response.

STEPHEN ROBBINS, HOT SPRINGS
Moore within the week[.] Time[.]
BRODY MITCHELL, Acting Sheriff Bunc Co

I showed the telegram to Prince, who wrinkled his brow and muttered, "What the hell . . . *time*?"

"Means that it takes time. Means that he'll cut him loose within a week and do it with as little noise as possible to keep him safe."

"You sure?"

I nodded. "I'm sure. You'd like Brody, Prince. He's as stubborn as you are."

THE NIGHTS GREW COOLER, AND EACH MORNING REvealed the hillsides painted more deeply with the palette of old fall. Oranges, fiery reds, yellow golds in the muted sunlight. First at the tops of the ridges and then lower down into the coves and hollows. Ancient colors new again in the present season.

And then one afternoon, Prince brought me the letter.

When he handed me the envelope on the porch at Rutland, I knew from the return address and the handwriting that it was from her, from Anna Ulmann. But in that flickering moment, my mind slipped a cog or two, and I wasn't sure what I was supposed to do.

"Are you listening to me, Stevie?"

"Hmmmm?"

"That means no. Look at me."

Which I did. Peered questioningly into his broad, dark face, one of the most familiar faces in the world.

"I said that I let her know you were alive, that you were . . . that Lucy had died."

"How did you do that?"

"The mails run both ways. I wrote to her in New York."

"You can write?"

"The hell with you. Go read your letter."

I CARRIED A TUMBLER OF APPLE BRANDY OUT TO A BENCH in the side yard and sat down there in the shadow of an ancient oak, the leaves having already turned a rusty brown above me. I sat my glass down on the bench and then used my pocketknife to slowly, carefully slit the top of the envelope. It felt like the beginning of a ritual, an approach to something significant like knowledge, or understanding, and I didn't rush.

Once the envelope was open, I took a sip of the brandy and closed my eyes. What did I want the letter to say? I didn't know . . .

I'VE PLAYED POKER OFF AND ON IN MY LIFE. USUALLY with men, though sometimes with women as well. At the old Mountain Park back before the war. Later with the round-table crowd at the Algonquin in New York. And here's what I've learned, time after time:

Life rarely offers up the hand you need—even more rarely the hand you want—in the first deal. Chips in the middle of the table. The cards go round, and you take a first, noncommittal glance at what the dealer has thrown your way. There's usually something but never enough. Oh, there's enough to entice you, keep you in, even seduce you into believing. But not enough to win.

You have to give up some cards in the second deal, sacrifice something you're already holding and ask for more. Believe in the possibility of more. And then there's a long, breath-held moment when your one or two new cards are on the table, and you reach out your hand to see what fate has to say to you that day.

Let's say you asked for one. Just one card to add to the four, highly suggestive cards in your hand. If the game is for nickels and dimes with your friends, and the dealer is your buddy, it doesn't matter.

But if your life is in the middle of the table, and the dealer is that dark figure shrouded in mist, then it matters. The air in the room is thicker, heavier, and you wish for a knife up your sleeve or a straight razor hanging by a cord around your neck in case things get ugly. The dealer is watching. Still and silent within the dark fold of time, the dealer is watching, already knowing. Sometimes the dealer has claws for fingers.

You reach for the last card. There's no other choice but to pick it up.

All that matters then is the curl of your lips, the span of your mind, the steadiness of your fingers . . . when you reach out. That's all that really matters because, most often, you lose. Then you must pay. Your palms are slippery with blood, and you must pay.

But then again . . . sometimes, perhaps a very few times in your entire life, it's *the* card. The only card that will complete the ones in your hand.

Dear Stephen,

How long has it been? Days and nights, weeks and months, years? Years, I think. Since I last saw you on that horrid night at the Anderson Gallery, when you ran away into the New York City rain and garbage. When I betrayed you and cheated you and you ran away. I was trapped, caught in a web, and couldn't follow you.

Please know that for me what happened back then meant nothing. Nothing except stupidity and selfishness on my part. And sorrow. The deepest and darkest sorrow of all is the pain that I caused you, for which I bow down and seek forgiveness. Through all this time, I have sought your forgiveness.

Prince tells me that you are alone now, except for your son. He writes that though you were wounded, you may live. And whether you know it or not, you need me.

It catches in my throat to think he might be right. That there is a world in which you would want me.

And so this brief letter is to say that I am coming to Hot Springs to visit. For your sake—I hope—and my sake. I will arrive the last week of the month. I'm telling you this in case you decide to go away. To take your son and flee. But my hope is that you will stay. So that I might touch your hand, and in touching you, become real again. Please stay for me if you can.

Always yours,

A

I read the letter twice. No, that's a lie. Three times. Refolded it carefully and slipped it back into the envelope. The afterimage of the letters burned in my eyes, along with the knowledge that she would be here—in this very place, perhaps sitting on this bench under this tree—next week. More than four years of absence suddenly reduced to a bare handful of days. I took another sip of brandy and considered. Life or death? Stay or go? The turn of a card . . .

CHAPTER FORTY-FIVE

THE LAST WEEK IN OCTOBER.

Monday the 27th dawned unseasonably warm, and I felt that more than anything else, I needed to get into the woods. Autumn was just past its full-dress parade, and thousands of fallen leaves were scattered over the fields and floating downriver. Color was everywhere. The woods seemed deep and very old.

Answers were buried in those depths, or so it seemed to me. Answers about the death of Ella Loving and the rebirth of Anna Ulmann. Answers about my own fractured heart and darkening mind. What of death? What of life?

Most years, I would have cleaned and loaded the deer rifle that Major Rumbough had given me before the war. I'd have gone up onto the higher ridges in search of venison for the pot, seeking sight and insight.

But when I got up that morning, I realized that by afternoon the temperature would be in the sixties and the breeze warm on the skin. I didn't have the heart for gunfire, even in the woods. I wondered if I would ever have the heart for it again.

So instead of the rifle, I took my old fly rod and fishing vest from the closet and followed the path along Spring Creek up to the west of town. There was a spot I loved, higher up where almost no one went except me, and I hadn't been there for a year.

A sandy, sun-drenched beach beneath some large boulders you have to clamber over to reach the creek. A small island above that splits the stream into two surging waves that flow over a rock spill and down into the pool that laps at the beach. And on all sides, the mountains rise majestically, proudly.

I DIDN'T STOP TO FISH THE CREEK ON THE WAY UP. RATHER, I walked and thought, walked and absorbed the yellow caress of sunlight and birdsong. Walked until I found myself climbing down over the rocks and standing on the sand below. Where the symphony of the creek fills the gorge with water music.

Without thinking, I lay my rod carefully against the rocks and stripped off my vest. I knew then that I hadn't come to kill a fish, not really. I'd come because I was dirty, soiled somehow on the inside. What I uncovered on the journey into Asheville had left something dark and desperate in me, something that doesn't wash away so easily as blood stains on a sleeve.

I was sweating, the light dazzling over my head and shoulders. First, I tossed aside my old fishing hat and let the sunshine pour down into my mind. But this wasn't enough. I unbuttoned my shirt, threw it aside. Shoes and socks, trousers and shorts. Until I stood naked in the bronze waves of light, bare before the singing world.

The water was frigid. Trout cold, aged in ice. It burned against the sheath of my skin. Nothing would do but immersion. Complete and wrenching. I sank deep at first, curling inside a womb of water. Then let my body relax and float to the surface. Face up in the swirling course of Spring Creek, my face and belly basking in the sun. Burning and freezing at once, the waves sluicing away the darkness left within me.

When I rose to face the shore, it was as if I had, for the first time, returned. As if, finally, I was *home*, and . . . Clean.

For her.

ACKNOWLEDGMENTS

FIFTEEN YEARS AGO, STEPHEN ROBBINS EMERGED FROM my imagination as the manager of the beautiful, old Mountain Park Hotel in Hot Springs, North Carolina. Despite his occasional despair and occasional drinking, he was retained as the Inspector General of the WW I German Internment Camp when it was constructed around the hotel. At the end of that novel (*A Short Time to Stay Here*), I assumed Stephen's story was complete, and he could rest in the arms of his beloved.

But as it turned out, he had much more to say and do.

This book, then, is the third installment of the Stephen Robbins Chronicles. As he tells us in Chapter Three, he's been married twice, once divorced, and once widowed. He's stood trial twice for murder and twice been acquitted. He's fathered two children, one of whom survives. He's killed three men. Like most great detectives of the night, he is in danger of being consumed by his scars, and yet each time he rises to face the enigma.

So, with regards to *The Devil Hath a Pleasing Shape*, I must first thank the teller of the tale. Perhaps only Stephen Robbins could do what must be done here. After all, this is a book about prostitution and politics—a timely topic—and it required a hard hand and true voice to find justice.

On a practical level, I would also like to thank Wendy Ikoku for her characteristic close reading of the manuscript and her advice about the ending. My agent, Margaret Sutherland Brown, championed this one, always with grit and grace. The team at

Turner—Amanda Chiu Krohn, Ashlyn Inman, Makala Marsee, Kendal Cliburn—have brought this Devil of a manuscript to life, for which I'm very grateful. And of course, Lynn watched it grow out of the wreckage of an earlier version and was ever wise and encouraging.

As you probably know, Asheville's Grove Park Inn is a real place; although, the current version bears little resemblance to the inn of one hundred years ago. Still, should you go there for a drink tonight, or sit down to dinner, you might spy the ghosts of Stephen Robbins and Ella Loving, talking and laughing quietly in the lobby.

ABOUT THE AUTHOR

TERRY ROBERTS IS THE AUTHOR OF FIVE CELEBRATED novels: *A Short Time to Stay Here* (winner of the Willie Morris Prize for Southern Fiction and the Sir Walter Raleigh Award for Fiction); *That Bright Land* (winner of the Thomas Wolfe Literary Award, the James Still Award for Writing About the Appalachian South and the Sir Walter Raleigh Award for Fiction); *The Holy Ghost Speakeasy and Revival* (Finalist for the 2019 Sir Walter Raleigh Award for Fiction); *My Mistress' Eyes are Raven Black* (Finalist for the 2022 Best Paperback Original Novel by the International Thriller Writers Organization); and most recently, *The Sky Club*, released in July of 2022.

Roberts is a lifelong teacher and educational reformer as well as an award-winning novelist. He is a native of the mountains of Western North Carolina—born and bred. His ancestors include six generations of mountain farmers, as well as the bootleggers and preachers who appear in his novels. He was raised close by his grandmother, Belva Anderson Roberts, who was born in 1888 and passed to him the magic of the past along with the grit and humor of mountain storytelling.

Roberts is the Director of the National Paideia Center and lives in Asheville, North Carolina, with his wife, Lynn.

Printed in the USA
CPSIA information can be obtained
at www.ICGtesting.com
JSHW021319251124
74264JS00002B/2/J